The kids all safe, Carlos ran to the 8x8 . . .

. . . even as the crows—those that weren't trapped in the bus by Betty's heroism—descended upon Kenny, who was already bloody and battered and still firing the flame thrower. Monique lay dead and bloody next to him.

As the crows overwhelmed Kenny, the flame thrower spun wildly around.

An arc of fire headed straight for Carlos.

He had only a microsecond to hope that his death would be quick.

Then, suddenly, the flame split, going around Carlos. He felt the heat on his face as the fire went around him, as if he was a rock in the middle of a river.

What the *fuck?*

Then the fire started to twist and spiral as if it had a mind of its own.

Or, rather, a mind controlling it.

Looking around, Carlos caught sight of the one person he knew who could do this sort of thing:

Alice.

RESIDENT EVIL: EXTINCTION

A novelization by Keith R. A. DeCandido
Based on the screenplay by
Paul W. S. Anderson
Based on Capcom's bestselling video games

POCKET STAR BOOKS
New York   London   Toronto   Sydney

Pocket Star Books
A Division of Simon & Schuster, Inc.
1230 Avenue of the Americas, New York, NY 10020

This book is a work of fiction. Names, characters, places, and incidents either are products of the author's imagination or are used fictitiously. Any resemblance to actual events or locales or persons, living or dead, is entirely coincidental.

First Pocket Star Books paperback edition August 2007

POCKET STAR and colophon are registered trademarks of Simon & Schuster, Inc.

Manufactured in the United States of America

10 9 8 7 6 5 4 3 2 1

For information about special discounts for bulk purchases, please contact Simon & Schuster Special Sales at 1-800-456-6798 or business@simonandschuster.com

ISBN-13: 978-1-4165-4498-2
ISBN-10:   1-4165-4498-4

*Dedicated to the fond memory of Pierce Askegren,
1955–2006.*

He would've really loved this . . .

Acknowledgments

Thanks to Pocket Books editor Marco Palmieri for bringing me back for a third go-round with the *Resident Evil* franchise; to Paul W.S. Anderson for the scripts that provided the foundation on which I built these three novels; to the good folks at Capcom who gave us the *Resident Evil* game that started this whole schmear; to S.D. Perry for her excellent novels based on the games, thus giving me a very tough act to follow; to the folks in the café who plied me with beverages during my marathon writing sessions; to GraceAnne Andreassi DeCandido for her usual fine first read; to my fiancée and my cats for encouragement and cuteness; and to all the actors in all three movies, but in particular Milla Jovovich, Sienna Guillory, Mike Epps, and the always-magnificent Oded Fehr, for giving me such vivid characters to play with.

Part One

Before and After

ONE

BEFORE

Dr. Jim Knable stood on the Ravens' Gate Bridge, with a seething tide of humanity heading straight for him. Knable was grateful for the presence of the Umbrella Corporation security guards and members of the Raccoon City Police Department who were stemming that particular tide, keeping him from being overrun.

Knable and a small medical station had been placed at the wall that had been hastily constructed around Raccoon City. The island metropolis had been completely enclosed by that wall, with the only opening at this bridge, the major artery in and out of Raccoon.

The outbreak of a virus that didn't just kill you but animated your corpse and gave it an instinctive need to feed on human flesh—thus transmitting the disease to more and more people—brought a fierce desire on the part of the surviving citizens to leave the city as fast as they could. But the risk of infection was quite high, so the Umbrella Corporation—the pharmaceuticals and electronics firm that paid Knable's obscenely high salary—physically quarantined the city and would allow only those who were uncontaminated to leave.

That morning, when the outbreak was first announced, Knable had been given the specifics of the virus and told to develop a quick-test that would determine if the virus was in a sample of human blood. Knable had pioneered many streamlinings of standard blood tests, the patents for which would guarantee him a comfortable retirement. But Knable was only in his late twenties, and he still wanted to practice. Umbrella, having purchased the rights to use his procedure for their Medical Division, which provided services to hospitals around the world, hired him to do just that.

The rumor around the lab was that Umbrella had actually developed this virus, though Knable didn't really credit rumors. It wasn't as if samples of tainted blood were hard to come by right now. Some of those rumors were that the virus had wiped out the Hive, killing all five hundred people who worked in that underground complex. Knable had a few friends down in the Hive, and he hadn't actually heard from any of them since yesterday—but then, he often went days without hearing from them.

However, that wasn't Knable's primary concern. He'd spent the better part of the day taking blood from people and running the quick-test, with only one food break, and then only because he was on the verge of collapse. Major Cain had been willing to let him take more breaks, but with *so* many people piling onto the bridge wanting to leave and unable to do so without Knable's express okay, the doctor couldn't bring himself to keep them waiting.

By the time darkness fell, he could barely stay upright. Sleep was building up in his eyes, and he tried to rub them, only to wince from the oily feel of the rubber glove on his eyelids.

The crowds had just grown larger with the onset of night. Knable had long since lost track of how many quick-tests he'd done. Whenever he was in danger of running out of anything—test tubes, gas for the Bunsen burner, rubber gloves, or the solvent he had developed—some black-suited person from Security Division showed up with a fresh supply before Knable even had the chance to ask.

At some point, he'd cut his finger. He'd barely acknowledged the trickle of blood that had been smeared as he removed the rubber glove, when a security goon handed him a Band-Aid. "Thanks," he said with a ragged smile as he applied the Band-Aid. He wasn't too worried about any infection—that was why he *wore* the gloves, after all. It would've been nice if he remembered how he actually *got* the cut, but that was a concern for another time when he wasn't in an emergency situation and exhausted beyond all reason.

Shaking the third of three test tubes over the burner, one each from a mother, father, and child who had come together, and seeing that they all came up green, Knable said, "They're clean. Let them pass."

So far, none of the blood had turned blue. The error margin for the test was that it often gave false positives but never false negatives. It might be inaccurate insofar as it would say someone clean had the virus, but it wouldn't say that someone who was infected didn't have it. As long as the blood turned green in the test tube when heated with Knable's solvent, the person was definitely free of the virus.

Knable would stake his reputation on it. And his reputation was considerable.

An old man and a young woman came up next. Even as Knable was drawing blood from the woman, the old man suddenly collapsed.

Panic shot through Knable. He stood up straight for the first time in about four hours. If this old guy was infected . . .

"Oh, my God, Daddy!" The teenager fell to her knees and started unbuttoning the old man's shirt. "He's not breathing! It's his heart—he has a weak heart!"

A heart attack wasn't what Knable was worried about. People who were infected with this virus could easily just collapse out of nowhere. The old man didn't have any visible bites, but Knable couldn't see his entire body, either.

The girl started to give her father mouth-to-mouth, which wasn't quite the stupidest thing she could've done but was right up there. "Get away from him!" Knable cried.

He was about to move to yank her off and found that

he couldn't. She *was* trying to save her father's life, after all. Knable took his Hippocratic Oath very seriously—even if he couldn't really remember all of it most of the time—and he couldn't just stop someone from engaging in a lifesaving procedure.

But he could get someone else to do it. Looking up, he saw that Sergeant Wells of the RCPD was nearby, along with an armed woman wearing a tube top and a miniskirt. Knable presumed she was an off-duty cop pressed into service.

To Wells, Knable spoke in his best order-nurses-around voice. "Get her away from him."

With a grunt, the sergeant did as he was told, though the girl didn't make it easy on him. "No, let me go!" she cried.

"He's saving your life," Knable muttered as he removed the test tube from the needle. He had a very bad feeling about what the quick-test was going to show.

Before he even had a chance to add the solvent, the old man's eyes opened.

They were a milky white.

Knable didn't need to run the test to know that the blood he had in the test tube was going to turn up blue.

The old man was infected.

As if to prove it, he immediately bit Sergeant Wells's leg, which meant the cop was going to turn into an animated corpse before too long as well.

Before anybody else could react, the woman in the tube top shot the old man right in the head.

While the girl was screaming that the woman had

killed her daddy, Knable felt a hand grab his arm. It was Anderson, the head of the security detail down here. "We're outta here, Doc," he said, guiding Knable rather forcibly toward the gate.

"Wait a minute, you can't—" Knable started, even as he was all but dragged toward the gate. He couldn't just *leave* these people; he'd been there all day, and—

"Giddings," Anderson said to the Bluetooth in his ear, "we've got an infected man here. I'm evac'ing the doc." He then nodded in response to whatever Giddings might have said.

Anderson all but threw Knable through the gate, forcing the doctor to stumble to the ground.

Only then did he realize he was still holding the test tube with the old man's blood, which he mostly noticed when it shattered on the pavement of the bridge.

Clambering to his feet, Knable looked down at the shards of test tube and infected blood, the latter spreading in rivulets through the asphalt. "Perfect ending to a perfect day," he muttered.

Another security goon, a woman whose name patch read ZOLL, led him toward a helicopter that was waiting on the far side of the bridge. Halfway there, he heard a thunderous bang that made him almost jump out of his shoes. Whirling around, he saw that the gate had been closed. "They can't just trap those people there."

"Not my call, sir," Zoll said. "We have to go."

As they approached the helicopter, Knable heard Cain's voice over a loudspeaker: *"This is a biohazard quarantine area."*

KEITH R.A. DeCANDIDO

Knable shuddered. He supposed that Cain was right. If one infected person had made it to the bridge, dozens more could have, and in that crowd, it would spread like a brushfire.

Cain repeated: *"This is a biohazard quarantine area. Due to risk of infection, you cannot be allowed to leave the city. All appropriate measures are being taken. The situation is under control. Please return to your homes."*

With a snort, Knable said, "Fat chance of that. He's never gonna get those people to move off the bridge."

As Zoll offered him a hand up into the helicopter, she smiled and said, "I think the major'll convince them, Doctor."

Knable sighed as he entered the helicopter. The main section had benches along both side walls—or bulkheads, or whatever they called them—which were mostly filled with fellow Umbrella employees and black-clad, well-armed Security Division folks. Glancing around, Knable finally found a spare space between someone he didn't recognize, who, like him, wore a lab coat, and someone from security.

As soon as he squeezed in between them, Zoll closed the hatch, and Knable felt a pull on his stomach as the helicopter took off. He shook his head, wishing he could have done more, but he wasn't about to resist someone with a gun telling him to get into a helicopter, especially since that gun wielder was carrying out the wishes of the people who signed his paycheck.

He just hoped that some of the people on this helicopter, or the others that had been used to evacuate peo-

9

ple in the Science and Medical Divisions, were working on a cure.

Lifting his arm to scratch an itch on his nose, Knable was surprised to see that the Band-Aid he'd hastily put on his right index finger had fallen off at some point. The cut was red with blood, but it didn't seem to be actually bleeding anymore.

Looking around, he asked, "Anyone have a Band-Aid?"

Two
After

The cameras recorded everything.

At present, they showed a large, beautifully appointed bathroom. It was all brass and marble, and the place was as large as some big-city studio apartments.

The shower, which was running, its staccato rhythm the only noise coming from the room, was a larger-than-average stall, with only a small lip and a shower curtain to keep the water contained. The curtain had been ripped from the rod and was draped over the shower's sole occupant: a naked woman.

She was unconscious or asleep. Her chest expanded and contracted slowly with each breath, the only sign of life she gave.

Then her blue eyes opened.

Slowly, she got to her feet. She looked very disoriented.

The cameras followed her movements as she turned the shower off and padded out into the bathroom proper. With one hand, she wiped the condensation from the mirror to take a look at herself. She gave the bruise on her right shoulder only a cursory glance—she seemed much more interested in what looked like a severe, and long-healed, knife wound on her left shoulder. As if she didn't know how she got it.

She looked around, but if the bathroom had any wisdom to grant her, she was unable to glean it. So she walked out the door into a large bedroom.

The cameras in that room winked into life and followed her.

The centerpiece of the bedroom was a huge double bed with two sets of pillows. Laid out on the center of the bed were a red dress, a pair of panties, and a pair of biker shorts. After staring at the clothing for several seconds, she put the panties and the biker shorts on and shrugged into the dress. A pair of thigh-high boots sat at the foot of the bed, and she slid them on.

Everything seemed to fit perfectly.

She looked at her left hand, noticed the gold wedding band on it. As with everything else, she seemed confused by it.

Wandering over to the window, she pushed back the thick curtains with the odd patterns on them to reveal a concrete wall.

This, more than anything, seemed to baffle her. Why

would someone put a set of curtains over a concrete wall?

Of course, the wall didn't match the rest of the décor. Perhaps that was the reason for the curtains.

The bedroom's furnishings also included a beautiful wooden writing desk right next to the window. A pad of paper sat at the center of it, and someone had written, "Today all your dreams come true," and then underlined it with an X in the center of the underline.

She grabbed the ornately designed pen next to the pad and started writing beneath the underline. She got as far as, "Today all your," then stopped when it became obvious that it wasn't she who had written it.

Frustrated, she moved out into the next room, the dining hall—though there was no dining table. It was simply a large, empty room with a few antique chairs and end tables, wood paneling, and a lot of space.

One of those end tables had a framed picture atop it. She picked it up, seeing her own face along with that of a handsome man. He wore a tuxedo, she a bridal gown. Again, she stared down at the gold band on her left ring finger.

A heavy thud startled her. She set the picture down and turned toward a statue that was just past the far end of the room, in a vestibule. The statue was, for reasons passing understanding, wrapped loosely in plastic. A breeze ruffled the plastic, making a low crackling noise.

"Hello?"

Curious, she set the picture down and walked toward the statue. Stepping through the entryway into the vestibule, she found a large, ornate wooden door. It had a brass pull handle that was at neck level for some reason. Reaching up, she pulled the handle downward, and the door swung open.

On the other side was a long, thin corridor with walls of glass that led to a giant metal door that looked as if it belonged in a bank vault. Bright lights behind the glass walls came on as she entered, and she averted here eyes from the sudden illumination.

Slowly, carefully, she walked forward, blinking a few times to adjust her eyes.

Once she was halfway there, the lights dimmed again.

She looked around quickly, not sure what was happening but getting into a defensive crouch, trying to be ready for what might come.

What came was a horizontal beam of light at about ankle height that sprang into being right in front of the metal door at the far end.

Then it started to move toward her.

She got lower in her crouch, preparing to jump, when the beam moved up to chest height. Seemingly running on instinct, she backpedaled and took a quick glance behind her to see that the big wooden door had slammed shut as well. Crouching low, she leapt up toward the ceiling, wrapped her fingers around an air vent, and levered her legs upward so that her body was parallel to the floor above the line of the laser.

As long as the laser didn't rise any higher, she'd be fine.

The red dress she wore was cut oddly: it extended to her ankle on the outer part of her right leg but was cut in a U shape, leaving her legs free. On the left side, the dress came only to her hips.

The bit on her right side hung down loosely from her position atop the glass corridor, extending below the laser line. The laser sliced cleanly through the fabric, the cloth fluttering noiselessly to the floor, smoke coming off the charred end of the part that was still attached.

Lowering herself back to a vertical position, she let go of the air vent and landed on the floor, bending her knees to lessen the impact.

Before she could decide on another course of action, the lights dimmed again, and another beam formed at ankle height at the far end.

This time, though, the beam didn't rise to chest height. Instead, it spread into a diagonal grid that took up the entire breadth and height of the corridor.

Nowhere to jump, nowhere to run, nowhere to hide.

With one exception.

Again she jumped to the ceiling. Again she grabbed the air vent. But this time, she didn't just level off but kicked upward at one of the other air vents, knocking it askew. Using her ankles to brace herself, she slid into the vent, barely ahead of the laser grid. Her head went in last, blond hair sliced at the ends and vaporized by the grid before it could reach the floor.

The air vent was tight, and she took a moment to get her bearings and squiggle around into a position where she could crawl through. Her only illumination came from the glass corridor below, and that was obviously not an option, unless she wanted to be diced.

So she crawled forward.

The cameras followed her here, too, transmitting in infrared, the heat source being the woman in the red dress.

She crawled.

Time was lost in the imperative of moving forward. All that mattered was finding a way out that didn't require staying in that glass corridor. She was moving in a direction that would put her back over the mansion. Perhaps she could get back in there.

The cameras found another heat source: a flicker of light that now came into her field of vision.

She crawled faster.

The light grew brighter, but it was also in the top of the air duct. Which meant it wouldn't lead to the mansion. But any port in a storm—she crawled to it, found another air vent much like the one she'd kicked in to get here, and lifted it slowly—just enough for her to see where it led.

It was a dark corridor. One not made of glass, which put it one up on the corridor she'd just left.

Throwing the vent aside with a loud clank of metal on linoleum, she climbed up into the corridor. While not as sterile as the glass corridor, it wasn't as homey as the mansion, either. Disinfectant tinged the air, which, along with the empty gurneys against one of the walls, identified this as a hospital—albeit an abandoned one. The only decorations were a few paintings that were probably meant to be soothing on the walls and the hexagonal red-and-white logo of the Umbrella Corporation on the floor.

Slowly, she walked forward, even more cautious after her last long corridor.

At the end of this corridor was not a forbidding hunk of metal but rather a set of glass doors. She could see the streets of Raccoon City beyond them.

Walking past the gurney, she suddenly stopped, looked around, as if sensing something wrong.

After looking up and down the corridor for several seconds, she grabbed the gurney and rolled it down the corridor.

Once the gurney made it to a fork in the corridor, a trip wire appeared and sliced the gurney clean in half. It would have done the same to her.

Shaking her head, she continued forward, carefully stepping around the spot that the gurney ran over to set off the trip wire.

And then she was thrown back several feet by a mine exploding.

She landed in a heap against one wall of the corridor, staring down in shock at the gaping, bleeding hole in her chest.

As the women breathed her last, Dr. Samuel Isaacs cursed.

Isaacs never used to curse. He had always prided himself on a fine vocabulary and a lack of need to resort to such crudity.

But the world had changed over the past few years, and Isaacs had been forced to change with it. Among other things, this meant that when things went wrong, he no longer shook his head, clucked softly, and said something bland like "What a pity" or "Back to the drawing board" or "Oh, dear."

No, he pounded a gloved fist on the table in front of him and said, "Shit!"

Then he turned to his team—who all, like him, were wearing white Hazmat suits—and said, "Let's move."

Yet another clone of Alice Abernathy had failed to make her way through the Cretan Labyrinth.

The other technicians and scientists went ahead in. Isaacs paused to close and seal the faceplate of the suit. The "Cretan Labyrinth" nickname had come a few months back from Moody, one of the techs, and it had stuck. Timson had suggested that they try to re-create Nemesis and use him as the Minotaur, an offense for which Isaacs might have fired Timson under other circumstances.

The Nemesis Project had been Isaacs's greatest success and greatest failure at the same time. He hated the very mention of it.

Once Isaacs's suit was properly sealed, he went in after Moody, Timson, and the others. He hated wearing the damn suit, as it was impossible to breathe properly in the thing. In the old days, he'd have delegated. Sadly, the growing unpleasantness had reduced the staff to the point that Isaacs had to be much more hands-on than a supervisor of his experience usually was.

Another change that had come in this new world they all lived in.

Not for the first time, Isaacs cursed the name of Timothy Cain. A German immigrant who served in the U.S.

Army before joining the Umbrella Corporation, Cain was singlehandedly responsible for destroying the world.

Worse, he was already dead, so he couldn't be punished. He died in Raccoon City shortly before it was vaporized by a tactical nuclear missile strike that Cain himself had ordered.

There was blame to spread elsewhere, of course. Based on the surveillance they'd been able to pull from the mansion attached to the Hive—the very same one that had been partially re-created in the Cretan Labyrinth—a former Umbrella security staffer, Percival Spencer Parks, had been the one to unleash the T-virus in the Hive, condemning five hundred people to death. After that, the Hive had been sealed, the only survivors being Alice Abernathy and Matthew Addison, who had been brought into the Nemesis Project.

Had the Hive remained sealed and been filled with concrete, it all would have been over. In fact, that had been Isaacs's very recommendation to Cain. As with most recommendations from anyone other than himself, Cain ignored it. Which was a pity, as Isaacs then would have been able to develop Nemesis properly, and no one would have found out about what happened in the Hive. True, the families and friends of five hundred people would have to have been told something, but they all lived in an underground complex that was filled with attendant risks. Surely Umbrella could have found a cover story.

Instead, Cain reopened the Hive, supposedly because he wanted to know what had happened.

If the human race survived, Isaacs was quite sure that Cain's decision would go down in history as humanity's greatest blunder, surpassing such classics as Napoleon's invasion of Russia and the introduction of the rabbit into the Australian ecosystem.

The infected corpses of the five hundred Hive employees—not to mention an entire Security Division team—had been animated by the T-virus, and Cain's re-opening of the Hive allowed them access to the world outside.

Within fourteen hours, Raccoon City was overrun. Each corpse was filled with an uncontrollable urge to feed on flesh, and when they did, their victims died and became hungry animated corpses themselves. Umbrella sealed off the city, just as it had sealed off the Hive, and then blew it up with a nuke.

That was only a temporary stopgap.

Isaacs looked down at the corpse. The dead blue eyes stared straight ahead. Blood pooled beneath the body from the gaping hole in its thoracic region.

He shook his head. "Take a sample of her blood. Then get rid of that."

Turning around, he went back into the lab. He had to get out of the damn suit.

Andy Timson watched as Isaacs retreated to the safety of the observation room. "Wuss," he muttered under his breath.

"Go ahead," Brendan Moody said next to him, "say that louder. I double-dog dare you."

"Aren't you supposed to build up to that?" Andy asked Brendan as the latter reached into the sterilized pouch on his suit and took out a syringe attached to a test tube.

"Huh?" Brendan asked distractedly as he put the point of the syringe into the pool of blood under Alice-85's body.

"You start with the dare," Andy said. "Then it's double dare. Then it's double-dog dare." He frowned. "I think. Been a while since I saw the movie."

"Oh, that's from a movie?"

"Christ, Brendan, did you have *no* childhood?"

Standing over them, the lone member of security assigned to the group, Paul DiGennaro, said, "Is there a chance that you two will ever shut the fuck up?"

"Not a big chance, no," Andy said with a cheeky grin that Paul couldn't actually see through the visor. Not that Paul needed to see it, since he knew it was there, and he probably shared it.

"Figured I'd ask. Maybe the nine-hundredth time'd be the fucking charm."

Brendan stood up, removing the test tube from the syringe. "We're all rooting for number nine-oh-one, Paul, trust me."

In the old days, Andy and Brendan never would have dreamed of bantering with the thug squad. They were the big, obnoxious apes who shot people and used words of one syllable; Andy and Brendan were the dumbshit geeks who couldn't find their asses with both hands. Neither side had any use for the other.

But that was the old days. These days, you couldn't

afford not to get along with the people you worked with. Because those were the people you lived with every day, probably for the rest of your life.

Generally, Andy tried not to think about it.

Brendan held up the test tube. "I'm gonna go run this through the machines and see what wisdom it provides."

"Probably the same thing the last eighty-four tests said."

"Yeah. *You* wanna tell Isaacs that? You can do it right after you call him a wuss to his face."

Before Andy could respond to Brendan's dig, Paul said, "C'mon, Timson, let's haul ass. I don't wanna spend any more time outside than I have to."

Sobering, Andy said, "Yeah. You want the feet this time?"

"Nah, I'll take the shoulders. Wouldn't want you to get blood on your precious Hazmat suit."

"Hey, at least this one got past the lasers." Andy shuddered, remembering the early clone who got sliced and diced by the laser grid. Andy couldn't eat steak for a week after that.

Not that there was a whole helluva lot of steak to be had these days. Umbrella had an impressive stockpile of food to keep its few remaining employees nourished, but guys like Andy and Paul usually didn't get the good stuff. Spam on rye was a typical lunch at the technician and security grunt level.

But at least they were getting food. That was all the payment they received, but it beat the shit out of the alternative.

Andy bent over and grabbed Alice-85's ankles, then waited for Paul to get a grip on her shoulders before straightening. He said, "Besides, I know the real reason— you get queasy walking backward."

"Hardy har har." Paul lifted her by the shoulders. "This one feels lighter."

Andy started backpedaling down the corridor toward the glass doors. "Half her chest was blown off. It's a great dieting program."

"Got her tits, too." Paul's leer wasn't visible, but Andy could practically hear it. "Probably lose a lotta weight there."

"Not with her tits," Andy said with a chuckle. "Dolly Parton she ain't."

"Yeah, I know—I trained with the real one, remember? Still, there's fat there, right?"

"Yah."

The two of them made it to the doors, which opened at their approach. The city view remained visible on the glass even as they parted—behind them was the the metal platform in the tube that led to the surface.

As Andy backed onto the platform, he shuddered, the same way he always did when they went topside.

Once they were in, Paul stepped on a big red button on the floor, resulting in the pneumatic hiss of the hydraulics that lifted the platform up out of the underground complex that had become home and work and refuge for Andy, Paul, Brendan, Dr. Isaacs, and a few dozen other employees of the Umbrella Corporation who had survived the apocalypse.

When he was a kid, Andy's mother had told him about what life was like in the 1950s during the early days of the Cold War between the United States and the Soviet Union, how they'd have drills to practice what to do in case of a nuclear attack. Those drills supposedly involved curling up under one's school desk, which left his mother with the impression until she was eighteen that wood was proof against nuclear fallout.

For so long, people assumed that when the world ended, it would be because somebody dropped the Bomb. Half the science-fiction stories that Andy had read or watched on television as a kid predicted a postapocalyptic future where some superpower or other dropped a bomb on their enemies, leaving only a few humans to keep the planet going.

As the hydraulic lift brought Andy, Paul, and the corpse of Alice-85 to the surface of Death Valley, Andy wondered if they would've been better off with bombs instead of *this*.

And didn't it just figure that Umbrella's super-secret underground base was located in Death Valley?

With a creaking sound, hidden doors parted in the floor of the weather station above to allow the platform to come to a halt on a level with the weather station's floor.

Located in the heart of the Death Valley salt flats, the station was built around the same time that Andy's mother had been hiding under her desk to stay safe from the bomb, and it hadn't been upgraded in almost that long. A tube filled with mercury indicated the temperature, a method of determining heat that Andy thought had gone out with cassette tapes. The equipment on the walls and cheap Formica tables still had dials on them, for crying out loud.

But it wasn't as if anybody needed to know the weather—especially here. It was the desert. It was dry, and it was hot.

Once the platform settled into place, Andy started backpedaling toward the open door. The Hazmat suit had its own temperature regulation, for which Andy was grateful, as the shift from the air-conditioned Umbrella complex to the great outdoors of the California desert was a transition Andy wouldn't normally be eager to make.

Stepping outside, Andy deliberately looked down at the sandy ground outside the weather station. He didn't want to see what lay beyond, he just wanted to dump the body and get back downstairs where it was safe.

"On three," Paul said. Before Andy could say anything, he added, "And if you ask me if it's one, two, three, and then go or go on three, I *will* punch you."

Realizing he was getting predictable in his old age, Andy just muttered, "People have *no* respect for the classics."

"I respect the classics. I don't respect you beating them into the ground."

Andy chuckled, grateful to the security guard for taking his mind off what they were doing and where they were doing it.

In unison, the pair of them started to swing the body. "And a one," Paul said, "and a two, and a *three!*"

On three, they tossed the body to the left into the big trench.

Without even thinking about it, Andy looked up.

What he saw, as usual, made his most recent meal well up into the back of his throat, and he almost doubled over from the nausea.

His immediate field of vision was the big trench into which they'd thrown Alice-85. The trench was lined with lime and filled with the remains not only of Alice-85 but of the previous eighty-four Alices as well. Eighty-four identical, red-dress-wearing corpses. Well, eighty-two, really. The one that had been diced by the laser grid was just an undistinguished pile of meat chunks. And then there was Alice-9, who, for reasons no one had been able to figure out, just went crazy in the bathroom right after she woke up and dashed her brains out against the bathroom wall before she ever even got dressed, so her corpse had remained nude.

That wasn't what made Andy want to lose his breakfast, however. He'd become inured to the multiple identical corpses. He suspected that if he ever met the real Alice Abernathy—"Ass-Kicking Alice," as Paul referred to her—he'd expect her to wander around mutely until something killed her, too.

No, it was what lay beyond the trench.

The weather station was surrounded by a fifteen-foot-high perimeter fence that was topped with razor wire. Pushing against it were literally thousands of corpses that had been animated by the T-virus.

Andy preferred to think of them as animated corpses.

Calling them zombies just brought to mind bad horror movies and also made it hard to take them seriously.

They all had learned the hard way to take these things seriously.

Once the fence had been electrified, but that proved to be more trouble than it was worth. The corpses were constantly shambling right into the fence, which meant that the current was nearly constant and not doing any good. Electrified fences generally were meant as a deterrent rather than a physical means of restraint. The subject would be shocked once and know better than to try again. But animated corpses didn't even have as much reasoning ability as your average wild animal, and so no matter how much you shocked them, they didn't die (being already dead), and didn't learn any better. So Isaacs killed the juice on the fence. As long as they couldn't get through— and they hadn't shown any signs of being able to do so yet—they were safe.

"Where the fuck did they come from?" Paul suddenly asked.

Andy turned to look at him, which was a relief, since even his Hazmat-suit-obscured features were an improvement on the hordes of corpses. "What do you mean?"

"We're in the middle of the fucking desert. What, these people wandered over from Vegas?"

"Tell you what, Paul, I'll see if Isaacs wants to run a study of zombie migratory patterns, okay?"

That got a laugh, and Paul said, "C'mon, let's get back downstairs."

"No problem," Andy said emphatically, turning back

toward the weather station. "God, I just wish we could get the original back. Dumping clones is starting to get a little tiresome."

"Fat chance," Paul said. "You don't know Ass-Kicking Alice. Isaacs couldn't keep her if he tried. In fact, he didn't try."

"I thought he had her in Detroit."

Paul smiled. "Not for long. Shit, he didn't even try to keep her in San Francisco."

Andy shook his head as they reentered the weather station and walked onto the platform. Paul stepped on the red button again. "I just don't see what we're accomplishing at this point. The results are always the same. Sure, she doesn't always die in the same spot in the Labyrinth, but she always dies eventually, and the blood work's all within expected norms."

Paul shrugged. "Long as it keeps us safe down here instead of out there, I don't give a shit what you guys do."

At that, Andy sighed. "Amen."

†HREE

BEFORE

Dr. Sam Isaacs stood in awe.

It had been three weeks since the Umbrella Corporation had destroyed Raccoon City with a tactical nuclear missile. The news media had been awash with reports, initially of some kind of virus that had spread through the city prior to its destruction, then of a catastrophic nuclear power-plant meltdown.

As ever, Isaacs was impressed with his employer's ability to manipulate the truth.

That, however, was not why Isaacs stood in awe.

Only a small handful of people got out of Raccoon alive. To Isaacs's great glee, his supervisor, Major Timothy Cain, was not one of them, but Alice Abernathy was.

She almost wasn't. When they found her in the wreckage of a C89 helicopter, she appeared to be one of two corpses, the other being Ian Montgomery, the copter's pilot. Montgomery had reported four other passengers—three adults and one little girl—but of them there was no sign.

Alice herself had been impaled by a large slice of metal. She should have been dead.

Now, three weeks later, she sat suspended in a tube filled with a nutrient bath, a breathing apparatus covering her nose and mouth.

And according to Dr. Kayanan, she was about to wake up.

"She's taking almost no nutrients from the system," Kayanan was saying, amazement in her brown eyes. "The regen seems almost spontaneous. It's like she's sucking energy out of thin air."

Isaacs turned to look at the monitors in front of Kayanan's workstation. Not only was her EEG almost normal, but her metabolism was actually hypernormal. Considering that she was little more than a corpse three weeks ago . . .

He walked over to the tube. Alice's blue eyes sprang open just as he approached.

"Can you hear me?" Isaacs asked.

After a moment, the blond head nodded yes.

"Good."

Now was the moment of truth. If past history was any indication, Alice would not take well to being studied, especially if she actually retained any memory of what had happened. But if she *didn't* recall what had happened, the possibilities were simply endless.

However, there was really only one way to find out.

Turning toward Cole, Isaacs said, "Begin the purging process."

Nodding, Cole started the sequence that drained the nutrient bath from the tank. Alice looked around as it happened, confused, not sure what was going on.

Once the liquid was purged, the front of the tank opened like a flap, bringing Alice into a prone position on the floor. Lang, one of the security people, handed Isaacs a lab coat, and he offered it to her. She wrapped it around her shivering naked form.

"Her recovery is remarkable," Kayanan was saying, "and her powers—both physical and mental, are developing at a geometric rate."

Isaacs did not acknowledge Kayanan—he'd read her reports, after all—but instead sat next to Alice, brushing wet blond hair out of her face and gently holding her hand. It was cool from the nutrient bath, but he could feel a vibrant warmth beneath. Alice shivered to the point of convulsion and kept looking around. Her mouth kept trying to form a word but couldn't get past a *wh* sound.

Assuming it was the beginning of "where," Isaacs asked on her behalf, "Where are you?" He stood up, trying to guide her to rise as well. "You're safe. Come on."

She got up slowly and stumbled once—she hadn't been on her feet in three weeks, after all, and possibly didn't remember *how* to stand. He guided her over against a pillar so she had something to lean on.

"That's it—there we are."

Alice's blue eyes looked lost. Isaacs had only seen

so blank an expression on newborns and animals before. It seemed as if she remembered nothing, which worked very much in Isaacs's favor.

Next to them, Doyle was looking at the readings on the nearby monitor and checking off items on a list on a clipboard. Alice started staring at Doyle's hands in fascination. Isaacs grabbed the clipboard and the pen and showed them to her.

"Do you know what that is?" He spoke slowly, as if to a child. "It's a pen." He started writing on the checklist to demonstrate the instrument's function. "See? You try."

He handed her the pen while holding the clipboard up toward her. She gripped the pen as if it were a dagger and started drawing squiggly lines all over the checklist.

"P—" Again, she could handle only the first sound of the word. "P—"

"Pen," he prompted.

"P—pen."

Just like a small child. Almost a tabula rasa.

But still, he needed to be sure. More tests had to be run.

First, the basics.

He took the pen away and handed it and the clipboard back to a nonplussed Doyle. Then he grabbed Alice's wet head and said, "Look at me."

She stared at him with baffled blue eyes.

"Can you remember anything? Hm? Do you remember your name?"

Blank stare. Glancing around furtively, as if trying to figure out what was wrong.

Sam Isaacs had met Alice Abernathy only a few times before the Hive incident, but while the person in front of him had the same facial features, it wasn't she. "Ass-Kicking Alice," as the cruder Security Division personnel had taken to calling her, was always in control of whatever situation she was in. Her sharp eyes missed nothing, and her body was like a coiled spring.

The wet, confused woman standing in front of Isaacs right now was barely in control of her own twitchy movements, her dull eyes weren't catching anything, and her body was like a wet rag.

"My name . . . my name . . ."

She was repeating the words, not entirely sure what they might mean.

Isaacs let go of her and walked toward Kayanan and Cole's workstations. He almost skipped, he was so giddy. He'd been living a nightmare for months, ever since that jackass Cain had been put in charge of his research. The Nemesis Project had been compromised beyond all recognition, the T-virus had gotten loose first in the Hive and then in Raccoon, the city had been destroyed, and Isaacs's best hope for Nemesis—not to mention that nascent Tyrant Program—had been impaled by a piece of metal.

"My name . . ."

But she'd recovered. Finally, he could move forward!

"I want her under twenty-four-hour observation. I want a complete set of blood work and chemical and electrolyte analysis by the end of the day."

"My name . . ."

"Sir—" Cole started.

Ignoring him—he couldn't possibly have anything of interest to say—Isaacs went on: "Advanced reflex testing is also a priority."

"My name . . ."

"I want her electrical impulses monito—"

"Sir!" Cole said more forcefully.

Sighing, Isaacs asked, "What is it?"

"My name—"

Isaacs whirled around. The previous times, she'd been muttering those two words almost as if they were a befuddled mantra.

This time, though, she spoke with a deeper, more resonant tone.

The tone of the head of security for the Hive.

"—is Alice." She flashed a smirk at Isaacs. "And I remember *everything*."

Isaacs quickly realized that Plan A wasn't an option.

Moving faster than any human should have been able to move, Alice grabbed Doyle's pen and stabbed him in the eye with it.

No! Though her arm's momentum had to be incredible, given the speed alone with which she moved it, she was able to stop the pen before it struck Doyle's eye.

Isaacs found he was almost giddy over the prospect of what he could do with her. His disappointment at her memory returning was ameliorated by his own foresight.

Alice then elbowed Doyle, knocking him to the floor.

After that, Isaacs could barely follow what happened. She took out one, maybe two more people, and then, before he could react, she grabbed Isaacs by the arm.

Then she flexed her wrist.

Isaacs had always thought stars forming in one's eyes from incredible pain was a fanciful creation of cartoon animators. Having his arm broken with but a flick of the wrist cured him of this misapprehension in short order. Glass cut into his hands and face as the tank shattered, and he fell to the floor covered in blood and glass.

With knives of pain slicing through his shoulder and arm, Isaacs blinked back tears and tried to focus on what was going on.

Cole and Kayanan had left. Doyle was still on the floor, as were Stolovitzky and Bruner. Lang had whipped out his taser and fired it at Alice. It struck her right in the shoulder.

The taser glowed with an electrical charge that would have sent a normal person to the floor, twitching. Alice didn't move—or even blink—as hundreds of amps shot through her body. She just looked at the sharp end of the taser, ripped it out of her shoulder, rending flesh but with no more effort than she would swat a fly, and then reared and threw the taser right back at Lang.

It had somewhat more of an effect on the security guard, who screamed as he fell to the floor.

And then she walked out.

Isaacs tried to focus past the pain. It wasn't easy, but he had a very important task to perform. He knew he wouldn't be able to hold Alice if she remembered who she was, so he had to do the next best thing: Let her *think* she was free.

It was the same principle that applied to animals. Why try to keep them trapped in enclosures when you could let them run free and keep track of them in the wild?

The advantage of working for the Umbrella Corporation was that one didn't have to rely on something so crude as a tag in the ear.

Looking up at the security monitors, Isaacs saw that Alice had not only made it outside but was now in an SUV, alongside several other people dressed as personnel from Umbrella's Security Division. Isaacs recognized three of them instantly. One was Angie Ashford, the daughter of Dr. Charles Ashford, one of Umbrella's top scientists and another casualty of Raccoon City. The other two were probably recognizable the world over as the fugitives who were allegedly responsible for the "false video" of strange, diseased people shambling through the streets of Raccoon City infecting the populace: Carlos Olivera, a former member of Security Division, and Jill Valentine, a former RCPD cop in their elite S.T.A.R.S. section.

With his good arm, he reached into his lab-coat pocket, took out his phone, and signaled the front gate.

Under other circumstances, Isaacs would have ordered security to stop them.

Instead, he said only three words: "Let them go."

After the guard disconnected, Isaacs switched his phone over to interface with the mainframe and said three more words: "Program Alice activated."

It would have been better if she had remained amnesiac, but Isaacs had known from the beginning that there was a better than even chance that she'd remember it all. After all, her mind worked better, faster than any human's. Unlike the other success the Nemesis Project had—Matthew Addison, who'd been mutated by the T-virus into a killing machine—Alice hadn't been changed by the T-virus. She'd changed *it*.

But he'd never be able to hold her as long as she still carried her tiresome animus for her former employer. Unlike the late Major Cain, Isaacs actually planned for every eventuality and didn't just let chaos reign and hope he could rein it in later.

A doctor came running in. "Are you all right?" she asked Isaacs rather stupidly.

Isaacs didn't dignify that with a response but instead allowed her to help him to his feet and bring him to the infirmary. As she led him off, he said to Cole, "We'll need to purge this base, relocate to the Detroit facility." They had gone to San Francisco more because of its proximity to what was once Racooon City than anything, but the Detroit facility had better tracking equipment and was also the nerve center for directing Umbrella's massive network of satellites.

He'd need them to keep track of Alice.

And eventually to bring her home.

FOUR
AFTER

In 1956, Congress passed the Federal-Aid Highway Act, a pet project of President Dwight D. Eisenhower. The act was designed to create a national system of highways that would make road travel throughout the United States faster and more efficient.

Traditionalists, of course, decried the notion, as traditionalists always will do. Allowing travelers to stay on lengthy stretches of highway meant they could, as John Steinbeck put it, "drive from New York to California without seeing a single thing." Route 66, famed in song and story as the road across America, became, if not obsolete, at the very least reduced in significance in a world that valued speed. Why have a long, dragged-out trip through the small towns of Kansas when you could zip through it at eighty miles an hour (sure, the speed limit was reduced to fifty-five during the gas crisis of the 1970s, but the cops don't even give you a second look until you approach triple digits) to get where you're going faster? Besides, they had to compete with airplanes, which really *could* take you from New York to California without seeing a single thing save a few clouds.

The main parts of the interstates were highways numbered with two digits according to direction and location. Odd-numbered highways ran north-south; even-numbered were east-west. The numbers increased as you went either north or east. I-5 intersected with I-90 in the Pacific Northwest and with I-10 in San Diego. I-95 crossed I-10 in Florida and I-90 in Boston.

Arguably the best-traveled interstates were the two longest: I-80, which went from New York to San Francisco, and I-70, going from Baltimore to Cove Fort, Utah.

Because part of the 1956 act's mandate was that the interstates go through all major U.S. cities, including through their downtown areas, there was an explosion in suburban populations. Suddenly, you didn't have to live in the city to work in the city, and towns outside cities became cities in their own right.

Of course, not every city developed in that way.

Take Salt Lake City, Utah. The capital of the desert state, it stood virtually alone. If someone drove west on I-80 through Utah, there was nothing until you reached the interchange with I-215, and then, all of a sudden, you were in a city, just like that.

Which was why Alice Abernathy was surprised, as she rode her BMW K1200 west on 80, to see a sign reading SALT LAKE CITY—CITY LIMITS. She'd been riding on the highway for quite some time, with very little signs of life. She hadn't realized she was so close to the city.

Then again, the whole world had very few signs of life these days.

The BMW was simply her latest ride. She'd had a chopper, but it washed out during a run-in with some undead back in Ohio. Alice had, of course, taken care of them, but it left her without a vehicle. She had had to walk from Youngstown to the Cleveland suburbs (she avoided going near Columbus; that was her hometown, and to see it now would be just too painful) before she found the BMW, left on the side of the road, its former owner decapitated and decomposing. Alice had seen no signs of the head, but the body was covered in bite marks, so it probably had been made undead and then killed by beheading.

Whoever he was, he had good taste in bikes. The K1200 was the biggest, most powerful road bike in production.

Until they stopped producing road bikes.

Or much of anything else.

Alice had made it all the way across the country on the BMW, scavenging supplies where she could. She had half a dozen saddlebags and gas cans—though the latter were mostly empty now—along with a radio receiver, all of which rattled about on the side of the bike as she weaved around abandoned, rusted cars and trucks.

As she approached the exit for Foothill Drive, she

found what she was looking for: the KLKB building.

Alice could see, as she got off the highway and headed toward the local independent TV station's parking lot, that the patch of overgrown grass and flowers in front of the building once was a well-mowed lawn, with the flowers arranged to spell out the station's call letters. Desert sand choked the flowers and the sprinkler system, making the entire patch look like something a kid had started on the beach and then abandoned by halfheartedly kicking sand over onto it.

Alice drove around three cars that were in various states of disrepair—and at different angles to the pavement—and parked the BMW near the station's front door.

Reaching up, she pulled the bandana down from her face. She didn't bother with a helmet. Ever since that bastard Isaacs had experimented on her after the Hive disaster, every wound, every injury, healed almost instantly. There was nothing a helmet could protect her from. She only wore the bandana because getting dirt, sand, and bugs in her mouth was irritating.

Reaching into the pocket of the duster that she'd taken off an undead she'd killed in Joliet (she'd gotten a pair of sunglasses from him, too, but they'd been broken in Cheyenne), she pulled out the digital memory stick she'd liberated from Umbrella's Detroit facility and put its earpiece in her left ear.

It played the file she'd downloaded from the radio receiver—another "gift" from her brief time in Detroit—yesterday when she'd left Cheyenne.

The voice she heard was that of a woman, one who

sounded desperate. Alice recognized the tone fairly easily. Most people had it these days.

"This is KLKB, transmitting on the emergency frequency. Can anyone hear us? We have seven people here in need of urgent medical attention. We've taken refuge in the TV station at the edge of town. We're surrounded, and we need help. Can anyone hear us? Can anyone help us? Please!"

Alice switched it off.

Then she looked around.

The woman had said they were surrounded, but Alice saw no evidence of the undead in the vicinity. Thanks to Isaacs—whom she intended to flense if she ever saw him again—she had a sensitivity to the T-virus, and she had only a faint whiff of it here. That could mean that the undead had come and gone or that they'd been killed.

Or that they were hiding.

Of course, it was possible that in the twenty or so hours since Alice first picked up this transmission, the undead who'd surrounded them had stopped surrounding and started feeding and then moved on to greener pastures.

She inspected the station visually. All of the windows and doors were boarded up, those boards riddled with bullet holes. Whoever was in there, if anyone was in there, probably felt they were under siege.

But then, a siege mentality was one of the few tenable strategies these days. And even a tenable strategy had only a fifty-fifty chance of succeeding.

Alice headed to the front door, knocking both door

and nailed-on boards down with one well-placed kick to the door's center. With a loud crack, the wood splintered at the impact of her boots, backed up by her T-virus-enhanced strength.

Inside was an empty reception area. Her noisy entrance drew nobody out. The desk was still intact, although it was covered in blood—some of which had been used to clumsily draw various religious symbols. Looking around, she saw that those same symbols—only a few of which Alice recognized—covered the walls as well, obscuring the posters advertising the station's programming. She'd been a lifelong agnostic before; the advent of the T-virus made it clear to her that if there was a supreme deity, he was an evil bastard who didn't deserve to be worshipped. More likely, to Alice's mind, there were no gods, just people.

And damn, but the people had fucked things up.

A whimpering sound caught her ear, and she moved slowly into the next room, pulling out her sawed-off twelve-gauge.

That next room was a studio, the set decorations scattered and shattered, with traces of dried blood everywhere, as well as more of the quasi-religious symbols sloppily drawn in blood on the walls and the equipment. Alice stepped over a battered, tipped-over camera as she moved to the corner of the studio where the whimpering noise was coming from.

"My baby—my poor baby."

Alice recognized the voice as the same one she'd picked up over the radio in Cheyenne.

"Please."

The woman was curled up in the corner of the studio, cradling a dirty blanket in her arms. Presumably, the baby she was muttering about was swaddled in that rather sad bundle. She looked up at Alice, tears streaming down a dirty face, and held out the bundle.

"Please help my baby."

Her shotgun still in one hand, Alice reached out with the other to take the bundle. It felt like a dead weight, and Alice feared that the baby was a corpse.

With a shudder, she wondered what would happen if the baby was infected. She'd seen plenty of small children who became undead, starting with the kids at Angie's school back in Raccoon, but never an infant, at least not yet.

Angie . . .

Shaking off those unpleasant thoughts, Alice pulled back the blanket to reveal a dead face.

Mostly because it was made of plastic. She'd been handed a doll.

Before she could start to formulate a response to this crazy woman, she looked up to see that the woman had a shotgun.

Alice dropped the doll to the floor and started to raise her own shotgun before she realized that they weren't alone.

Without even looking, she knew that there were five other people surrounding her, all armed, all with their assorted weaponry pointed right at Alice. Based on the clicks, they were all cocked and ready to shoot.

"You bitch," the woman said with a nasty smile. "You dropped my baby."

"Yet now you stop crying." Alice shook her head. "Must be getting old—should've seen this coming."

"Yeah, you really should've. Murph?"

One of the men, whose face was pockmarked, lowered his pistol and walked over, holding a half-rusted pair of handcuffs. "My pleasure."

He grabbed Alice and whipped her arms around. "You've done this before," Alice said calmly.

"Used t'be a state trooper. Till they fired me, anyhow. Said I was poorly socialized. Least, I think that's what they said—don't remember much, on account of I wasn't listenin'. That was my other problem—I don't listen too good." Once he slipped the cuffs on, he slammed her over what Alice figured was a news desk. "You're the prettiest fish we caught in a while."

That confirmed what Alice suspected as soon as the trap was sprung. This was standard operating procedure for these people. She wondered what they did with their "fish." She also figured she'd get the answer in fairly short order.

As if to confirm, the woman put on the same tone she'd used over the radio. "We're surrounded. We need help. Can anyone hear us? Can anyone help us? Please!"

They all got a good laugh at that. All except for another of the men, a short one who also looked to be the youngest of the bunch. He was checking out Alice's twelve-gauge, as well as her other weapons.

"Look at these," the kid was saying.

Murph walked over to take a closer look at the twelve-gauge. "This fish is packing."

A big man came over. Alice's eyes widened as she saw the two Kukri blades in the large man's hands. She'd seen the Nepalese knives only once before, as part of the collection belonging to one of Umbrella's security higher-ups, who went by the code name of One. One had been killed during the Hive mess, diced by the laser grid protecting the Red Queen computer, and his collection presumably was destroyed along with the rest of Raccoon City.

Now these scavengers had themselves a pair. Alice wondered if they belonged to one of them or if they'd taken them off a previous "fish."

Either way, she was looking forward to adding them to her arsenal once she killed these people.

Because she fully intended to kill every one of them. While she had walked into the KLKB station fully intending to rescue whoever was trapped inside from the undead, now that she knew she'd been set up, Alice had marked every single one of them. Not just for fooling her but for distracting her from her real work.

Alice was responsible for what had happened to the world.

True, technically, it wasn't her fault. Technically, it was Spence who let the T-virus loose in the Hive in order to cover his tracks while he stole the virus to sell to the highest bidder on the international market.

But Alice had been partnered with Spence. They'd been assigned to run security at the mansion, which served as the primary access point to the Hive. Not only had they been working together, they'd been sleeping together. Alice originally had trained with the Treasury Department, intending to be part of the Secret Service, before the institutionalized sexism of Treasury drove her to Umbrella, and part of that training was to be able to observe people and events. She *had* worked out that Lisa Broward, who ran security for Umbrella's computer system, was working to bring Umbrella down and had worked to recruit her to join Alice's own efforts to bring Umbrella down.

However, she missed Spence completely.

And that nagged at her. If she had just figured out what Spence was up to and stopped him, most of the world's population still might be alive today.

So she was determined to do what she could to help the few people who were left.

Or, at least, those who deserved it. These fuckers didn't qualify, as far as Alice was concerned.

The big man held up one of the Kukris. "Let's see what else she's packing."

He put the tip of the blade under Alice's duster.

Looking the big man straight in the eye, Alice said, "I wouldn't do that."

That got her a slap across the face. "Shut your mouth!"

It barely stung, and Alice hardly moved from the pathetic impact. If she weren't manacled, she could've taken these fuckers down back when she was just a Treasury agent, much less now.

She was definitely going to enjoy killing these people. Bad enough that there were so few people left, but they had to lure others for—what? Their sport?

The others seemed to think that the slap meant something, though. "That's it, Eddie!" one of them cried. "You show her!"

"You show the bitch," the woman with the baby added.

Eddie smiled and once again positioned the Kukri to slice open Alice's duster.

Before he could start to do so, Alice reared one foot back and brought it up with a powerful kick right to Eddie's nose.

The woman ran toward him as he fell to the ground. "Eddie! Eddie!"

She knelt down next to Eddie, felt his neck, then looked up, giving Alice a murderous expression. "Jesus Christ, he's *dead*."

Alice shrugged as best she could while handcuffed. "I warned him."

At that, the woman raised her own shotgun. "You fucking *bitch!*"

"Hey!" Murph said. "None'a that, Margie. We do this same way we always do." Murph smiled then. "And this time it'll be *fun*."

Margie nodded, lowering the shotgun. "You're right, Murph. Bitch probably did that so we'd shoot her. Put her outta her misery quick-like. But she ain't that lucky."

That got a snort from Alice. She did it because she wanted Eddie dead. Period.

Murph grabbed her arm and started leading her to another room. "Let's go, pretty fish. We gonna have us a
show, boys 'n' girls!"

Chris Murphy was gonna *enjoy* this.

The world had gone into the toilet, yeah, but hell
with that, he was having *fun*. Lot more fun than he'd
been having since before it all ended, that was for *damn*
sure.

Murph's daddy had been a state trooper, and his
granddaddy before him, and his great-granddaddy before
him. Where Murph grew up, it was like that Springsteen
song, they bring you up to do what your daddy done, so
Murph—who used to like Springsteen's music until he
got all political—applied to be a trooper when he turned
eighteen.

At first it was fine. Murph wasn't all that great at paperwork on account of he couldn't spell all that good, but
neither could any of the other deputies, so he didn't fuss
over that.

But the sheriff, he fussed right good over the fights.
They weren't nothing at first—just the usual brawls that
happen when folks get into disagreements—but for some
reason, Murph was singled out. Just 'cause that damn
fool whose leg he broke turned out to be the mayor's
kid—that wasn't hardly Murph's fault. Ain't like the little twerp was goin' around with a sign on his chest
sayin', "I'm the mayor's dumb kid." If he had, Murph
probably wouldn't've popped him one for talkin' trash
about Richard Petty.

Or maybe Murph would've anyhow. Didn't nobody make fun of Richard Petty in his presence. Just wasn't done.

Murph hadn't been a trooper long enough to get a pension worth a damn, and he didn't have no skills that nobody could use. His wife hit the road pretty much the minute he turned in his badge and gun. He moved to the city, figuring there'd be jobs in Indianapolis you couldn't get out in Carroll County, moving into some flea trap and taking jobs as a bouncer at a strip club. That worked out fine till one of the girls charged him with sexual harassment. Murph thought she was crazy, since all he was doin' was appreciatin' her finer qualities, but didn't nobody believe him.

So he strangled the little whore and left Indiana for good.

Eventually, he wound up in Montana, and there he met up with some right-thinking folks who saw that the world was going into the toilet 'cause of those big companies messin' with the world. Their leader was a fella named Raymond. Murph had never gone for that pinko Greenpeace stuff, but this Raymond guy made sense, and he invited Murph to his bunker, so they'd be ready for when the world ended.

Then the plague happened.

Murph had never seen nothin' like it. People'd get sick and die and then just get back up again and start eatin' people. They took down Raymond, and Murph got the hell outta Montana before they took him, too. A bunch of Raymond's people came with, and they wandered around, trying to stay alive, until they met up with Eddie.

Eddie was strong and smart. He knew the only way to survive in this new world was to take what you wanted. Salt Lake City was a ghost town after the plague wiped it out, so Eddie set up shop in an old TV station. Margie was real good at sounding all hysterical and stuff, so she'd get on the radio and call for help, and sure enough, some nutbar like this pretty lady would come to "help." Murph had always liked Margie, going back to Montana, and she'd even let him bone her a few times, which was very neighborly. Weren't much by way of companionship these days, and you couldn't be fussy.

Not that Murph ever had been. He'd bone anything with tits, even when he was married.

Folks who were still alive and inclined to give aid to strangers these days were usually well stocked with food and medical supplies and the like, so the scam'd been workin' pretty good, even nowadays with so many people gone.

Murph didn't care, though. Only thing he missed was NASCAR. He'd seen on TV—back when TV was still running—that the entire Petty family'd been taken down by the plague. It was a sight that would haunt Murph's nightmares till the day he died, seeing his hero brought low like that. It was a real shame.

And now he missed Eddie. He was the leader, same as Raymond was back in Montana, same as the sheriff was back in Indiana. Murph had lost all of them, and he was still kickin', so maybe he didn't need people like that. In fact, maybe he'd be takin' over this little to-do now that Eddie was dead.

But that was for later. For now, he got to have *fun*. He grabbed the blond fish and dragged her to the next room, then threw her headfirst down the hole.

The hole'd already been there when Eddie and the rest of them took over the studio, and since it led to the basement, it was the ideal place for the main events.

Spiff, the kid, bent over and called down the hole, "Think you're pretty smart? Well, you'll see—you'll see!"

From up here, Murph could barely make the fish out. Only light down there came from topside through the hole. Made it more dramatic-like, Eddie'd said. Murph decided that when he took over, he'd make the hole bigger. It was more fun to see the whole thing. Electrical wires hung around near her, dangling from the ceiling. Murph figured that whoever was in the station before Eddie set up here had taken a bunch of the equipment and the fixtures with 'em, leaving a lot of loose wires hanging around. Luckily, there wasn't no power to any of 'em.

The fish looked around, and she saw the bones of her predecessors. Usually that was when they got all freaked out, but this fish was a cool customer. She just stared at the human remains for a second, like she saw skeletons every day (and who knew, maybe she did), and then looked around some more. Murph supposed that shouldn't've been all that surprising, since she was cold as ice when she killed Eddie.

But he figured that'd just make for a better show.

Margie walked up to the edge of the pit and dropped down the keys to the cuffs, which Eddie thought was overdoing it a little. "There you go, bitch," Margie said as the keys hit the floor with a jangle. "Wouldn't want it to be over too fast."

Murph was about to object but then conceded the point. Besides, if this woman could do what she did to Eddie while tied up, she'd probably put up a good fight, and it'd be better if she had full use of her hands.

The fish started crabwalking backward toward the keys. She moved pretty good for a lady all handcuffed. Usually—and Murph had experience in this regard—folks could barely stand up right, much less move, once their hands were behind their backs. It was why hand-cuffs was so effective that nobody'd ever changed how you manacled prisoners since back to Roman times, that's what Daddy'd always said. Murph didn't know if Daddy was right—somehow, Murph couldn't picture Roman soldiers in their sissy skirts and brushy-top hel-mets actually cuffing some guy in a toga—but he defi-nitely believed in the power of the handcuff.

With a clanging sound, the fish backed up against what she probably thought was a wall. Murph smiled. He loved this part.

A snarling face with a bloody snout rammed into the cage, startling the fish. She backed away right quick.

Murph muttered, "Was startin' to wonder if *any-thing'd* spook her."

"Don't worry," Margie said. "She'll be spooked enough in a minute."

"Damn right." He looked over to Spiff and Avi. "Let 'em loose!"

The pair started pulling on the ropes that were attached by pulleys to the gates that kept the pooches in check.

With a whining sound, the rusty metal gates opened, and Murph heard the sound that never failed to give him a thrill: the clacking of sharp paws on concrete.

When they first got here, Eddie had five of the pooches. They were like the plague-ridden people, except they moved a lot faster, and they were, y'know, dogs. One of 'em died three months back when one of the fishes managed to snap its neck. That was the same fish who busted Avi's leg, and Avi'd been limping something fierce ever since.

Murph had no idea how Eddie'd managed to capture the pooches, but he did, and they'd been the source of entertainment for all of them for goin' on a year now. Watchin' them chew up the fishes was almost as much fun as NASCAR.

The four that were left looked like hell, but that just made it more fun. The first one that came out was showin' its entire rib cage, and its teeth were half broken and also covered in blood. At the right angle, you could see clean through its body, though the intestines got in the way of the full view.

Next one to come out was even bigger, and missin' more skin, but that didn't stop it from clickity-clacking on the concrete toward the fish, who was scrambling with the keys Margie'd thrown down and stepping on bones with her boots.

"That's it!" Margie cried. "Fuck her up!"

And then the fish went crazy.

The handcuffs clattered on the ground, and the fish got up and started doing some *serious* kung-fu fighting. The pooches leapt right at her all at once, and she jumped out of the way, runnin' along the walls, looking like Spider-Man or somethin'. She did her some backflips, some side jumps, she even swung around the support beams like the dancers used to at the strip joint.

With snarls and barks, the pooches kept jumpin' and leapin', but they couldn't get her. At one point, two of 'em came at her from opposite sides, and she went and ducked at the last minute. The two pooches collided headfirst and went to the floor, whimpering all sorry-like.

But they kept getting closer each time. Murph bet that the fish could feel the pooches' hot breath on her pretty face, and sooner or later they'd get her.

Spiff had come over from the ropes and was watching alongside Margie and Murph and the rest of them. "The fuck she doin' with them cables?"

Murph hadn't noticed anything about the cables; he was just enjoying himself. Nobody'd lasted this long without getting bit, not even the big guy who broke Avi's leg.

Heck, this fish might be better than NASCAR.

And then Murph realized what Spiff was talkin' about. The way she was jumpin' around reminded him of the girls in the club for a reason. Back then, he'd taken the job 'cause he thought he'd get to see nekkid girls for free. But the novelty wore right off, 'cause they was all doin' the exact same routine around the pole like fifty times a night. Got borin'.

This fish was also doin' the same thing over and over with the support pillars and the pooches, and once Spiff started yappin' about the cables, Murph figured it out.

She was tyin' them *to* the cables, like they was on leashes in some backyard.

Them pooches started yowlin' somethin' fierce, tuggin' at the cables, but they wasn't goin' nowhere.

Murph frowned. Somethin' was wrong.

The fish leaned against a wall, breathing a sigh of relief.

Margie grinned. "Get her now, get her *now*."

Then it finally hit Murph: only three of them were tied up. The other pooch was lurkin'.

Definitely as good as NASCAR.

Out of nowhere, the last pooch leapt at the fish's back.

A thrill of excitement ran through Murph. This always happened right before the big moment. He'd felt it when he beat up the mayor's kid, when he strangled that stripper, and every time the pooches got first blood.

Except this one didn't.

At the last second, faster than Murph had ever seen a human being move, the fish whirled around and slammed the heel of her hand into the pooch's head. It fell to the ground, and it didn't move.

It was dead for real now.

Damn.

Now they had only three. And they was all tied up.

Murph found himself torn between excitement at watching this all happen and worry about what they was gonna do next. This fish had already lasted longer than anyone else had in the pit, and she'd tied up three pooches and killed the other one.

"We may have to shoot her," Margie said, like she was readin' his mind.

Reluctantly, Murph nodded. Heck, he might've asked her to join 'em—she'd be great at luring folks here, he bet—but after her killing Eddie, he doubted the others'd go for it. He wasn't sure he was too keen on the idea, neither, but damn—she was somethin'.

Then the ground shuddered.

"What the fuck?" Murph blurted without thinking. Then he put his hand to his mouth.

Aw, hell, this was disastrous.

About two years back, when everything went to the toilet, Murph made a promise to the Lord. He knew he was a sinner and that he was goin' straight to hell when he died—for the stripper, if nothin' else—but for whatever reason, the Lord had seen fit to let Murph live. In gratitude, Murph had promised Him to go the rest of his days without cussin'. He figured it was the least he could do.

But when the ground shook like that, he spoke without thinkin' and cussed for the first time since he got to Utah.

The ground shook again, and he looked down to

see that the pooches were pulling against the support pillars—and them pillars, they was *movin'!*

Murph cried, "Get back, get *back!*"

Then the floor gave way under him. He jumped up, trying to grab at something, anything, that would keep him from falling down into the pit. His meaty fingers managed to curl around a lighting fixture that was hanging from the ceiling. Clutching it for dear life, he looked frantically around, his feet dangling in midair, and then pushed himself off the light to a solid piece of ground a few feet from where he'd been standing.

He looked around. Spiff, Margie, and Avi were all at various points in the room. Avi was on the floor, massaging his bad leg. "Y'all okay?"

They all nodded. Avi said, "I'll live. What the *fuck* happened?"

"Shit, *look!*" Margie was pointing down at the floor.

Murph looked over and saw that the floor where he'd been standing had collapsed, falling downward at an angle into the hole that led to the basement. The fish could probably run right up that!

Sure enough, that was what she did a second later. Murph scrambled around trying to find his semi-auto. Or, shit, Margie's shotgun, the fish's sawed-off, even those sissy blades Eddie carried, *anything* he could use as a weapon against that woman.

Before he could find it, she ran up, her boots slamming onto the wood. Murph was sure she was gonna take him out the way she took out Eddie, but instead she grabbed the same light fixture he'd used and swung up to the grid on the ceiling. He lost sight of her a second later.

"Shit," he said, shaking his head. He'd already broken his promise to the Lord, so what the fuck. Besides, this struck Murph as a situation that called for some *serious* cussin'.

Especially when he heard a familiar clicking sound. Oh, fuck.

All of a sudden, the pooches came running up the ramp, cables trailing behind them but not really slowing them down.

One of them leapt right at Murph, snout glistening with blood.

Murph's last thoughts as the pooch's teeth sank into his throat and ripped it out were that he never should've started cussin'.

Alice sat crouching in the light grid of the KLKB television station and watched as her captors were torn apart by the very dogs they'd tried to kill her with. One tore apart Murph, the guy with the pockmarked face. Another chewed off the arm of Margie, the woman with the baby doll. All of them were literal dog food after a few minutes. Alice wondered how they had managed to keep them in check in the first place and then realized that the one she'd killed—Eddie—was probably the ringleader, or at the very least the dog wrangler.

Once they were out of people to munch on, the dogs wandered around the television station for a while and then headed out, instinctively moving to a place that was less empty of living human flesh to feed on.

When they were gone, Alice jumped down, her knees bending with the impact as she landed on the damaged studio floor.

Trying not to slip in the blood of her captors, she walked back into the room where she'd found Margie and took her bike keys and her weapons back. She also grabbed the Kukri blades. They were priceless and could be useful, particularly against the undead.

Just as she stepped back out into the daylight, her watch beeped.

Looking down at the battered Timex, she saw that she had only a minute before the satellite would be overhead.

Fuck.

As the watch beeped down—59 . . . 58 . . . 57 . . . 56—she ran to the BMW and pulled a desert camouflage tarpaulin out from one of the containers that dangled from the side of the bike. After laying the bike down on its side, she whipped the tarp out to full size and draped it over the bike. Then she threw some of the sand that had blown into the parking lot and the grass onto the tarp to make it look less conspicuous. Between that and the bike being on its side, it wouldn't jump out as being a bike.

25 . . . 24 . . . 23 . . .

Shrugging out of her coat, she ran to the doorway to KLKB, dusting the ground behind and in front of her to eliminate any evidence of footprints.

10 . . . 9 . . . 8 . . .

Finally, she crouched in the doorway, covering herself with the duster, hoping it would look only like someone's coat that had been blown into the doorway by the wind.

3 . . . 2 . . . 1.

Then she waited.

She hated this part. Time slowed to a crawl, and she was afraid to move. True, she'd been trained to stay absolutely still if need be—training that went back to when she started taking karate as a teenager in Columbus and which the T-virus enabled her to do with ridiculous ease—but her ability to rid her mind of all thought the way *Sensei* had taught her had lessened of late.

There was simply too much in her mind to clear it all out.

And most of it was death.

After several dozen eternities, the watch beeped again. That meant that Umbrella's satellite was no longer overhead. She could come out.

Within minutes, she was back on her BMW, the tarp having been folded back into its carrier and the Kukris now alongside her other weaponry.

Firing the bike up, she got back onto 80 and headed into Salt Lake City. Big cities were dangerous—they had many enclaves of undead hidden in buildings and other odd places—but they also had lots of supplies that might still have gone unlooted. It was certainly worth a look, since she was already in town.

FIVE

BEFORE

They told Jill Valentine she was insane.

They told her she was rumormongering. That what she was telling everyone was truth was, in fact, the realm of video games and action movies, not real life. That she was seeing things, that she was mistaken, that she was overreacting.

Then, when the truth came out, when the same undead creatures she'd fought off in the forests of the Arklay Mountains invaded Raccoon City proper, to the point where the Umbrella Corporation had had to seal the city, Jill had made damn sure she got out. Alongside two former members of Umbrella Security—Carlos Olivera and Alice Abernathy—as well as Angie Ashford, the child of another Umbrella bigwig, and a street thug named L.J. Wayne, Jill had gotten out. She even had video footage, taken by the late Terri Morales, the Raccoon 7 weather reporter.

She had thought that having video proof—not to mention a nuked city—would be enough to bring those Umbrella fuckers down.

Carlos and Alice both had warned her that Umbrella's reach was long, that it was more powerful than any world government, that it could even make the nuking of a city go away.

And they were right.

Worse, Jill and Carlos had been named as fugitives. Umbrella used her suspension after reporting the zombies in Arklay against her, not to mention Morales's own history of faking footage to get a story. Morales had been a news reporter until she showed footage of a councilman taking a bribe that turned out to be fake, thus relegating her to the weather. Like all the best liars, Umbrella used a grain of truth to make its falsehood more convincing.

Carlos had managed to forge papers that would allow them to get Alice out of the San Francisco facility—something Angie had insisted they do—but they had to get out of California as fast as possible after that, as there was no way Carlos's forgery would hold up for more than five minutes.

So they wound up in the middle of nowhere in Idaho. Jill knew it was the middle of nowhere because they'd gone through a considerable patch of nowhere before finally arriving at the middle of it.

They'd checked into some dump—L.J. had jokingly

called it the "It'll Do Motel"—and plotted out their next move while sitting in one of the rooms. It was barely big enough to fit the two double beds and a bureau with a battered television on top of it. The end table between the beds had a lamp with a flickering bulb, a remote for the TV, and a Gideon Bible next to the phone book in the drawer—both books had many pages ripped out. Besides the door leading outside, there were two other doors—one to the adjacent room, which Carlos and L.J. were sleeping in, and one to the tiny bathroom. The toilet made strange gurgling noises every few minutes, which Jill just knew was gonna keep her up all night. The walls were covered either in stained puce wallpaper or large, awful abstract paintings. It was even money as far as Jill was concerned which of the two hurt her eyes more.

Still, it was cheap, and they took cash. L.J. insisted he had plenty of credit cards they could use, but Jill found herself strangely unwilling to commit credit-card fraud until they got *really* desperate.

L.J. had snorted and said, "Once a cop, huh?"

The motel also had a back alley between two long buildings that provided a handy escape route, if one was willing to crawl out through a dirty, old sealed window that Alice had managed to force open. A quick escape was something they might need. They did their best not to get noticed on their way here from San Francisco, but with the number of people after them and with the resources those people commanded . . .

Now they sat around on the two beds in the women's

room, plotting out their next move. Carlos's contact who'd gotten them the forged papers had stopped answering his cell phone. "I've got a bad feeling that they made him disappear."

"They're good at that," Alice said.

"We need to get this information out to someone Umbrella can't touch," Jill said.

"And who would that be, exactly?" Carlos asked. "Umbrella made significant campaign contributions to the chair of every important committee in Congress and each of the last four presidents. Umbrella lobbyists are all over D.C. rewriting laws to suit them. They—"

Jill exploded. "They blew up a fucking *city,* Carlos!"

"No, a nuclear plant melted down," Carlos said snidely. "Didn't you see it on the news? The very same news outlets that we gave copies of Terri's tape to? Umbrella owns half the TV news outlets and three-quarters of the print ones."

"They don't own all of it, though, do they?" L.J. asked.

"There are a few independent stations," Alice said, "but Umbrella has at least a piece of most of them. It'd be impossible to get this done through the mainstream press. I'm surprised you even bothered trying—all it did was put you two on the most-wanted list."

Jill ignored Alice's criticism. She hated to admit it, but L.J. was on the right track. "So fuck the mainstream." She pointed at the laptop that sat next to Angie. "Put the video online."

"That whole shit with Clinton and the blow job," L.J.

said. "That happened 'cause a some motherfucker online, right?"

"Matt Drudge," Alice said.

"Drudge is a jackass with delusions of grandeur," Carlos said.

"Maybe," Jill said, suddenly feeling energized, "but it's people like him who'll get this story out—the people who don't give a fuck about corporate sponsorship."

"The numbers are meaningless," Alice said. "A few thousand people, maybe."

For the first time, Angie spoke. "It's a few thousand more than know now, though—isn't it?"

"Girl's got herself a point," L.J. said.

Alice shrugged and got up from the bed. "Fine, we put it online. That can't be all we do, though." She thought a moment. "Treasury."

L.J. grinned. "What, we gonna rob Fort Knox to finance the revolution? I'm down with that."

"Is a felony your answer to everything, L.J.?" Jill asked.

"Nah—I'm strictly misdemeanor."

Jill shook her head. L.J. was a cockroach, a two-bit hustler who made his living on small-time shit. He'd gone through the Raccoon City Police Department in handcuffs half a dozen times a month, and he usually got kicked by dropping a dime on someone. L.J. had his fingers in many pies and knew to give up little enough so that he didn't piss off the people on the street but not so little that it wouldn't be worth the cops' time. It was a delicate balancing act, and Jill knew that several uniforms were looking forward to the day that he lost his balance and they could bust him proper.

That day would never come, of course. Jill was the only member of the RCPD still alive, while L.J., like any good cockroach, survived the holocaust.

She was amazed he hadn't bailed yet.

Alice was explaining herself. "What I meant was, I still have some friends in the Treasury Department. It's not much, but those guys are pretty autonomous. If we bring this to the FBI or Congress, the White House could come down on them like a ton of bricks, but even Umbrella's not gonna fuck with the money or with the Secret Service."

Carlos shook his head. "Yeah, but this isn't Treasury's jurisdiction."

Jill was about to agree, when her face suddenly broke into a wide smile. "Sure it is."

"No, he's right," Alice said. "I don't see how we can—"

"Secret Service's job is to protect the president, right?" Jill asked.

Carlos and Alice both nodded.

"So," Jill went on, "only the president is authorized to fire our nuclear weapons, yes?"

"Technically," Alice said, "but—" Then she broke into a smile of her own. "I like it. It's a stretch, but it's a start."

Carlos looked confused. "I don't get it."

Alice turned to Carlos. "By firing a nuclear missile on American soil in a situation that was not a test, they usurped the power of the president of the United States. It's possible—*possible*—that we can convince Treasury that this brands them a threat to the president."

"Which *is* their jurisdiction."

L.J. shook his head. "Knew I shoulda been watchin' *The West Wing* and shit—I dunno *what*ch'all're talkin' 'bout."

"It's a long shot," Alice said.

"What's the alternative?" Jill asked. "We can sit on our asses and run from the feds. The longer we wait, the easier it'll be for Umbrella to cover this up. We gotta get people picking at the scab before it has a chance to heal."

"It's done." That was Angie. Jill and the others all turned toward the bed to see that she had opened the laptop and was using it.

"What's done?" Alice asked.

"I put the video online—all the footage of Raccoon City and your confession. I had to put it in two separate bits, since the website I'm using only lets me put up videos up to two minutes at a time."

"Angie," Alice said in a panicky voice, "if they can trace it—"

"They can't." Angie spoke with the classic give-me-a-break tone that all children knew instinctively. Jill, God knew, had used it on her parents often enough when she was Angie's age. "I used an untraceable e-mail address and used one of my father's programs to mask the IP address. No one'll know where it came from."

"How'd you get online?" Carlos asked. "Don't tell me this place has wireless?"

Angie grinned. "No, but someone who lives nearby does, and they never changed their network key from the default."

Alice grinned right back. "Your father teach you how to do that?"

"Actually, I taught him."

They all got a good chuckle out of that, even though Jill didn't entirely believe it. Whenever she'd used that know-it-all tone at Angie's age, she was usually about a hundred percent wrong—but, like all kids, she didn't realize it until she was a grown-up and discovered how much more complicated the world was.

Then again, Angie had a pretty good idea about that. Like Alice, she was swimming with the T-virus, which had regenerated her legs. Those limbs were atrophied at birth, a hereditary condition she got from her wheelchair-bound father, but the T-virus—along with a regular dose of the anti-virus, both of which Angie kept in a Spider-Man lunch box that never left her side—had regenerated the limbs to working condition.

Dr. Charles Ashford's own body was too far gone for the T-virus to help him, but his daughter was young enough to be able to regenerate the muscle and nerves that needed strengthening.

Then, according to what Alice and Angie had both told them, the research was taken away from Ashford. He had wanted to use the virus as a tool for healing. Umbrella—which owned the patents of anything Ashford (or anyone else) created while working for it—took it away from him and turned it into the basis of a wrinkle cream that they could sell for millions and a bio-weapon they could sell for billions. According to Alice, the project had been given over to two younger, more malleable doctors in the Hive named Mariano Rodriguez and Anna Bolt, who had been refining it into something more fitting with Umbrella's corporate mandate.

Bolt and Rodriguez had been infected when one of Alice's coworkers, Spence Parks, let the virus loose in their office. Their legacy, however, lived on in Raccoon.

Jill took some solace in the fact that, if nothing else, Umbrella nuking Raccoon meant that the virus had been stopped. The only infected people were Alice and Angie.

"If we done yappin'," L.J. said, grabbing the remote off the end table and leaning back against the headboard, "I ain't seen *Oprah* in a month, an' I'm sufferin' withdrawal."

When he switched on the TV, it showed the motel's menu options—including a pay-per-view selection that Jill suspected was mostly of the adult variety—and he flipped forward to the first channel.

Before he could flip further, Carlos said, "Stop. Hang on, L.J."

It was a news report, the words "Outbreak in San Francisco" under the anchor's concerned features. *"The Mission Hill District has been quarantined, and representatives from the Centers for Disease Control will be on the scene shortly."*

"What's the big—" Jill started, then she noticed the image over the anchor's shoulder, showing someone who looked suspiciously like one of the infected people in Raccoon.

The anchor went on: *"The cause of the disease is unknown; however, the symptoms include delirium, a milkiness to the eyes, and a desire to—well, bite people. There is concern that those infected might transmit the disease through biting, hence the quarantine."*

Jill almost said, "Fuck me," but the last three times she did, L.J. offered to take her up on it, so she just shook her head.

"The fuckers let it out," Alice said. "That has to be it."

"No," Carlos said. "Even Umbrella wouldn't—"

"They did it before," Alice said. "Cain reopened the Hive, and—"

"Cain's dead," Jill pointed out. "And Umbrella wouldn't deliberately infect another city. They wouldn't be able to pull the same trick twice." She looked at the television, seeing a street reporter interviewing a San Francisco cop. "But they didn't have to. Think about it. Tons of people were plowing through the Ravens' Gate Bridge. Maybe somebody got through who was infected—or maybe somebody got out before Umbrella sealed off the city, or somebody else broke through like we did—or maybe it's some stray employee who got through the screening. Who the fuck knows?"

"And made it all the way to San Francisco, which just *happens* to be where Isaacs relocated his lab?"

Jill sighed. "All right, maybe they fucked up an experiment. Who gives a shit? The point is, we've got something now. We—"

"We've just received word that the RPC—the Reserve Physician Corps—is also sending medical assistance to aid local medical personnel in identifying and containing this disease."

"That's that," Alice said.

"What's what?" Jill asked.

Carlos sighed. "RPC is a division of Umbrella. They're already going in with a syringe in one hand and whitewash in the other."

"Maybe, but it may not work this time. Raccoon was isolated—a small company town on an island, but San Francisco?" Jill smiled. "There's too much city there, and Umbrella doesn't have the same pull that they had in Raccoon. This might be just what we need."

Angie said in a small voice, "So people dying is a *good* thing?"

Jill winced, a heaviness in her chest. "Angie, I didn't—"

"I know, Jill," Angie said, sounding almost depressingly mature.

The light flickered again, just as the toilet made its gurgling noise, and suddenly, Jill had a tremendous need for air. "I'm gonna go smoke," she said.

"Actually," Carlos said, "we could use some food. I saw about twelve different fast-food joints when we drove in."

Jill nodded. Now that Carlos had said it out loud, she realized she was starving. Her stomach gurgled for good measure, in almost perfect harmony with the toilet. "Fine. Burgers, fries, and chicken for everyone."

"Yeah," L.J. said with a grin, stretching the word to three syllables. "I be *livin'* on grease, yo."

"Why am I not surprised?" Jill said with an exaggerated sigh.

As she went outside to the small covered walkway that bordered the motel parking lot, she pulled her cigarette pack out of her pocket.

Only one left. Fuck.

Hoping that there was a deli or something with all those fast-food joints Carlos mentioned, she took out her matchbook.

Only one match left, too.

She folded the matchbook shut for a second and stared at it.

The stylized logo of McSorley's Bar and Grill stared back at her.

For a second, she was scared to strike the match, as if the act of doing it would cut off her last connection to Raccoon City.

Jill had been born and raised in Raccoon. A lot of her youth was misspent at McSorley's, hustling pool. While her friends were waitressing or working at fast-food joints for their pocket money, Jill was in McSorley's, drinking Diet Cokes so old Eamonn McSorley wouldn't lose his liquor license, and fooling guys into thinking that the cute teenage brunette didn't know an eight-ball from a tennis ball right before she took them for all they were worth.

Once she got into the Police Academy, she had to stop hustling, of course—or, as she preferred to call it, "educating." Eamonn had given her a neon Budweiser sign as a going-away present in gratitude for all the business she'd brought to the bar (once she got a rep, everyone wanted to take down the "pool girl").

The bar was gone now. So was McSorley's. So, presumably, was Eamonn himself—if the T-virus didn't get the cantankerous old bastard, the nuke did—and so was her Budweiser sign.

The matchbook was all she had left.

It was funny—Jill had been set to leave Raccoon altogether. If Umbrella hadn't put up a wall on Ravens' Gate, she would've driven right out and not looked back—not at her brownstone, not at her job, not at anything. Not that she was all that hot to return to the job in any case; they had told her to fuck off and die. And she had no family anymore anyhow, so the only things she left behind in Raccoon were things that, she had told herself, could easily be replaced.

And yet, where would she find another McSorley's matchbook?

Suddenly, she burst out laughing. The matchbook was, after all, the absolute least of her problems. The U.S. government wanted her for questioning in the perpetration of a fraud on the American public and slander against a fine American corporation. The same fine American corporation whose orders forced the RCPD to fuck her up the ass and suspend her when she had the temerity to tell the truth about thost *things* in the Arklay Mountains.

Shaking her head, Jill lit the last match and took a long, wonderful drag on the last cigarette.

The really funny part was that right before she was suspended, she was considering trying to quit smoking. So much for that crazy idea . . .

She walked down to the first fast-food place that presented itself and went in once she was done with her cigarette. As she waited in line, she decided to buy enough burgers, fries, and chicken for ten people. Sure, there were only five of them, but Angie was a growing girl, God knew what Alice's metabolism was like now, and L.J. struck her as the type who could eat for four.

During the whole time she had walked in and stood in line, something had been nagging at the back of her brain. But she couldn't figure out what.

Then, finally, just as she got to the front of the line, she caught it.

There was somebody in the fast-food place, a short guy in a big coat that was too warm for the weather but just the right size to conceal a shoulder holster, as well as a ball cap and sunglasses. He looked outside right when a car drove by that slowed down as it passed the fast-food place. Right when he did that, the car headed off in the same direction as the hotel.

Jill had been made.

She cursed herself up, down, backward, and sideways. If they'd traced the SUV to this podunk town, the first thing they'd do is check fast-food places, since it was the ideal location for people on the run, seeing as how you could get quick food for cash. Jill remembered a lecture given to the Academy while she was there by a member of the Fugitive Squad from an East Coast PD—she could no longer remember which one—who said that the best way to find someone who's hiding is to track the pizza joints, fast-food places, and Chinese restaurants.

There were at least three of them—one here and two more in the car. Probably a bunch in the other joints.

Calmly, Jill ordered the food, but only enough for herself. There was a cigarette machine outside the place, so she set the bag down there and bought herself another pack, which conveniently came with a matchbook. Then she pulled one out and lit it up.

She did not rush. The worst thing she could do right now was give the appearance that she knew she'd been made. If they knew the others were in the motel, nothing she could do would help them.

And if they didn't know for sure, she needed to lull them into a false sense of security. That was why she only got enough food for herself.

It was possible she was being paranoid, of course. That it was just some guy and the car slowed down for some other reason.

But every instinct Jill had said that she was made, and Jill's instincts had been wrong only once before: when she reported the creatures in the Arklays, assuming that Captain Henderson would back her up.

Calmly, she walked back to the hotel room, slipping in quickly enough that no one could see who else was in the room.

"Shit, bitch, that ain't enough to feed a bird!"

To L.J., she said, "Shut up. I got made. There was someone watching in the fast-food joint, and he signaled a car here."

"You sure?" Alice asked.

"Not a hundred percent but sure enough."

Carlos got up and grabbed his nine-millimeter. "We've got to get out of here."

"Yeah, *you* do."

Alice stared at Jill. "What's that supposed to mean?"

"You know what it means."

"Fuck that," Carlos said. "We're not letting you—"

"You don't have a choice," Jill snapped. "They know I'm here. They don't know you're here. If they barge in and find nobody, they'll keep looking. If they barge in and find me, I can stall them, make them think I was here alone, and that'll give you more time." She smiled grimly. "Just leave me the tape."

"You flippin', bitch?" L.J. said as he started packing up what gear he had. "Without that tape—"

"You've got copies—Angie has it on her laptop, and we've still got some DVDs and VHS tapes with it. Take those, but leave me the original."

"It's too risky," Carlos said.

"No," Alice said, "she's right. If those are the feds out there, they can verify that the tape's real. Best to do that with Terri's original."

"And then Umbrella will waltz right in and—" Carlos started, but Jill wouldn't let him finish.

"Maybe they will, but there's a *chance* they won't. If they don't get their hands on the original, though, there's *no* chance they will. Which do you prefer?"

Jill stared at Carlos for several seconds. Finally, he nodded.

Within seconds, everyone had gathered up everything and slid out the window that Alice had busted open—L.J. first, followed by Angie, whom he caught.

Carlos was next. "This is crazy."

"No crazier than anything else that's happened to us the last three weeks. Besides, this *needs* to be done, and I'm the best person to do it."

"Yeah. Be safe."

After Carlos clambered through the old window, Alice walked up to Jill and put a hand on her shoulder. "Thank you."

Someone pounded on the door. "Federal agents, open up!"

"You're welcome," Jill said. "Now get your ass outta here."

As soon as Alice was through the window, Jill closed it and jammed it shut again. With luck, they wouldn't be able to tell that someone had climbed through it.

Forensic technology might reveal that the window had been used in due time, but by then, Carlos and the others would be long gone. A quick eyeballing of the room wouldn't reveal anything untoward, which was all that mattered.

Jill called out, "Hang on, I'm in the bathroom," as she ran over to that place and flushed the gurgling toilet.

Then she walked to the front door to see four men wearing blue jackets and Ray-Bans—one of whom looked a lot like the guy in the fast-food place—holding guns at the ready.

She smiled sweetly. "Can I help you guys?"

Six

After

Claire Redfield had long since stopped noticing when the Hummer ran over one of the zomboids.

Otto had started calling them that as an alternative to L.J.'s nickname, which was *zombie-ass motherfuckers.* Given that they had kids in the convoy, not to mention the excess number of syllables, it was generally felt that a better neologism was required. Claire had nixed *zombies,* simply because you couldn't take the word seriously. It conjured up images of bad movies and worse comic books. Zombies were fictional.

The walking, lumbering, feeding corpses were very real. And they were growing in numbers, in direct proportion to how the human population was shrinking.

A part of Claire was convinced that the thirty of them were the last humans left alive.

She looked up briefly at the sun visor. The picture she'd clipped there was ragged at the edges and had faded after a few years of exposure to sunlight, but it was still clearly a picture of Claire and her brother Chris from their trip to Florida.

Then she fixed her eyes back on the road. Not that it was necessary. Aside from the occasional zomboid that the Hummer smashed into, they were alone on the road, which, in the California desert, was pretty straight.

Claire wasn't entirely sure that *zomboid* was a better alternative, but Otto used it once, and it stuck.

The Hummer bounced slightly. The suspension was such that a simple pothole wouldn't have been that noticeable—although, given that the roads hadn't been maintained in a few years, even simple potholes got pretty large—so Claire figured it was another zomboid.

That was fine with her.

Quickly, she checked the side-view to make sure everyone was there. She could see everything except the 8x8, bringing up the rear. And she could only see the news truck because of the gigunda antenna poking up past even the oil truck.

But, assuming Carlos hadn't veered the 8x8 into a ditch without telling anyone, they were all there: the ambulance they'd found abandoned in Dallas, furbished with medical supplies they'd looted from everywhere they could; the school bus from the Omaha public school system, which served as the main living accommodation and had been tricked out with gun ports and armor plating taken from both the San Diego Naval Yards and Fort

Irwin; an Enco oil tanker that was jackknifed on I-70 somewhere in Missouri, three zomboids at the wheel, and full when they'd liberated it; and a news truck from a Denver TV station.

Bracketing these vehicles in the front and rear were two more gifts from Fort Irwin: a Humvee leading and an 8x8 guarding their backs. By the time they had reached Irwin (at that point, the convoy consisted only of the school bus, the ambulance, and the news truck), these two were the only vehicles that weren't wrecked or stolen—or, in one case, blown up in order to stop the zomboid soldiers that had overrun the place. Claire would have preferred a tank, but there wasn't one available. She also would've preferred that Otto and L.J. had used some of the base's munitions to blow up those zomboids instead of one of the three remaining working vehicles, but beggars and choosers and all that.

Claire was just grateful to be alive.

She looked up at the sun visor and wondered again what had happened to Chris.

Then she shook her head, as she always did, and told herself to stop thinking about it. There was no way to know and no sense beating herself up about it. Thirty people were counting on her and Carlos to keep them alive, and she couldn't do that if she was moping about Chris.

Keeping her left hand on the steering wheel, she palmed sweat off her forehead. Aside from the news truck—which needed to keep the equipment inside cool—none of the vehicles in the convoy used air conditioning anymore, as it used up the gas too quickly. As it was, the Enco truck wasn't much more than a big metal can of air storage. They needed to find a refill of gas, and soon.

Their difficulty in doing so was one of the things that gave Claire hope that there were other humans still living: somebody else was looting the remains of human civilization besides them. How else to explain the number of small towns they'd gone through that had already been stripped clean of gas and food and weaponry, like bones after the vultures were done?

But all they saw were more zomboids. The convoy had been as many as sixty people at one point, but every time they came up against some zomboids, they lost someone—or several someones. Occasionally, they'd pick up new people—the last hospital they'd raided, in Bakersfield, also had a paramedic and a med tech still alive, and they'd joined up.

The zomboids weren't the only danger. Having an ambulance was all well and good, but they didn't have any doctors. The paramedic and the med tech were handy in a pinch, but they were recent additions, and Emilio, the med tech, had died soon after joining. Carlos had field medic training, but that also wasn't particularly helpful when someone needed surgery.

Like Lyndon.

Lyndon Barry was a good, kind soul who'd been the camera operator for Denver's KT3. He worked alongside a reporter named Heidi Ellis and a driver named Ross Vincent. They'd been driving all over Denver, reporting on what was going on. When KT3 stopped broadcasting, they put their stories online for as long as they could.

By the time the convoy found them, they were in Boulder, being overrun by some zomboids. Carlos and L.J. had made quick work of their attackers—they'd had more experience killing these things than anyone else in the group—but not before one bit Heidi. They didn't know that until she died and went zomboid on them, biting Ross and infecting him as well.

Claire herself shot both of them in the head.

Lyndon hadn't let any of it get to him, remarkably enough. He'd watched the world fall apart around him, dutifully recording it for whatever posterity was left. He'd stood and watched as his best friends and colleagues turned into zomboids, and still he was always ready with a joke or a cheery word.

Truly, Claire had envied him that talent.

Then, one day, they were going through a ramshackle old house that had some canned food and old ammunition in the basement, and one of the ceiling supports came crashing down right on Lyndon's leg.

They all did the best they could for him, but nobody had the skill actually to fix his leg or even keep the wound clean. No one in the convoy had had a proper shower in years, and there was simply no way even to approach antiseptic conditions. Eventually, Lyndon got gangrene.

This was the world they all lived in now, when a sweet, cheerful man could die of a broken leg.

Depressed, Claire reached for her pack of cigarettes.

The pack collapsed in her grip, empty.

"Dammit!"

She looked into the rearview to see Kmart applying makeup for whatever stupid reason. "Have you been smoking my cigarettes?"

Claire had no idea what the girl's real name was. When they had found her in the Kmart in Athens, Georgia, she had refused to provide her name, saying she'd never liked it anyhow, and the people who gave it to her were dead. L.J. started calling her Kmart, and she took to it.

The fourteen-year-old wore electrical wire on her left wrist as bracelets. Otto had called it "apocalypse chic." She had liberated the entire makeup supply of the Kmart where they'd found her and still insisted on using it every day, even though her face, like everyone else's, was filthy.

"I don't smoke," Kmart said, not bothering to look up from applying eye shadow.

"Well, don't start," Claire said, crumpling the pack into a tiny ball. "Don't need the competition. Carlos is bad enough."

She flung the pack out the window, then grabbed the Army-issue PRC that came with the Hummer. All the convoy vehicles were equipped with them. Radio had become the communications medium of choice, since telephones depended on either wires or satellite towers, which were not reliable anymore.

If nothing else, she could make sure that Carlos was still there. "Carlos, this is Claire—got any smokes?"

Carlos Olivera had a pleasant, reassuring voice. It had enabled him to do well in the Air Force, before he resigned his commission to join the Umbrella Corporation, and it had enabled him to be a strong team leader in Umbrella's Security Division. Carlos had been one of the first people to tell the truth about what was happening in the world, and he had led several military operations that had saved hundreds of lives. For a time, he was in command of a ragtag group of armed forces and police personnel as a sort of last stand against the undead. They called themselves *the strike team*.

Eventually, though, the tide of zomboids was just too strong. Carlos and L.J. were the only survivors of the strike team left.

Claire had been one of the refugees Carlos's team had rescued, and eventually she grew into a leadership role.

Now Carlos said in as sincere a voice as he was capable of, "I'm out."

However, Claire wasn't having any of it. "I'm supposed to believe that?"

"Would I lie to you, Claire?"

Dammit, he wouldn't, either. Carlos was honest to a fault, which was one of several reasons why Claire didn't understand how he could work for Umbrella. For his part, Carlos never had been able to provide a good answer to that question—and he'd certainly been asked it enough times.

Sighing, Claire said, "L.J.?"

"Claire Redfield," L.J. said in his usual boisterous tone from his position behind the wheel of the Enco tanker. "Now how can I help you?"

Nobody knew much about L.J.'s past, mostly because he kept making up different ones. Every time someone new came into the convoy, L.J. would spin some yarn about who he was—a haberdasher, a shoe repairman, a computer programmer with IBM, a minor-league baseball player, a cop, a drug dealer, a federal agent, a deli clerk, and a veterinarian.

He had been with Carlos when he had the strike team, and his job was to help out with all the nonmilitary stuff—including keeping the refugees safe. While Claire owed Carlos her life, she owed L.J. her sanity. His crazed sense of humor had kept her going through the worst of the despair, especially after she realized that she probably would never see her brother again.

What little Claire did know about L.J. was something that only one other person in the convoy knew: that he, like Carlos, was a survivor of Raccoon City.

It was for that reason that Claire hadn't pried about his past. If it was connected to the city that started the apocalypse, she was just as happy not to open up that old wound.

"Got a smoke?" she asked him now.

"We talkin' regular tobacco or alternate substances?"

L.J. had shown an affinity for pharmaceuticals that led one to think that his claim to have been a drug dealer in the past was pretty close to the mark, and he had managed to scrape together a supply of drugs that weren't FDA-approved.

Not that there was an FDA to approve it or a law-enforcement structure to enforce it.

"Regular," Claire said. Getting high sounded appealing, but not while she was driving.

"No can do," L.J. said quickly.

Frowning, Claire asked, "How about alternate?"

"Sorry to say, we're out of that, too."

Somehow, Claire wasn't surprised.

Betty Grier, the paramedic they'd picked up in Bakersfield, was driving the ambulance, and she chimed in: "You gotta be shitting me! Otto?"

From the school bus, Otto Walenski said, "Sorry, campers. Smoked the last of it back in Salt Lake."

They hadn't been in Salt Lake for almost a month, so Claire was rather amazed that Otto'd been able to hold out this long. He'd been a high school history teacher in Omaha, and he'd been using the bus from his own school system to protect his kids and later other kids who'd been abandoned or orphaned by the growing plague of the undead.

"Damn," Betty muttered.

"Yeah, people," L.J. said portentously, "it really *is* the end of the world."

Otto snorted. "Ladies and gentlemen, our morale officer, L.J. Wayne!"

Betty said, "There better be some damn cigarettes in the next town."

"So speaketh the medical professional," Otto said. "An inspiration to us all."

L.J. said, "Motherfucker, lung cancer ain't exactly high on the list of shit I'm concerned about, you feel me?"

Claire interrupted the bantering. "Speaking of the next town, shouldn't we be close to something?"

"Maybe," Carlos said. "If I remember right, there's a small town coming up soon. If we see a video billboard for Vegas, we're close."

"A video billboard," Otto said. "And you expect it still to be working why, exactly?"

"It's solar-powered," Carlos said.

When she noticed moving images on the road ahead, right before the road angled downward into a valley, Claire asked, "Does the billboard say WHAT HAPPENS IN VEGAS STAYS IN VEGAS?"

"That's the one," Carlos said.

"Then everyone pull yourselves over, 'cause we're coming up on it now."

Claire pulled the Hummer onto the shoulder of the highway, decelerating at a leisurely pace to give all the other large vehicles time to shed momentum. A car crash would be beyond disastrous.

From the back, Kmart said, "I hope this is a real town. Not like Pahrump."

"You keep mentioning Pahrump. It's not like it's the only town that was abandoned and half buried in dunes." A lot of the towns that they'd come across had been half buried in sand, as if the desert was reclaiming them. In a few more years, there might not have been any sign of Pahrump, or Kettleman Station, or Bakersfield, or Lebec, or any number of other places.

"Yeah, but I just like saying it. Pahrump, Pahrump, Pahrump. Who names a town that?"

"The people of Pahrump, apparently," Claire said as she switched the ignition off and opened the door.

L.J. and Carlos had already gotten out and were running ahead to the billboard, which stood about thirty feet high, in the hopes of getting a better vantage.

Claire leaned against the side of the Hummer, Kmart standing next to her. Imagining that she was smoking a cigarette, Claire reached in to grab the PRC so she could talk to Carlos and L.J. The pair of them were climbing up the billboard as if it was a set of monkey bars, Carlos moving a bit faster than L.J.

Once they got to the top, Carlos took out a pair of binoculars. "This is another one the desert's trying to take back," he said.

"Latest in a motherfuckin' series—collect 'em all," L.J. said. "Shit." That last word was stretched out to about four syllables.

"However," Carlos added, "we got us a motel, complete with restaurant, gift shop, and, best of all, gas station."

"Eu-goddamn-reka." That was Chase MacAvoy, who'd been riding shotgun with L.J. in the tanker.

A pause. Claire looked up to see that Carlos was taking in the entire view.

Finally, he said, "Seems quiet."

L.J. put in, "Don't they always?"

Claire sighed. "Your call."

Otto then said, "Whatever you guys decide, can you get a move on? I got a yoga class at seven."

That prompted several chuckles. It was also code: the kids were getting restless, and stopping for a while wouldn't be a bad thing. Stopping in a place that at least once was part of Western civilization would be an even better thing.

Finally, Carlos said, "I think it's worth a look. I'm not seeing any signs of life or unlife, but as long as we're careful . . ."

"Fine," Claire said. "You two go on ahead and scope out the joint."

"Copy that."

As Carlos and L.J. started climbing back down off the billboard that continued to extoll the virtues of Las Vegas—a place they'd all been afraid to visit, having learned the hard way that big cities were *not* safe—Claire hoped and prayed that there would be something left in the gas station. She had very little expectation for food— anything still left in the restaurant had probably long since spoiled, though the gift shop might have had some jerky or canned food.

But what they needed more than fuel for the body was fuel for the convoy. The best way to stay safe was to keep moving. The biggest advantage that the living had over the dead was speed—the zomboids ambulated at a fairly leisurely pace and weren't capable of the motor functions necessary to operate a moving vehicle.

So staying mobile was key, and that required gas.

Her last words to Carlos before signing off were: "Good luck."

SEVEN
BEFORE

The face of Dr. Sam Isaacs stared angrily through the computer screen at Dr. Jaime Cerota. She tried not to be intimidated by him, but the way he stared was just demoralizing. It was as if she was in college all over again, with Professor Krapovsky glowering at her in anatomy class. Sweat beaded on her brow, which she was unable to wipe, because she was wearing a Hazmat suit. She was still in the containment area for the San Francisco outbreak, in the special tent Umbrella had set up for her upon her arrival.

"How could this have happened, Doctor?"

"Right now, we're a little more focused on containment. Besides, the CDC guys are all looking at me funny."

In a tight voice, Isaacs said, *"I'm not interested in how you socialize with the Centers for Disease Control, Doctor. I'm interested in how the T-virus has spread to the Mission Hill District of San Francisco."*

Jaime sighed. "As best as I can tell, sir, it was Dr. Knable."

Isaacs frowned. *"Knable? What does he have to do with this?"*

"He's one of the people infected, sir."

"What?" Isaacs yelled the word loudly enough that Jaime feared it would blow out the speakers on her laptop. The connection was spotty, so the camera providing Isaacs's face refreshed only every second and a half or so, which meant his expression went from glowering to screaming with his mouth open in an instant. Jaime had to suppress the urge to giggle.

Isaacs continued: *"Knable was tested before we put him on the bridge—with, I might add, his own foolproof test."*

"It wasn't foolproof, sir—sometimes it gave false negatives."

"But not false positives. So how—"

"My guess, sir, is that he got it while he was on the bridge."

"That's not possible. The virus wasn't airborne yet, and—"

"We don't know that, sir," Jaime said emphatically. "We don't know the precise vector of the virus, because we abandoned Raccoon City before we could track it properly. We don't know how long it incubates, how quickly it becomes airborne or gets into the ground. We're spitting in the wind here, sir."

"*All right,*" Isaacs said after a distressingly long pause. "*Your primary purpose there remains the same: stop the spread of the virus by whatever means are necessary.*"

"Yes, I know. I was standing right there next to you when you told me that," Jaime said angrily. "Unfortunately, I don't know that I can."

"*Why not?*" Isaacs said angrily. "*You've been granted executive authority over this by the order of the governor.*"

"Yeah, and that went over *real* well." She winced, recalling the confused, angry, and hurtful—but mostly angry—looks from her fellow doctors when she handed the governor's order over. She'd overheard Dr. Bousquet, one of the locals, refer to her as "some private-sector diva with pull."

"*How it 'goes over' is comparatively irrelevant, Doctor.*"

"The problem is, one of the CDC doctors is making the connection to what happened in Raccoon."

"*That's impossible.*"

"Sir, the *dead* are walking. I think we seriously need to revise our notions of what constitutes impossible."

"*Oh, you have no idea, Doctor. But that's neither here nor there. How can one of those doctors connect this to Raccoon City?*"

Jaime shuddered in her Hazmat suit. She'd heard rumors about Project Nemesis and Project Alice and the odd bioengineering that Isaacs's office had been spearheading.

"She downloaded Valentine and Olivera's video."

"That's not possible—we had that removed from the site that was hosting it, and we're trying to trace the uploader now. We also confiscated all the copies."

"Well, however long it was up before you took it down was long enough for some people to see it. Dr. Yu-Chin has it on her hard drive, and she's noticing that the people we have restrained look *just* like the people on the video. Not everyone believed the meltdown story, you know."

"The ravings of conspiracy theorists are not to be taken seriously, Doctor."

"Dr. Yu-Chin isn't a conspiracy theorist; she's an intelligent woman with a medical degree who recognizes parallel symptoms when she sees them. Also—" She hesitated. This was the main reason she had come into the Umbrella tent to contact Isaacs, and she'd been dreading it.

Isaacs obviously noticed the hesitation. *"What is it, Doctor?"*

"I've managed to hold them off from sending the test results outside the quarantine area, but I don't know how much longer I can do that."

"You can do that as long as you like, Doctor. You're in charge."

"I can wave the governor's signature around all I

want, but I don't think I can push it too far before they start ignoring me. And the cops are on the side of the locals."

"That's ridiculous."

"Not really, sir. These are the same doctors the cops see in the ER all the time. They know each other. They trust each other. And cops don't trust private-sector divas like me."

"We cannot risk infected blood leaving the quarantine area," Isaacs said stating the obvious. Jaime already *knew* that. What she needed was instruction on how to stop that from happening.

After a moment's thought, Isaacs said, *"Obviously, we must contain this situation. Dr. Cerota, use your authority granted by the governor of California, and order all the blood samples destroyed, the patients terminated, and their bodies burned. There must be no evidence left."*

"Not even for testing?"

"There is nothing to test," Isaacs said slowly, as if speaking to a child. *"We know that this is the result of the T-virus."*

"Oh, fine—can I tell Dr. Yu-Chin and the others that?"

"Of course not."

"Fine—when *they* ask why there's nothing to be tested, what do I tell them?"

Still impatient, Isaacs said, *"Tell them it's classified by order of the governor."*

"And what happens when they call the governor's office and ask him?"

"He'll say exactly what we've instructed him to say. How do you think he got reelected?"

All of a sudden, Jaime's nose started to itch. She tried to ignore it.

"Oh, and if you can degauss this Dr. Yu-Chin's hard drive, that wouldn't be untoward, either."

Jaime shook her head. "I'll try my best. But I don't think this is going to work."

"Why not?"

"Because this might not be an isolated incident. If it is, great, we incinerate the blood and the bodies, and we're fine, but this isn't the only place Knable was after he left Raccoon. True, he didn't break out with symptoms"—*and die,* but Jaime found she couldn't add that part for some reason—"until he got here, but we're not even sure how he was infected, or if it really was him, or if he's the only one. We can't keep this to ourselves, sir. If we let the CDC in on this, then we can—"

"No."

"Sir—"

"I said no, Dr. Cerota. If you persist in this, you will be recalled, and we'll send someone who can do the job properly."

Isaacs didn't bother with the rest of the threat. She'd be fired and would never be able to work in her chosen field again, as Umbrella would blackball her.

"Yes, sir. I'll—"

Before she could finish the sentence, a loud crashing sound came from outside the tent.

"What is it?"

"I don't know." Jaime walked over to the tent flap and pulled it back—

—to reveal three infected corpses shuffling down the street where they'd set up their command post and several Hazmat-suited personnel trying and failing to restrain them.

One of the corpses was Jim Knable.

Jaime's heart leapt into her throat. Jim was a good guy, and a brilliant one. He'd done amazing work in the streamlining of blood-testing procedures, which—in the age of high-tech crime labs, not to mention rampant disease and drug testing—had made him a very rich man at a very young age. But he'd never let it get to his head.

He deserved better than this. Especially since his last act in Raccoon City was trying to help people get out.

Dr. Yu-Chin was running down the street. "They got loose! We've got to restrain them!"

Two of the uniforms from the SFPD—who were also wearing Hazmat suits—came running, weapons out. "Police, freeze!"

One of the corpses grabbed a Hazmat-suited doctor— after a second, Jaime realized it was Bousquet, the one who'd called her a diva—and bit through the suit. The doctor screamed.

"I said freeze!" one of the uniforms yelled. Both had their pistols aimed at the scene.

Jaime appreciated their dedication to the letter of the law, but now was not the time. "They won't respond. You need to shoot them in the head."

One of the cops said, "This may not be the best time to tell you my range scores."

The other cop just fired, hitting one of the corpses in the leg.

"That won't do it. The *only* way to harm them is to shoot them in the brain or sever the spinal cord. That'll short out the impulses the virus is sending to their brains, and they'll die for real."

"The fuck? You sayin' they're dead?"

Yu-Chin shot her a look. "How the hell do you know all that?"

"Not now," Jaime said.

"Then soon, *Doctor.*"

The cops continued to shoot. One managed to get in a head shot, but the other two corpses, including Jim, kept shambling forward.

One shot flew wild and hit Bousquet. A moment later, he got up and started shuffling forward, too.

"Oh, my God," Yu-Chin said, her pale face growing more ashen behind the Hazmat visor.

Jaime ran back into the tent.

"What's happening?" Isaacs asked.

"Three of the subjects got loose." She was looking for, and then eventually found, her nine-millimeter pistol.

Jaime Cerota probably had better range scores than that cop did. Her father had taken her hunting as a kid, along with her two brothers, and she was the only one who ever got anything, a fact that always pissed her older brothers off but made her dad proud.

Her entering medical school had been more of a disappointment, but her salary paid for his new house in Florida after he retired, so he didn't complain all that much.

"Doctor, you need to—"

Uninterested in what Isaacs thought she needed to do, Jaime exited the tent just as Jim and the other corpse overwhelmed the two cops. Jaime took aim and shot one of them in the head.

Jim was feeding on one of the cops, and the officer's flailing spoiled Jaime's shot.

A scream from behind her got her attention. Whirling around, she saw two more corpses coming down the street and also that Bousquet was feeding on Yu-Chin. She shot Bousquet in the head, the nine-millimeter bullet easily plowing through the Hazmat headgear, then did the same for the other two.

Then, after hesitating for only a second, she shot Yu-Chin in the head, too. The bullet was slowed only a bit by the faceplate, which was stronger than the rest of the headgear. True, she wasn't dead yet, but it was only a matter of time. And Isaacs had wanted her out of the way, and this worked, too.

Cold-blooded, perhaps, but it wasn't as if Yu-Chin had a chance in hell now.

Three more corpses were coming down the street. Jaime figured that they'd been tugging against the restraints for more than a day now. They didn't tire, they just kept pushing, and sooner or later, even the strongest material gives in if pressure is applied long enough.

Then a hand touched Jaime's protected shoulder, and she whirled around, trying to raise the pistol once more, but the corpse of Jim Knable was already on top of her, his mouth craning open. Jaime tried to push him off, but Jim was a lot bigger than she, and he was literally dead weight. They both collapsed to the ground.

Pain cut through her right shoulder as Jim bit down on it, his teeth easily ripping through the Hazmat suit. Jaime imagined she could feel his infected saliva intermixing with her blood.

She kicked upward with her left foot, which got Jim off her. Clambering to her feet, she held up the pistol, supporting it with her left hand, pain slicing through her wounded shoulder, and she shot Jim in the head.

Then she turned around and tried to shoot the others, but she couldn't hold her arm up any longer.

"Dammit."

She stumbled back into the tent. "Sir, we've lost containment."

"What? What happened to—"

"Sir, the infected corpses have broken free. I've stopped some of them, but there are others that I've been unable to terminate. And I've been infected, so it's only a matter of time before I join them."

"Dr. Cerota, I need you to—"

"Sir, there's nothing I can do for you now. I've reported the breach, and that's the last duty I can perform for the Umbrella Corporation." With her left hand—her right was now pretty much useless—she undid the fastenings on her Hazmat suit's headpiece and removed it. "I'm sorry I couldn't get the job done, sir."

Then she put the pistol's muzzle under her chin and pulled the trigger.

EIGHT
AFTER

Sam Isaacs mostly blamed Timothy Cain.

He was a handy scapegoat, the deceased major. For starters, he was deceased. It was always preferable to have someone to blame who was unable to defend himself.

Not that Cain would have been able to mount much of a defense. Cain had reopened the Hive, violating every protocol the company had—not to mention simple common sense—just to satisfy his own curiosity. Pretty much everything that had happened since could be traced to that event. If the Hive had remained sealed, Raccoon City wouldn't have been infected, and it wouldn't have had to be purified. The larger the infected area, the more difficult containment became—that was elementary mathematics, after all. Raccoon City proved too much, as the infection got out, presumably through Dr. Jim Knable.

And San Francisco—a major city located on a peninsula—was far more difficult to contain than a smaller city located on an island. In fact, it was impossible. The media had painted that California city as ground zero of the infection, but Isaacs knew better.

Not that it mattered now.

As he went up the hydraulic lift with two of the security people—DiGennaro and Humberg—he thought about how much better things would have been if Cain wasn't such an idiot. He could have done the Nemesis tests on Addison and Abernathy in relative peace, instead of having them dropped into the infested Raccoon City to engage in some kind of boxing match—again, for no other reason than to satisfy Cain's own curiosity. Not that he had any kind of scientific interest. Cain's was the same morbid curiosity exhibited by a child who pulled the wings off flies.

Isaacs walked toward the mesh fence at the perimeter. He wasn't entirely sure why the undead all congregated here, but there were certainly a lot of them—hundreds, it seemed. They carried the stench of rotting flesh, overripe fruit, and moldy dust. It was almost as if they saw that there was a fence here, and that meant that there was flesh they could feed on.

Certainly, this facility was the only place in the vicinity where there was human life.

Hundreds of undead shuffled forward, slamming into the fence, pushing harder and harder against it, trying and failing to get through. The ones closest to the fence had been slammed against it so many times they barely had faces left. One person's head was little more than a cracked skull with two eye sockets dangling in front, thinly attached by fraying optic nerves. Their hands also were pounded to mulch, trying and failing to plow through to where the living were so they could feed on them.

How did they know, though? That was one of many mysteries, but it was one that pointed to a possible conclusion: there was more to these walking corpses than simple electrical impulses being fed to the brain in lieu of blood.

Plus, there were the dogs.

While humans were barely able to walk in this state, canines appeared to be fully functional. They could run and jump and do pretty much everything they could do when they were alive—yet they were not alive, given that they could neither respire nor procreate. Still, they functioned far better than their human brethren, and among the many tasks Isaacs had set about to accomplish was to find out why.

And now there was some evidence to show that there was at least a rudimentary intelligence to go with the instincts. The undead had all congregated here, even though there was no evidence that there was life here except for the occasional person who came up the lift. The T-virus that the late Dr. Ashford had developed might have been able to cure far more than a degenerative nerve condition.

The bad news was that more tests needed to be run.

The good news was that he had an infinite supply of test subjects right outside the fence.

To DiGennaro and Humberg, he said, "We need a fresh one. Prepare the tower."

"Okee dokee," DiGennaro said.

"Can you really call someone who's dead fresh?" Humberg asked.

DiGennaro smirked. "Long as none of 'em grab my ass."

Isaacs had long since lamented the possibility of maintaining discipline. Inappropriate humor was the way his people got through the day. Most of those headquartered here and still working for the Umbrella Corporation had lost most of what they had held dear to the T-virus. They continued to work here, not for money—that was a useless commodity now—but for survival. They continued to do their jobs, and Umbrella provided them with food and shelter.

But the fact that most of the world's population had succumbed to the T-virus was of very little moment to Sam Isaacs—he had his research, he had resources, and he had a problem to solve, so he was content. Most of humanity was dead, but Isaacs had never cared much for most of humanity, made up as it was of dolts and dunderheads who got in the way of allowing Isaacs to do his work.

Thanks to the Umbrella Corporation, Isaacs had lost nothing when the world ended. He still had his research, and he was content with that.

Isaacs turned away from the undead and followed Di-

Gennaro and Humberg to the guard tower on the other side of the weather station. The scent of lime wafted across his nostrils—which, oddly, was a palliative after being so close to the undead—but he didn't even look at the pit where the Alices had been dumped. They represented failure, and while Isaacs was a firm believer in learning from failure, these corpses had gone beyond the point where anything could be learned from them.

Besides, he was getting well and truly sick of the sight of that face.

If only he'd been able to keep her in Detroit . . .

He entered the guard tower, where another hydraulic lift took him, DiGennaro, and Humberg up fifteen stories. Upon arrival at the top, Isaacs stepped into the basket. It was akin to those used on hot-air balloons, except that this one was attached to an extendable metal bar, similar to those used by firefighters.

DiGennaro said to the guard at the top, "How's life treatin' you up here in the nosebleed seats, Robertson?"

"Just fucking peachy, Deej. It's nice and toasty warm up here. Heat rises, y'know."

Humberg and DiGennaro followed Isaacs into the basket. At a nod from Isaacs, Robertson activated the bar, which cantilevered out over the mesh fence and above the undead.

This activity was far from covert, as the metal made a horrible noise when it moved—keeping the hinges oiled wasn't a priority, as oil was needed for far more critical purposes in these dark times—and so all the undead looked up at the sound. They started jumping up, grabbing and clawing at the underside of the basket, sensing that there was fresh flesh for them to consume.

Robertson, however, kept them above the fray.

Since the project required a particularly strong specimen, Isaacs ruled out the women he saw. While he had known plenty of women who could hold their own in a physical conflict—up to and including Alice Abernathy, even before Isaacs got to experiment on her—when one was looking for a sample of humanity with the brute strength Isaacs required, the male of the species was far better suited.

He looked down, and eventually his eye caught a particularly fine one. In part, he stood out because of the brightly colored hockey shirt he wore with a number emblazoned on the back. It was impossible to tell at the stage of decay the clothes were in whether or not it was a legitimate hockey uniform or simply a store-bought facsimile, but what mattered to Isaacs was the broadness of the man's shoulders.

Pointing at the man in question, he said, "There—that one at the back. He'll do."

DiGennaro nodded, and he and Humberg pulled out their carbon-fiber nooses. The former whipped the noose around his head with a goofy grin on his face.

Humberg rolled his eyes. "John fuckin' Wayne, you ain't."

"Yeah, but that motherfucker's dead, and I'm alive."

"Big deal. Dead, he's still more of a man than your ass."

They threw the nooses down onto Hockey Jersey, each nabbing an arm. It was easy enough to accomplish, as he, along with all the other undead, reached upward, trying in vain to grab the basket.

Both security men pulled, hauling the undead up, even as Robertson moved the metal arm back toward the tower.

Grinning ear to ear, DiGennaro said, "Ride 'em, cow-zombie! Who's John Wayne now, asshole?"

Isaacs held in a sigh. It didn't do to antagonize those tasked with keeping Isaacs and the others safe. Thus far, Umbrella had been able to buy their loyalty with its stores of foodstuffs, but there was always the chance that the best-armed employees might take it upon themselves to take over. And since they had the guns and knew how to use them, they stood quite an excellent chance of succeeding.

If they got the notion into their heads. One sure way to make that happen was to antagonize them by, say, complaining about their endless half-witticisms. Isaacs, however, was no fool. He let them carry on.

Besides, he was going to need them for his long-term plans. One of history's finest lessons was that the strongest emperors were the ones with the most powerful armies.

Upon their return to the top of the guard tower, Robertson had the shackles ready. The large metal bar covered the occupant from neck to knee and was more effective than any straitjacket. They had disabled the function that shot a blast of electricity into the subject if he moved, simply because it was a waste of energy with the undead. The electricity wouldn't slow them down. In fact, there was some evidence to suggest that it would make them more active.

Humberg and DiGennaro held the undead in place while Robertson applied the restraints.

"This guy smells like ass. Like *dead* ass. Any chance we can take him for a shower, first?" Humberg asked.

"Go right ahead," DiGennaro said. "I assume you're volunteering to scrub those hard-to-reach areas?"

"Blow me, asshole."

"Later, if you're good."

They rode back down to ground level, then took the lift in the weather station back into the complex. Isaacs closed his eyes as they descended, enjoying the feel of the air conditioning wafting over him. He had never cared much for desert air, particularly when it was perfumed by the aroma of decaying corpses.

As soon as he got to the bottom, he saw Slater. This time, he didn't bother to hold in the sigh.

Alexander Slater's post as second in command of Umbrella's Science Division was most assuredly *not* Isaacs's idea. However, there were fewer places to assign personnel these days, and Slater was qualified to be Isaacs's right hand. Most of his staff from San Francisco and Detroit had died, and he couldn't afford to be choosy, nor could he afford to complain to the Committee about Slater's appointment.

At least, not yet.

And while he had no choice but to acquiesce to Slater's placement, Isaacs certainly had no reason to treat him with anything other than contempt.

"We're late," Slater said without preamble.

"I'm sorry?"

"The Committee meeting started five minutes ago. Where the hell've you been?"

Ignoring the question, Isaacs turned to DiGennaro. "Put that in my lab. You know the drill."

"You betcha, boss-man." DiGennaro turned to Hockey Jersey. "C'mon, Gretzky, let's stick you in the goal."

Isaacs turned and walked toward the meeting room, not bothering to see if Slater followed. Reaching into his lab-coat pocket, he touched the button on a device held therein.

As he approached the room, Isaacs could hear the conversation from down the corridor. The French accent and nasal tone indicated that Jacques Mercier, the head of the French Division, was giving his report. "—ualties. Biohazard numbers increasing."

A moment later, the clipped British tones of the head of the United Kingdom Division, Colin Wainwright, could be heard. "London facility: food supplies down to twenty-eight percent, seventeen casualties. Biohazard numbers increasing."

Isaacs entered just as Chairman Wesker's authoritative voice could be heard. "Thank you for your reports."

Upon entering the large room, Isaacs saw a large dark table in the center of the dimly lit space. A holographic representation of the globe rotated over the tabletop, with the hexagonal Umbrella logo indicating the location of Umbrella's headquarters on five continents.

On the far wall, several screens showed footage of cities around the globe: London, Paris, Lisboa, Amsterdam, København, Antananarivo, Srinagar, Tokyo, Beijing, Berlin, Moscova, Johannesberg, New Delhi. All of them were being overrun by the undead in much the same way Raccoon City and San Francisco had been years ago.

As ever, Isaacs blamed Cain.

"Gentlemen," he said as he walked in. Heads all turned.

Or, rather, the illusion of heads. While Isaacs saw the faces of all eight of Umbrella's division heads, as well as that of Chairman Wesker, he knew that none of them was actually in the room. Every Umbrella facility had a meeting room just like this one, and they were all showing the same information on the holograph above the table and the screens on the wall. They also all appeared to have the same eight people sitting around the table, and they all saw an image of Isaacs and Slater walking into the room.

The Holography Department had done its work well. Travel was too risky these days, and while it was difficult to coordinate a meeting that would occur across assorted time zones, that was preferable to risking the lives of the corporation's most important people.

Wesker looked over at Isaacs. At least, Isaacs assumed he did. It was hard to tell, as the chairman insisted on wearing mirror shades at all times. Wesker still wore the same crew cut he'd affected as a Marine, he still had multiple scars from that time, and Isaacs wondered if he wore the shades because of some ocular affliction or if he was just a pretentious ass.

If there were still money in this world, Isaacs would have bet all of it on the latter.

"How good of the Science Division to join us," Wesker said dryly.

Isaacs heard Slater exhale through his teeth, but he ignored it as he ignored most of what came out of Slater's mouth. He simply said, "I have been busy."

Wesker lowered his shades and stared at Isaacs with a penetrating pair of eyes, leading Isaacs to understand a bit more why he wore them. "That's most interesting, Doctor, because we were just about to discuss the results of your 'experiments'—or, rather, the lack of them."

"Is that so?" Isaacs asked, for lack of anything better to say. He'd been expecting something like this, which was why he hadn't been eager to show up on time for the meeting in the first place.

Wainwright spoke next. "On the subject of the biohazard, what does the Science Division have to report?"

Not for the first time, Isaacs marveled at his employers' capacity for making the appalling sound commonplace, though he wondered who, precisely, they were trying to impress at this point. "Biohazard" sounded as if someone had been putting anthrax through the postal system or a flu strain was going around. The T-virus was several orders of magnitude worse than a "biohazard."

But then, Wainwright had a much bigger population

of living humans left to be concerned with. Europe and Asia were still comparatively well off—while the Americas, Africa, and Australia had been almost completely overrun, the spread of the T-virus had been slower in the other two continents. Wainwright and the other Eurasian division heads no doubt harbored some illusion that they could beat this back.

Unfortunately, Isaacs was not about to give them the answers they wanted. "We now know conclusively that they have no real need for sustenance. They hunger for flesh but do not require it."

A rumble of discontent went through the room. The one benefit to the undead so greatly outnumbering the living was the hope that with a shortage of flesh to feed off, the undead would simply die out on their own. Isaacs had said all along that this was unlikely—after all, what use did the dead have for nourishment?—but the Committee had clung to the possibility as if it were a life preserver.

Isaacs went on: "Unless exposed to extremes of temperature or environment"—or, he didn't bother to add, all shot in the head—"my research indicates that they could remain active for decades."

Wainwright stood up at that, pounding his fist on the table as he rose. "Decades! We are to be trapped underground for *decades?*"

Wesker raised his hand and stared at Wainwright, whose face contorted into a more meek expression, and he sat back down.

"What news of Project Alice?"

Here Isaacs knew he could provide that life preserver. "Our goals remain unchanged. The original Project Alice was unique. She bonded with the T-virus on a cellular level, somehow managing to overcome it. Using antibodies from her blood"—the one aspect of Alice he'd been able to hang on to after the disaster in Detroit—"I will develop a serum that will not just combat the effects of the T-virus but potentially reverse it." Isaacs started to pace around the table, being sure to make eye contact with each Committee member as he spoke. "The power of this serum would go far beyond the weak anti-virus we have now. For those not yet infected, the serum would offer *complete* immunity. And for the"—he hesitated, then looked right at Wainwright—"biohazard themselves, a partial reversal of the process. Giving back these creatures a measure of their intelligence, their memories— and curbing their hunger for flesh."

The ripple that went through the Committee this time was far more positive. Wesker asked, "You're confident you can domesticate them?"

In fact, Isaacs was confident of no such thing. That was the goal, yes, but there were many roadblocks. However, appearances needed to be maintained. "Why not?" he said matter-of-factly. "They are animals, essentially. We can train them—*if* we can take away their baser instincts."

Behind him, Isaacs heard Slater mutter, "And if my grandmother had wheels, she'd be a wagon." Slater had been against this entire program from the start, viewing it as a waste of time. "Sure," he had said once, "*if* you can take away their baser instincts, but it's not like that's something you can just carve out of their brains. In fact, you try that, you lose them."

Isaacs, however, was more sanguine. To the Committee, he continued: "They'll never be human again but would provide the basis for a docile workforce under our guidance. We would return to the surface and create a new world order in our image."

Some of the Committee members seemed to like the sound of that. Mercier, however, was not one of them. "Pipe dreams!" the Frenchman said, flicking his hand in a scoffing motion. "After months of experiments, you have nothing to show, and we are left to rot underground!"

"Without the original Project Alice," Isaacs said testily, "progress has been difficult. We have been forced to try and replicate her using cloned genetic models whose growth has been accelerated by Dr. Wiegand. It's laborious, and the results are unpredictable."

Wainwright snorted. "Eighty-five failures, Doctor."

Shrugging, Isaacs said, "This is not an exact science."

"I don't see much *science* at all."

Before Isaacs could reply to the slander—as if this idiot bureaucrat knew anything about science in the first place—Wesker again held up a hand.

"Project Alice, and the subject of domestication, is of the *highest* priority." Then, suddenly, the image of Wesker froze for a second, his face in a comical position for half a second, before he went on, the signal having been reacquired, his gaze now suddenly fixed firmly on

Isaacs. "You will concentrate on this to the exclusion of all other research. We will expect an updated report within the week."

For about the nine-thousandth time, Isaacs said, "Simply demanding results will not guarantee them." This was something else he blamed Cain for—he always blithely gave timetables for accomplishments that had no bearing on reality but were fast enough to suit the whims of the Committee. Science didn't actually work like that.

However, it seemed that Isaacs had used up whatever reassurances he could provide, because this was the first time that Wesker responded to his rational explanations with a threat.

"Then perhaps we should place someone else in charge. Someone"—again, Wesker's signal was interrupted, then it picked up again, but the audio was now out of synch with his mouth—"who can give us the reassurances we require." Wesker looked like one of those badly dubbed martial arts films that the security staff seemed to get no end of enjoyment in watching over and over again during their downtime.

Suddenly, Isaacs was very much aware of Slater standing behind him. Slater was just stupid enough to tell the Committee what they wanted to hear rather than what they needed to hear.

"Continue with your research, Doctor." Wesker's image hadn't yet caught up to his voice. "And be quick about it while it still is *your* research. This meeting is adjourned."

The images of the Committee members, as well as the footage on the wall screens and the holograph of the globe, all winked out as one.

Were Slater not still in the room, Isaacs would have pointed out, if only to the empty air, that it would be *his* research no matter who administered it. But he saw no reason to give Slater more ammunition. He had been fairly certain that Slater was making his own reports to the Committee, even though technically the only person Slater was supposed to send any reports to was Isaacs himself.

Still, that was a problem for another day.

Isaacs turned around to see Slater grinning stupidly. "That went well."

"I have work to do," Isaacs said as he strode past Slater.

"Yeah, you do. And you'd be wise to do it quickly and not piss Wesker off."

Continuing to ignore Slater, Isaacs proceeded to his lab. Only when he'd shut the door behind him did he allow himself to speak. Doing an exaggerated impersonation of Wainwright's London accent, he said, "'I don't see much *science* at all!' Imbeciles."

With a glance, he saw that DiGennaro and Humberg had secured Hockey Jersey to the wall, a collar around his neck and shackles binding his wrists. The undead— or "biohazard," to use the Committee's preferred euphemism—struggled mightily against those restraints as soon as Isaacs walked into the room, but he ignored the creature as easily as he'd ignored Slater.

Isaacs reached into his lab-coat pocket and took out the device he'd been running since before walking into the room: a digital recorder.

He placed the recorder on the docking station attached to his computer. Using the mouse and keyboard, he instructed the program that ran as soon as he docked the recorder to isolate Wesker's voice print.

"Continue with your threats, Wesker," Isaacs muttered, "while it's still your corporation to run."

Hockey Jersey pulled harder against his restraints. Isaacs finally looked at him. "In due time."

Then he turned to look at the lab's far window.

And he smiled.

Officially, the only two projects that were currently active in this facility were Project Alice and the research into the domestication of the "biohazard." Clone 86 was being prepped even now for the former, and Hockey Jersey was the latest subject to facilitate the latter.

But there was a third project that was just as active and even more important than those two, as far as Sam Isaacs was concerned.

It was only because that project was so much closer to fruition that Isaacs had taken the risk of bringing a digital recorder into the Committee meeting. But he would need Wesker's voice to accomplish his goals.

And nobody would stand in his way.

NINE

BEFORE

In all her years as a cop, the thing that amazed Jill Valentine more than anything else was that every single person they ever brought in for questioning didn't ask for a lawyer.

It was remarkable, really. Ever since the *Miranda* v. *Arizona* case in 1966, cops were *legally obligated* to tell you up-front that you could have legal representation present when you were questioned by the police or if you were under arrest. Without the lawyer present, you were on your own, a civilian who probably didn't know nearly enough about the law sitting in a room full of people who worked with the law every day. Only a complete fool would go in there without an advocate, especially one they knew they were entitled to.

It wasn't as if *Miranda* was a big secret. The most

popular television shows on the air were cop shows, and had been for as long as there'd been television, and on every one of them since 1966, they saw cops telling people they had the right to an attorney. The second most popular television shows involved lawyers.

And yet Jill always saw perps brought in, or witnesses, or whatever, and they always passed on having an expert in the law whose purpose in life was to protect them when they were in a room with cops who had absolutely no interest in doing so.

Every cop knew that an interrogation was all but finished as soon as the perp lawyered up, so they did everything possible to discourage it. And when cops themselves were brought in, you couldn't get the union lawyer into the room fast enough.

So when Jill Valentine was taken into custody in Idaho by federal agents and did not ask for a lawyer, she knew that the agents in question found this behavior odd.

What they didn't realize, of course, was that she *wanted* the interrogation to go on for a long time. For one thing, the more she had their attention, the fewer people they had looking for Carlos, Alice, Angie, and L.J. For another, she wanted to cooperate completely with them. Protecting her rights was of comparatively little interest just at the moment—it was protecting the lives of millions of people who'd be exposed, not to mention speaking for the millions who had already died.

They flew her in a helicopter to the Boise field office, and then—before anybody could talk to her—they remanded her to the main office in Washington.

On the one hand, Jill was glad to be getting the attention of the big boys. On the other, it meant the locals would still keep looking for the others.

But she knew the job was dangerous when she took it.

When the jet landed in D.C., they put her, still handcuffed, as she'd been from the moment they busted into the room at the It'll Do Motel in Idaho, in a bland interrogation room. That was almost a redundancy—there was no such thing as an interesting interrogation room. You didn't want any distractions, after all. Nor did you want, say, a window or anything else that indicated a way out. Back in Raccoon, there was one local district house that had windows in every room, but they'd put bars on them.

It wasn't a jail cell, but it had all the right aspects of one. Once they got you in here, you were trapped.

However, that was precisely what Jill wanted.

They'd kept her sitting for about an hour—another standard tactic but one that generally worked. Let the perp sit and stew with her own thoughts for a while. If nothing else, it served to frustrate and annoy the perp.

Unless, of course, the perp in question was expecting it, as Jill was. So she sat quietly, occasionally picking at a fingernail, and waited for her interrogators to make their presence known.

The one difference between this room and the typical RCPD one was the table at which Jill currently sat. It was a pristine metal table. Back home, they were partial to Formica, and it was battered within an inch of its life, covered in nicks, cuts, and scrawls of various perps who would spend their time alone in the room doodling, if the cops bothered to leave a pen.

Television also had taught everyone what was on the other side of mirrors in interrogation rooms, and as a result, many places had done away with them. This room had nothing, but there was a video camera in one ceiling corner that was no doubt recording everything in the room for potential future evidence. The video made everyone's life easier, especially since nobody was really surprised that people other than those in the room were watching and listening.

Finally, two men walked in. One was the very model of a modern federal agent: tall white guy in his thirties, very short dark hair, with the beginnings of male-pattern baldness. The other was an African-American man who looked barely old enough to shave. Both men wore dark suits with white shirts and dark ties. All they needed were trenchcoats and Ray-Bans to complete the stereotype. They sat in the two chairs that faced Jill.

"Ms. Valentine," the white guy started, "or, rather, I should say Officer Valentine."

"Well," the black guy said, "she's not an officer anymore. I mean, she was suspended, and the city she was supposed to serve and protect's a radioactive crater, know what I'm sayin'?"

The white guy nodded. "Fair point. Still, she's a member of the community, y'know? Anyhow, Officer Valentine, I'm Special Agent Hicks, this is Special Agent Graves."

"Fuck this," Graves said. "I ain't callin' her Officer shit."

Jill finally spoke. "If you prefer to call me Ms. Shit, I'm okay with that, Agent Graves." She added a sweet smile.

"Oh, you're funny." Graves got up and started pacing. "This is bullshit. Let's just toss the bitch in a cell and—"

"On what charge?" Jill asked.

Hicks smiled at her in as insincere a manner as possible. "Don't tell me you don't know, Officer Valentine."

"Honestly, I don't. I was placed under arrest, I've had my rights read to me, and I've filled out paperwork saying I waived my right to an attorney. By the way, you guys should look into streamlining, 'cause our paperwork takes maybe half the time. I mean, I know, the higher up the food chain you get, the paperwork metastasizes, but damn—it shouldn't take twenty minutes of me doing my chicken scratch just to say, 'I don't want a lawyer.'"

Graves sat back down, folding his hands together. "We like to be extra careful with law-enforcement types. You know the system, so you're more likely to try to fuck with it."

"Now, why would I do that when I let you guys catch me?"

To their credit, they didn't react at first. Then Hicks chuckled. "C'mon, Officer Valentine, you really expect us to believe that—"

"I made the guy in the fast-food joint, not to mention the signal car that had been driving past every fast-food joint in the area trying to find me or one of my alleged co-conspirators. You know, the guy wearing the black North Face coat big enough to hide his piece, the ball cap from a local minor-league team, and sunglasses—all newly bought, I might add."

Hicks and Graves exchanged a glance. "Maybe you're right," Hicks said. "Maybe we should just toss her in a cell."

Jill leaned back in her chair and tried not to smile. Hicks was trying to get Graves to agree so they could leave the room and regroup. Jill hadn't been what they expected, and she hadn't been following the script they laid out. These guys were pathetic—a *good* interrogator would be able to go with the flow if a perp went off-script, but these guys obviously weren't the FBI's finest. She was almost insulted.

"Hang on," Graves said, modulating into Good Cop. "I'm curious—let's say you did let yourself get caught. Why?"

"You play the tape?"

"What tape?"

"Oh, cut the shit, Agent Graves. I only had one thing on me when you guys slapped the bracelets on. The tape. The digital tape. The one that looks just like the ones that were on various West Coast news stations before Umbrella 'exposed' them as fakes." Although it was an affectation that annoyed her when other people did it, Jill made little quote marks with her fingers when she said "exposed."

"Funny you shoulda done that," Hicks said. "See,

that's the main piece of evidence against you on the fraud charges. That's what you're being charged with: fraud."

"Gawrsh," Jill said with a smile. "In Raccoon, frauds are taken care of by the gomers—the test takers who managed to get a gold shield thanks to the written but aren't really *detectives,* know what I mean? It's the low-priority shit."

"Yeah, so?" Graves asked defensively.

"So I get flown across the country for just fraud? Cah-*mon,* Agent Hicks, Agent Graves—there's gotta be more to it than that."

"Oh, there is," Graves said, leaning forward and grinning. "See, you pissed off some really important people. People who don't take kindly to slander."

"Slander?" Jill leaned back and put her hand over her heart, as if aghast. "Agent Graves, I am shocked. I have committed no acts of slander. If the tape I released to various news stations is false, then, yes, I admit to aiding in the perpetration of a fraud. But slander? That would require my bearing false witness, and you have no evidence to support that. The only person a slander case could be made against is Alice Abernathy—*she's* the one on the tape, after all. All *I* did was provide a videotape—which, by the way, also included some fascinating footage of people with some kind of awful disease walking the streets of Raccoon City. Funny how they look just like the people in San Francisco. What's happening there, anyhow? I've been kinda cut off."

A knock came on the door before Hicks could reply to that. An older man with a steel-gray crew cut and horn-rimmed glasses poked his head in. "Gentlemen, may I see you a moment?"

Graves started to say, "Sir, we're in the middle of—"

"Now, Agent Graves." The older man didn't change his tone, but something in it made Graves cease his objection.

He and Hicks left.

Jill wasn't sure how much time passed after that—no clocks in the interrogation room, since you never wanted perps to know how long they'd been in there—but eventually the crew-cut guy came back alone.

He sat down at the desk in a very studied manner, placing a manila folder on the table in front of him. "Officer Valentine, first of all, let me apologize for Agents Graves and Hicks. They were simply doing what they were told."

"It's not a problem," Jill said, matching the older man's politeness.

"Can you tell me, please, Officer Valentine, where you obtained the tape that was found on your person yesterday?"

"From a handheld video recorder owned by Terri Morales, now deceased."

Unlike Hicks and Graves, this guy was actually taking notes. "Mr. Morales worked—"

"Ms."

"I'm sorry, Ms. Morales was a local reporter?"

Jill smiled. "She used to be. At the time we met, she did the Raccoon 7 weather. She used to be a field reporter until she was demoted."

"She was demoted for airing a fraudulent videotape, yes?"

Nodding, Jill said, "That's what I heard, yes."

"You don't know?"

"Don't care—I met Morales a few times before that last time, and she never impressed me overmuch. And the doings of TV reporters were never something I was overly concerned with."

At that, the man smiled. "I can understand that." Then it was back to all business. "Officer Valentine, you were suspended from the Raccoon City Police Department. Why?"

"Excuse me, sir, but are you a U.S. attorney? 'Cause I gotta tell you, this sounds more like court testimony than my giving a statement."

"Do you wish to give a statement, Officer Valentine?"

"I wish the truth to be revealed," Jill said in an even voice, "and I wish to know who I'm talking to."

"I'm a federal agent, like Hicks and Graves."

"And yet you're not carrying an ID badge like everyone else in this building."

"I left it on my jacket, which is back in my office. I can go back and get it if you want, Officer Valentine."

Jill wondered whether to believe this man or not. Whoever he was, he got Hicks and Graves to jump.

And he seemed genuinely interested in what she had to say. But then, so did Captain Henderson until Umbrella exerted its pressure. Who *was* this guy?

"Shall I continue with my questions, Officer Valentine?"

After a second, Jill nodded. "I don't suppose I can get a cigarette."

"No smoking in the building, I'm afraid."

Jill chuckled. "World really is going to hell in a handbasket." She let out a long breath, as if she was puffing out cigarette smoke. "To answer your question, I was suspended without cause. I reported some kind of biological contamination that I saw in the Arklay Mountains."

"Are the Arklays part of the RCPD's jurisdiction?"

"Technically, that's the domain of the county police. I was there hiking, and I stumbled on some—infected people. Later on, I learned that they were corpses that had been animated by a virus."

"Who informed you of this?"

"I was told by a woman named Alice Abernathy, but even if she hadn't, I'd seen it for myself. People would die and then start walking around again. The only way to stop them was to shoot them in the head."

"What were the symptoms of these—these infected people?"

"Lack of breathing, lack of blinking, lack of beating heart . . ." At the older man's look, she grew serious. "Milky white eyes, lack of coordination, inability to speak, and an apparent hunger for living flesh." She closed her eyes. "They got Peyton." Off another look, she said, "Sergeant Peyton Wells, my commander with S.T.A.R.S."

"That would be the Special Tactics and Rescue Squad?"

Jill nodded.

The door opened, and a young man wheeled in a large black stand on which was a large television and, on the shelf below it, a combination VCR/DVD player, as well as a projector. They were all plugged into a power strip, which the young man plugged into a socket in the wall.

After the young man left, the older man continued: "What happened to Sergeant Wells?"

"He was bitten by an old man who died of a heart attack on the Ravens' Gate Bridge. After he died, he got up and bit Peyton on the leg. Peyton's wound wouldn't clot. It just got worse. Then he was killed by—by gunfire." She didn't get into that Nemesis creature that Alice fought—it would shoot them off on an unproductive tangent, and besides, Nemesis wasn't a danger anymore, which was more than could be said for the T-virus. "A few minutes later, he was trying to chow down on me, and his eyes had gone milky."

"And the footage on the tape you provided, these were examples of those infected people?"

"Yes."

The old man leaned over to the stand and pulled a remote off the second shelf. He turned on the TV, which lit up with a solid blue screen and the number 3 on the upper-right-hand corner. Then he hit another button, and the blue switched to black.

A moment later, Jill saw the very familiar sight of zombies wandering down streets. Just like in the graveyard, just like at the school, just like at City Hall.

And just like in the Arklays.

Except that Jill recognized the street they were shambling down: Lombard Street. Located on a particularly steep hill in a city famous for them, the steepest section of Lombard twisted and turned, surrounded by beautiful flower beds.

Those flowers were now being overrun by the same zombie creatures that had run rampant through Raccoon and through the Arklays. The same creature that Peyton had turned into.

"Is this what they looked like, Officer Valentine?"

Jill found she couldn't keep looking at the screen. She'd been a cop all her adult life, had seen things as a member of S.T.A.R.S. that would send most civilians hiding under their beds and not flinched, but this—

There was only so much of this she could take.

"Officer Valentine, what I'm about to tell you is something you are technically not cleared to know about—but I suspect that you actually know more than we do. You see, there has been an outbreak of some kind of virus in San Francisco that kills people, animates their corpses—as ridiculous as that sounds—and sends those corpses on a feeding frenzy. Everyone they bite is similarly infected. We have no means of stopping it."

"You may not, but the Umbrella Corporation does. They created the virus. The section of the Arklays where I went hiking was owned by Umbrella." She smiled sheepishly. "I only was there by accident. I got turned around on one of the rocks and went north when I should've gone south."

The old man returned the smile. "That's why you're supposed to pack a compass, Officer Valentine."

Jill wondered how much different her life would've been if she had packed that compass, then decided that she just would've gone about her duties and been nuked along with the rest of Raccoon. Her foreknowledge of the zombies was what had kept her alive long enough to be evacuated thanks to Dr. Ashford's crazy plan.

"In any case," Jill said, "Umbrella sealed off Raccoon City after the outbreak—put a big wall around the entire island, cutting off all the bridges and tunnels out of town. The only egress was Ravens' Gate, and they had armed guards there who fired on the crowd. If I remember right, that's on the tape, too—Morales was there when it happened."

The older man made a few more notes, then stood up. "Officer Valentine, we will have more questions for you—and we may need to fly you to San Francisco."

Jill frowned. "Why?"

"The governor has called in the National Guard, but we're completely at a loss. You've actually dealt with this, and the Umbrella Corporation thinks enough of you to engage in a smear campaign."

"That has nothing to do with me," Jill said. "They needed a cover story after they nuked the island."

For the first time, the old man was nonplussed. "Excuse me?"

She couldn't believe that they hadn't connected these particular dots. "The meltdown was a cover story."

"We received telemetry from the power plant for

hours before the meltdown. We were warned that it would—"

"That was to cover their tracks. It's why they waited most of the night to hit with the nuke. They needed to lay the groundwork for the cover story. There *was* no meltdown!" Jill almost stood up but decided to stay at the same level as this man and look him straight in the eyes.

He was the first to look away, which Jill considered a rather pointless moral victory.

"I'll be back," he said after taking a few more notes. He rose from his chair and moved to the door.

After he opened it, he said, "My name, by the way, is Deputy Director Kirby Johnson."

With that, he left.

As soon as the door closed, Jill tried to contain a whoop of delight. The video camera was still on, after all, and it wouldn't do to show her enthusiasm.

But she had just been vindicated in her choice of action once she saw the schmuck in the ball cap in the fast-food joint. From the look of things, the feds weren't just going to roll over for Umbrella—not with what was happening in San Francisco right now.

For the first time since her hiking trip, Jill Valentine allowed herself a glimmer of hope.

†en
After

As Jill Valentine drove her Prius through the remains of Baltimore, she found herself without a glimmer of hope.

She had been lucky to salvage the Prius—a hybrid gas/electric car—as it got her much farther on less gas than the SUV she'd been in before. True, the SUV had a stronger cage, which made for better protection against scavengers—whether human, undead, or animal; the world was awash in all three—but with more and more gas stations coming up empty, the Prius made it easier for her to keep moving.

Sooner or later, she supposed she would have to settle somewhere, try to wait this whole thing out, but she'd yet to find anywhere worth staying.

She'd done what she could—helping out the occasional enclave of humanity—but eventually they were overcome by the zombies, and Jill quickly got out while the gettin' was good. Those instincts had enabled her to be one of Raccoon City's few surviving citizens, and they'd kept her alive since Raccoon's legacy had all but destroyed the world.

As time went on, she'd worked her way east. She'd hoped to find Alice or Carlos or even, God help her, L.J. She'd heard that Angie had been killed, though that was secondhand.

As if there was any information that *wasn't* secondhand anymore.

The last time she'd seen Carlos was when she bumped into that convoy he and L.J. and some woman named Claire Redfield had put together back in Atlanta. Jill had collected a bunch of refugees of her own, like ducklings. She had gratefully left them with Carlos and his people, L.J. relishing the notion of more people to take care of.

Even as the death toll increased, even as the government collapsed under the weight of the zombies, Jill kept surviving, kept moving. She could have stayed with Carlos and Claire and L.J., but after so many betrayals, she could not bring herself to trust anyone.

She'd lead, but she would never follow again.

Jill navigated the Prius down a road that she knew would lead to the Inner Harbor. Once a thriving shopping district, according to more of that secondhand information, it was the headquarters of a group of humans who'd managed to tough it out against the zombies. If nothing else, it might have been a good place to share intel and trade supplies. The backseat, passenger seat, and trunk were full of assorted items Jill had scavenged or traded for.

As she went down the road, she saw numerous skeletons and dead bodies—all, she noted, with severe head trauma. She had no interest in examining the bodies, but she was willing to bet that they all died of various and sundry causes and were all shot in the head postmortem, either as a preventive strike against the T-virus or in response to its posthumous effects.

The road took her past the convention center, but before she could reach that, she saw a barricade staffed by armed guards. The number of bodies and skeletons got considerably higher the closer she got.

Jill took a glance at the Prius's passenger seat, which held her own weapon collection. The only one she couldn't use was the MP5, as she hadn't been able to find any proper rounds for the thing. However, the MAC-11, the nine-millimeter, the sawed-off shotgun (which always made Jill think of Alice), and the rest all were fully loaded.

She stopped the car about fifty feet from the barricade. Two of the guards ran forward, their own guns at the ready. After a second, Jill recognized them as police-issue nine-mills, much like her own. Probably used to belong to the Balto City Police.

One took aim at Jill's head, while the other, shorter one spoke. They were dressed shabbily but seemed much better fed than most of the living people Jill had encountered lately.

"This is how it's gonna be!" the short one said. "You give us y'car and everythin' in it, we letcha go on y'merry! You *don't* give us y'car and everythin' in it, we shoot your ass and take the shit anyhow! We're only bein' so considerate on account of how we don't wanna be makin' more zees, but we *will* shoot y'ass down if you don't—"

Whatever else he might have said was cut off by Jill shooting him in the head. She only waited that long because she had been moving her arms toward her weaponry slowly under the dashboard so neither of the guards would notice.

After she shot the short one, she shot the tall one. His finger spasmed on his trigger, but his shot went harmlessly into the air.

Jill turned the steering wheel around as she slammed her foot on the accelerator and headed back the way she came. Her route was a bit more haphazard this time, and skeletons and bodies cracked and squelched under her tires as she ran over the remains that she'd carefully avoided on the way down.

Gunfire reports sounded behind her, some ricocheting off the Prius, but they stopped after a few seconds. Whoever these assholes were, they didn't seem interested in giving chase—or didn't have the means. That may have been why they wanted her car.

Now the large number of bodies made sense.

After she made it to a street corner far from the harbor, she stopped the car.

The street was deserted, of course. Up and down

each block were brick row houses with the three-step stoops that Baltimore was famous for.

No, wait—not deserted. Three zombies were shuffling out of one of the alleys.

Jill took aim and shot each one in the head in succession. They all fell to the ground.

The reports of the nine-millimeter echoed down the quiet street like thunder.

Flipping down the sun visor, Jill looked at herself in the mirror. Her dark hair had grown down to her ass, as she'd had no inclination to cut it. She kept it tied back in a ponytail that was more like a horse tail at this point. The bruise on her cheek from that run-in with the zombie dogs in Virginia Beach was finally starting to heal. She wore the battered Umbrella Security Division uniform that Carlos had given her in Atlanta, body armor that served to protect most of her. Her thighs were a bit more exposed, as the now-deceased previous owner was apparently much taller than Jill. He was likely bulkier, but the torso piece still fit fine. Jill had abandoned the pants, though she kept the boots, which were a size too big, but tissue paper solved that problem.

Once, she would have tried to look her best—not out of any vanity but because it made people underestimate her. Look at her; she's gorgeous; she's wearing a miniskirt; she's wearing a tube top; she's some ditz, a pair of tits whose brain was there just to make sure basic body functions worked.

That made it more fun when she kicked their asses.

Now, though, it hardly mattered. Nobody cared what

she looked like, least of all her. The zombies weren't likely to be impressed by her exposed legs, except as something they might want to munch on. So she kept covered up.

The sound of creaking wood interrupted her self-examination. She looked out the Prius window to see someone sticking his head out the row-house door across the street from where she'd parked the Prius.

"You just shoot those zees, lady?"

She aimed her nine-mill across the cracked pavement. "Shoot you, too, if you give me reason."

He came all the way out, hands raised. "Nah, s'a'ight. I'm cool. Don't be shootin', lady, s'a'ight."

Like the guards, this African American man was shabbily dressed. However, he most assuredly wasn't well fed. What she could see of his arms were thin as rails, and his face was sunken and sallow.

"Listen, lady, don't be shootin', but—well, you best be gettin' somewhere that ain't here, a'ight? Them boys, they be takin' fuck-all, an' then you ain't got shit, a'ight?"

Assuming that "them boys" were the fellows she'd just shot, she said, "You mean those assholes at the convention center?"

The man nodded. "You wanna keep that car an' that gun an' fuck-all else you got, you best be leavin', a'ight?"

Jill finally lowered her weapon. "My name's Jill."

"Andre. Pleased t'be meetin' you, an' all that shit."

"You alone, Andre?"

Shaking his head, Andre said, "Nah, I gots me some peoples here. Them boys don't be lettin' us in, so we be hidin' here. Survivin', you know, and hidin' from the zees. Thought those zees'd be doin' us in, but you went and shot 'em. Pretty neighborly, y'ask me, so, y'know, thanks an' shit." Andre still had his hands up, even though Jill was no longer actively threatening him.

"How many of you are there?"

"Five. Plus me, so, y'know, six an' shit."

Jill opened the door to the Prius and got out. Andre still stood on the three-step stoop, hands raised.

"Tell you what, Andre. I got some food in the trunk. I'll share it with you and your five friends, on one condition."

"What's that?"

"You tell me *everything* about those guys at the convention center."

Interstate 80 hadn't really gotten any better for Alice after Salt Lake City.

The city itself had been stripped down. Every gas station in town was dry as a bone—or, at least, the ones she could get to were. Plenty were overrun with so many undead that even Alice didn't think she could get through them.

Leaving aside any other considerations, she didn't have that much ammo. She wasn't sure there was that much ammo left in the world.

So she continued westward on 80 toward Nevada. After a time, just before she reached the border, she caught site of an Enco gas station on one of the nearby local roads.

Just as she was getting onto the off-ramp that would lead to the road in question, her watch beeped.

59 . . . 58 . . . 57 . . .

She had modulated the Timex's beep to be on a high enough frequency that even if she couldn't hear it over the engine of the BMW, she could still feel the vibration of the beeping in her skull.

Another legacy of Dr. Isaacs and his experiments on her.

She was really looking forward to the day when she could repay him for that.

Not to mention Angie.

44 . . . 43 . . . 42 . . .

Pulling onto a ridge overlooking the Enco station, she took out the camouflage tarp and put it over herself and the bike, just as she had at the Salt Lake TV station, this time with almost thirty seconds to spare.

Then she waited.

Eventually, the watch beeped again, and she clambered out from under the tarp.

After stowing the tarp, she removed her binoculars and peered through them at the Enco station.

She saw an undead shuffling back and forth between the gas pumps and a rusty old Chevy pickup truck. His face had long since decayed past recognizability, but he wore a gray jumpsuit with the word STEVIE emblazoned on the breast.

There was no other sign of life. Or unlife.

Replacing the binoculars, she opened another of her many "saddlebags" to remove the parts of a crossbow. She'd found this in an abandoned fallout shelter in Minnesota about a year back. The shelter's doors had been opened sometime previously by an explosive of some sort, and most of the useful supplies—like food and gasoline—had been looted long ago. The only useful things Alice had found were the programmable Timex that had just warned her of the Umbrella satellite's pattern of flight and the crossbow. The former probably had been left behind because no one cared what time it was anymore. As for the latter, it was an esoteric weapon, one few people were capable of using properly. No doubt, it had been abandoned as being archaic.

But sooner or later, the bullets would run out. A crossbow could fire pretty much anything that was long, skinny, and hard, and the world had a lot more of that lying around than refined metal.

So Alice took the crossbow.

Now she assembled it and aimed a bolt right at the former gas station attendant's head.

"Sorry about this, Stevie," she muttered as she fired.

The bolt nailed Stevie right between the eyes, the tip coming out the back of his skull and pinning him to the bodywork of the pickup truck.

Confident that the place was now free of undead, Alice got back on the BMW and drove into the gas station.

She tried each pump in succession. Nothing. Nothing. Nothing. Then half a cup before nothing.

"Damn."

Looking over the station itself, she saw that it included a minimart, which was boarded up from the inside. Probably Stevie's coworkers had barricaded themselves inside to protect themselves from Stevie and his fellow undead. She grabbed one of her guns, pretty much at random, and kicked open the door. Wood splintered easily at the impact from her boot.

The stench hit her nose a lot harder than her foot had hit the door. Alice would have thought that after all these years, she'd be inured to the smell of decay and death, but no such luck. The Enco's minimart was overwhelmed by a miasma of rot.

A lot of the smell came from the refrigerator units, which were full of liquids that hadn't been kept cool. Her nose refused to inhale, and she breathed through her mouth as much as she could without hyperventilating. What food was still on the shelves had gone an unfortunate green color. Tons of empty containers—cans, bottles, and more—were littered about the floor.

Slowly, Alice moved through the minimart, peering into the shadowy darkness—the only light was what came in through the door she'd kicked open—her gun cocked and ready. Whoever was in here certainly didn't starve. Based on the buzzing sound, there were plenty of flies, but they couldn't have opened the cans, so there had to have been a human being in here once.

The flies' buzzing grew louder as Alice moved further inside.

She leapt aside and whirled the gun around before

her conscious mind was even aware of the clattering sound.

The metallic clinking of pennies falling on the floor was all she heard. Looking down, she saw that she'd up-ended the penny tray by the cash register with her elbow.

For a brief moment, Alice barked a laugh. "Ass-Kicking Alice" reduced to being startled by knocked-over pennies. If One could see her now, he'd laugh in her face.

Well, no, that wasn't his style. He'd just look at her disapprovingly.

The sad thing was, One would've thrived in this new world. He lived for this sort of seat-of-the-pants, every-one-for-themselves life that the remnants of the human race were now stuck with. Instead, he had been reduced to a pile of cubed meat in the corridor that led to the Red Queen's CPU in the Hive. An ignominious end.

But given the way life tended to end for people these days, he was probably better off.

Alice turned around—

—and smacked into a thigh with a meaty thud.

Again, she leapt to the side, raising her gun, but it was unnecessary. The thigh belonged to a body that was hanging from the ceiling. The rotting clothes, which looked similar to those worn by Stevie outside, covered rotting flesh. In the dim light, Alice couldn't make out what this guy had hung himself with, but it had obviously snapped his neck quite well. And people with broken necks couldn't be revitalized by the T-virus.

Sighing, Alice turned to leave. There was nothing of value here. Probably this poor bastard had holed himself up in here until the food ran out, then hung himself.

Just as she started toward the broken door, she noticed a flash of red. It was a notebook, lying on the counter shelf next to where the body hung.

She grabbed it and started flipping through it. It looked to be a journal of some kind.

A wave of nausea overcame her, and she decided that she'd find somewhere else to read this guy's last will and testament, or whatever the fuck it was.

After stuffing the journal into one of her bags, she hopped on the BMW and high-tailed it back onto 80.

Eleven

Before

"It looks different."

Tom Hoyt, the Umbrella Corporation's chief liaison to the federal government, looked over at Dr. Emily Love. They were sitting in the lobby of the White House, a place Hoyt had been several dozen times before. However, it was Love's first trip. They were supposed to be meeting with the president, as well as several key members of his staff, to discuss the T-virus issue. Hoyt hadn't wanted Love to be with him for this meeting. It was going to be difficult enough to calm the president on his own, but this deranged old woman would probably undermine his every attempt at placation.

However, he'd been overridden. For starters, the White House had made it abundantly clear that someone from Umbrella's Science Division needed to be present. Chairman Wesker himself had agreed to this stipulation, and Hoyt wasn't stupid enough to countermand Wesker. Besides which, Love was the company's leading expert on the virus.

Well, the leading expert still alive, anyhow.

They'd been sitting in the lobby for ten minutes. There was very little activity in the place, which was unusual. Hoyt knew that with the country in a state of emergency, a lot of government business was being done over the phone. People were being encouraged to stay in one place, after all.

Hoyt had ignored Love's comment, but she kept talking anyhow. "I mean, from television. It's so big on there—this massive space with columns and stuff. This—this just feels like a doctor's waiting room. Did you ever watch *The West Wing?*"

Since it was a direct question, Hoyt reluctantly answered. "No. The guy who wrote it was a drug addict. I don't watch TV shows written by drug addicts."

Love smiled, showing very expensive dentures. "You must not watch any television, then."

A young man came through a door. "Mr. Hoyt, Dr. Love, my name is Al Cowan. I'll be taking you to the Oval. Come with me, please."

Getting to her feet, Love's smile widened. "Thank you very much, Mr. Cowan."

"Is this your first time in the White House, Dr. Love?" Cowan asked as he led them through the door and down the hallway.

"Yes, it is, actually. I must admit to being a bit nervous."

Cowan gave the world's most insincere smile. "You've got nothing to be nervous about, Dr. Love."

"I appreciate your encouragement, young man, but in fact, everyone in the world has a great deal to be nervous about. The fact that I'm about to talk to the president of the United States is not why I've bitten my fingernails down to the nubs, I can assure you."

Hoyt sighed. At least he knew that Love was taking this seriously.

Cowan brought them past a curved wall, meaning that they were nearing the Oval Office. He opened one white door and held it for them.

With the greatest reluctance, Hoyt entered. The president was sitting at his desk, reading a report, with the vice president, various staffers, cabinet members, and all of the joint chiefs either in the chairs or on one of the two striped couches.

"Mr. President," Hoyt said, "it's good to see you—"

"Please spare me the usual glad-handing Umbrella bullshit, Mr. Hoyt," the president said.

Hoyt sighed. The president was obviously in one of his moods. The public never saw this side of their leader, and it was a good thing, as the man had a vicious temper. Hoyt had sat in this room with four different presidents, and no one had ever given him a tongue-lashing like the current one.

The chief of staff stepped in quickly. "Mr. Hoyt, we asked for a meeting with all of Umbrella's experts on this virus. We were told you had a *team* working on this, and we were supposed to meet with *all* of them."

"I'm sorry, but Dr. Love was all we could spare." Hoyt walked to stand between the two couches and the president. Love lagged behind.

"Love?" The president snorted. "You actually brought someone named Dr. Love?"

The doctor stepped forward. "Actually, Mr. President, it's my married name. I was born Emily Johannsen."

Moving his gaze from Hoyt to Love, the president asked, "Very well, then, Dr. Johannsen or Dr. Love or Dr. Feelgood or whatever your name is—what the *fuck* is happening to my country?"

Hoyt started. "We're working to contain—"

"I didn't ask you, Mr. Hoyt. See, when I ask you, I get bullshit. The reason I wanted your *team* here was to get some real answers."

The secretary of defense spoke up. "I'm sure Mr. Hoyt is—"

"Shut up, Mike," the president said. "Dr. Love?"

Love looked nervously around the room first. "I'm afraid, Mr. President, that we haven't the slightest idea how to combat this virus. We have an anti-virus that works on people who are infected, and it will keep them safe for a while, but only if it's administered on time, and the number of infected people is simply too over-whelming. We've been coordinating with CDC to dis-tribute, but we're swimming against the tide."

The president shook his head. "I've already declared a state of emergency on the entire West Coast. California, Oregon, and Washington are completely cut off from the rest of the nation. Now, can we—"

"Sir?" The chair of the joint chiefs interrupted. "I'm sorry, sir, but I'm afraid I've got some bad news in that regard."

Glowering at the man in the Navy dress uniform, the president said, "Mr. Chairman, I've had more bad news in the past few months than Nixon had after Watergate."

"Yes, sir, I'm sure you have, sir, but—" The admiral hesitated, then finally said, "We've had reports of outbreaks of this T-virus in Oklahoma, in Michigan, and in Baltimore."

Hoyt put his head in his hands. He hadn't known about this, and he wondered if anyone at Umbrella did. He had a sinking feeling that they did and just neglected to tell him.

Holding up a manila folder, the president said, "Mr. Hoyt, according to this report, this virus was originally developed as a wrinkle cream. Would you mind explaining to me how a wrinkle cream turns my country into the hot zone?"

Love raised her hand. "Uh, sir, if I may?"

"By all means, Dr. Strangelove," the president said, waving his hand back and forth. "You're supposed to be the expert."

"Thank you, sir. The T-virus was originally developed by Dr. Charles Ashford as a way of revitalizing dead cells. It was meant to be medicinal."

Another staffer, whom Hoyt did not know, asked,

"Have you seen the state of California lately, Dr. Love? Doesn't look all that medicinal to me."

"I'm aware of that," Love said in a tight voice. "I wasn't part of the development team."

"Then why aren't they here?" the staffer asked.

Love hesitated. Hoyt stepped in. "They're all dead. Most of them were killed when the reactor in Raccoon City melted down, and—"

The president actually laughed at that. "Are you *still* trying to sell me that bill of goods, Mr. Hoyt?" He held up another manila folder. "This report is from the investigation into the meltdown. An investigation that only happened because I signed an executive order, one that got half of Congress coming through this office telling me not to sign that order or they'd grind government to a halt, that the Umbrella Corporation has been such a huge help in this crisis, and a whole lot of other bullshit. See, until recently, I actually *believed* that about your company, Mr. Hoyt. But then I read this report, not to mention a report made by the FBI, not to mention a report made by the Secret Service, all leading me to believe that your company was actually *responsible* for all of this, from unleashing this virus on the country to firing a nuclear weapon on American soil."

"Mr. President—" Hoyt started.

Getting up and walking around his large wooden desk, the president wagged his finger back and forth. "Don't give me that shit, Mr. Hoyt, we're past that."

Love was staring at Hoyt with her eyes wide as saucers. "What is he talking about, Tom?"

"Nothing, Doctor. The president has been given false information about Raccoon City. Sir, it was a meltdown of—"

The president was now standing almost face to face with Hoyt, and there was betrayal and anger in his eyes. Umbrella had been a huge contributor to his campaign, after all. He had supported every piece of legislation that Umbrella's lobbyists had rammed through Congress. This president had been a friend to Umbrella, and Umbrella had been a friend to him. There was no betrayal quite like that of a friend.

"No, Mr. Hoyt, it wasn't. It was a missile, one that Umbrella owned illegally and which has a pattern of destruction that's completely different from that of a power-plant meltdown. I didn't understand a lot of what was in this report, but I got the gist: Raccoon City was destroyed."

Another denial was on Hoyt's lips, but he abandoned it before he could speak. The cat was out of the bag anyhow. "Yes, sir, you're right."

A ripple went through the room.

"You realize," the chief of staff said, "that you've just admitted that the Umbrella Corporation committed treason."

"I don't recognize that, sir," Hoyt said, "because I'm not a lawyer and because no charges have been filed."

"They will be," the chief of staff said.

"Rest assured," the president said tightly, "I fully intend to bring your fucking company down. You've made me out to be a fool, and history's going to remember me as the person who sold the United States out to the people who nuked a city and poisoned a population. Kids'll remember me as the president who got everyone killed, and I'm *damned* if I'll let you get away with that unscathed, Mr. Hoyt."

"Be that as it may, Mr. President, I think we have bigger problems. Right now, *we're* the only ones who know anything about this virus, and if you decide to engage in criminal proceedings against the corporation, that help will *not* be forthcoming."

"Oh, *please.*" That was one of the joint chiefs, a bald pale man, who looked as if he was sweating. "You've been so much of a help so far that this disease has made it all the way across the country, and all your best experts are dead. Exactly how much do we lose if you're not involved?" He wiped his brow with his hand as he stood up. "Your company, sir, is a disgrace to the United States, and I'm right with the president on this. You will be made to pay for what you've—"

Suddenly, the general's eyes went extremely wide, his arm extended straight out, and he fell to the carpeted floor, his face landing right on the eagle in the presidential seal on the rug.

Chaos reigned in the room. People called for doctors; Secret Service agents came running in; people shouted.

Love took advantage of the chaos to pull Hoyt aside. "What the hell did he mean, Tom? We *nuked* Raccoon City? That's crazy! How could we do that?"

Hoyt tried to formulate something in his head that would satisfy the doctor, when he heard a strangled scream.

Whirling around, he saw that the general who'd collapsed was biting the chief of staff on the ankle.

"Oh, my God," Love said. Then she looked at one of the Secret Service agents. "Quickly, you've got to quarantine this building!"

The agent looked befuddled. "What?"

Hoyt realized what she meant. The T-virus had gotten loose in the White House. The general's eyes had gone milky. He had the virus, and now he was trying to bite everyone in the room.

"Shoot him in the head, quickly!" Hoyt cried at the agent.

"Are you insane?" the president asked. "He—"

Love interrupted. "Mr. President, the general has the T-virus, and he'll kill everyone in this room if *somebody* doesn't shoot him in the—"

The general leapt into the air, making a strangled noise from his dead throat, and landed right on Dr. Love, ripping into her shoulder with his teeth.

People were screaming and yelling, and Hoyt felt the world tilt around him, because this wasn't supposed to happen. Sure, there was what happened in Raccoon, though Hoyt wasn't present for it, and he knew there were problems in California, but it shouldn't have affected *him*. He was just doing his job, and he was three thousand miles from where this mess started.

The report of a gunshot ripped through the chaos, silencing the room. The general fell forward on top of Love, who started screaming again.

Lowering his weapon, the muzzle still smoking, the Secret Service agent cried out, "Crash the building! Crash it!"

Hoyt knew that meant they would seal the building so no one could get in or out.

But he wondered if it would do any good.

The White House had been infected.

†WELVE
AFTER

L.J. looked up at the sign: DESERT TRAIL MOTEL.
"Truer motherfuckin' words . . ." he muttered as he and
Carlos headed toward the motel's entrance. On the side-
walk in front of the place—which looked like it used to
be a truck stop of the type that L.J. wouldn't have had
his ass caught dead in for *no*-fuckin'-thing—was a big
pole with signs pointing in different directions. Looked
like that motherfuckin' thing on *M*A*S*H*. It pointed to
Alaska, Denver, Vegas, Rome, Paris, Mexico, Berlin,
London, and a buncha other places L.J.'d rather be than
here.

Well, except Vegas. Only motherfuckin' *fools* went
to Vegas.

The motel itself was half covered in sand, just like
half the other places they went to. The desert was taking

the city back. Well, the desert could have it, soon as they were done with it.

L.J. hated the desert. Raccoon City was a cool place, literally—never got too hot in the summer or too cold in the winter. Sure, they had a heat wave right before it went boom, but L.J. was okay with that.

But the desert was some crazy-ass shit. If it was up to L.J., they'd stay far away from it. He didn't get a vote, though. It was Carlos and Claire, with L.J. just following orders, like usual. Not that L.J. minded—he'd never been much for doing that drill-sergeant shit. He just did his business.

Like now, when they walked into the Desert Trail Motel, Carlos going first. He had the training and shit. L.J. was schooled on the streets, and while he bowed to no one in his ability to take out zombie-ass motherfuckers, he still deferred right to Carlos. He had the skills for *damn* sure.

He grinned as they approached the front entrance. "I'm going to get me a room with a water bed, take a Jacuzzi, maybe check out the porn channel."

Carlos chuckled and shook his head. For his part, mentioning the porn channel just reminded L.J. how long it had been since he had himself some snatch. Too fucking long, it came to that.

He thought about asking that paramedic when they finished checking out this joint. She was *fine*.

The lobby looked just like every other motel lobby in the world. He'd seen plenty back in Raccoon when he needed a place to take the ho's—you didn't take ho's to your crib, that just wasn't *done*—and plenty more lately, since they was good places to loot. There was a big poster that said NEVADA—LAND OF LEISURE. It was funny, but L.J. couldn't bring himself to be laughing.

L.J. didn't even need Carlos to give signals anymore, they just *knew,* like through telepathy or some shit: he'd go left while Carlos went right. He went down a corridor, but the sand was all piled up in back, and lights sure as shit wasn't working, so he unhooked his flashlight.

For some reason, it amused the shit out of him that he had a flashlight to unhook. Back in the day, he just had his nickel-plated Uzis, a deck to deal three-card, and his lucky ring that said LOVE.

He lost the ring somewhere in that school back in Raccoon, when they were rescuing Angie.

Angie . . .

He shook it off. L.J. couldn't afford to be dwelling on old shit. If he started thinking about all them people who died, he wouldn't think about nothing else.

L.J. passed by eight rooms and didn't hear nothing, but behind a room with a tarnished golden 9 on it, he heard a noise. Tucking the flashlight under his arm— he wasn't letting go of the gun nohow—he grabbed the door handle and pulled it down.

The door budged a little but wouldn't open all the way. Was probably all warped and shit from the heat.

So L.J. threw some weight into it. This time, it budged a little more. Not letting no door beat his ass, L.J. hit the door with his shoulder.

That knocked it loose. L.J. quickly held up his nine-mill Beretta. Not as cool as the nickel-plated Uzis, but he lost them a while back. Besides, it was easier to find ammo for the nines.

'Course, it was dark in Room 9, so L.J. shined the flashlight in so he could see what the fuck—

BAM! Something slammed into L.J.'s back, knocking him into the room.

Not something, some*one*. L.J. knew what the zombie-ass motherfuckers smelled like, and even as his ass fell to the floor, he started crawling across the ugly carpet to get away from it.

Quickly getting to his feet, L.J. saw that this guy was po-po—a highway cop, complete with those fucking aviator glasses. In fact, L.J. could see his own damn face in those shades, and *damn,* but he looked scared.

He raised his Beretta to shoot, but the cop was too close—and too *big,* the motherfucker was six-three at least and had shoulders wider than Claire's Humvee— and he barrelled his cop ass up into L.J., knocking them both down onto one of the two beds. L.J.'s piece went flying across the room and under the desk. L.J. tried to get up to get it, but the zombie cop wasn't having none of that shit.

L.J. had always had a simple philosophy when it came to fights: run his black ass away. That was why L.J. wore the LOVE ring—he wasn't about the violence. Sure, he armed himself, 'cause he wasn't no fool, but given a choice, L.J. always went for the run-the-fuck-away option. Folks who ran away lived longer, and L.J. planned to live for-fucking-ever. Shit, he'd survived Raccoon being nuked and zombie-ass motherfuckers taking over the world; he could survive any goddamn thing.

Unfortunately, he was trapped in a shitty motel room with Officer Zombie blocking his only way out. He tried to fight, but the zombie cop was too big, and he knocked L.J. on his ass.

Then he used his big-ass hands that were the size of fucking *hams* and started choking L.J.

No fucking way. As it got harder and harder for L.J. to breathe, he thought that there was no *fucking* way he was going out this way. No-fucking-how. He was Lloyd Jefferson Wayne, and this was how he do. He was a fucking survivor.

But nobody told Officer Zombie that. L.J. started seeing stars in front of his eyes as the zombie-ass motherfucker's grip tightened.

In his reflection in the cop's mirror shades, L.J. saw tears running down his face and into his beard. That was just fucking *wrong.* L.J. didn't play that. He had to do *something,* but his motherfucking Beretta was under the motherfucking desk.

Suddenly, it hit him. This was a *cop*—he had a piece of his own. Glancing down, he saw that there was a revolver in the holster.

L.J. paused for only a second to wonder who the *fuck* still carried a *revolver*—didn't this motherfucker know it was the twenty-*first* century?—then grabbed for the gun. Any port in a fucking storm, that was L.J.'s motto. Or, at least, it would be if he got out of this shit.

One of the things L.J. loved about zombie-ass mother-fuckers was that they didn't multitask. A real cop would've noticed L.J. going for his piece. 'Course, a real cop would've gone for it his own self, instead of choking a poor, defenseless Negro.

Problem was, the gun was strapped in, and L.J. couldn't undo the fucking thing, especially what with the world getting all hazy and shit.

But he could slide his finger into the trigger.

The first shot fired down into the sandy floor. Officer Zombie didn't even flinch.

He didn't flinch the second or third time, either.

L.J. was starting to feel all woozy, and he needed to get this shit done. He pulled on the revolver so it was pointing at the zombie cop's leg.

Fourth shot went clean through the foot. Mother-fucker didn't even blink. Or maybe he did, wasn't like he could tell through them shades.

With L.J. pulling harder so the gun was at a sharper angle, the fifth shot went through the shin.

Still nothing.

Only one bullet left. L.J. was having a bitch of a time focusing.

Come on, pull the fucking trigger, nigger! The rhyme gave him focus, and he pulled the trigger.

The sixth shot blew off the motherfucker's kneecap. Officer Zombie stumbled and loosened his grip. L.J. grabbed his head as he buckled and turned the head violently the way Carlos had taught him, snapping the motherfucker's neck.

Zombie Cop fell to the sandy floor, and L.J. fell back onto the bed. "Son of a *bitch*."

Looking down, he saw his Beretta under the desk. He reached down for it—

—and saw something move!

Fuck, L.J. forgot that he saw something moving up in here. He looked up and saw another zombie-ass motherfucker, and he shot at it.

Glass shattered as the mirror L.J. had just shot fell to pieces—and the zombie-ass motherfucker who'd been reflected in it jumped L.J.

Jumping back on the bed, L.J. tried to avoid getting bit. He wasn't turning into one of them, *no fucking way!*

The report of another gun echoed through the room, and blood splattered on L.J. He knew it wasn't his own on account of it being all coagulated and shit.

Then the zombie-ass motherfucker fell onto the floor on top of the cop.

Looking up, L.J. saw Carlos.

"The fuck you been, yo?" L.J. asked.

Carlos smiled. "Figured you could handle it." He looked down at the splintered glass on the floor. "The mirror piss you off?"

"Nah, man, this asshole"—he pointed at the second zombie-ass motherfucker with his gun—"was reflected in it. Shit, I thought they wasn't supposed to have reflections."

"No, that's vampires."

"What-the-fuck-ever, yo." He put his hand down on the bed to brace himself so he could get up, only to have his wrist collapse and pain slice through his entire forearm. *"Fuck* me!"

"What is it?" Carlos asked, grabbing L.J.'s arm.

Quickly, L.J. said, "Just, uh, my wrist. Probably sprained or some shit." He gently eased out of Carlos's grip—he didn't need the man's help, though it didn't pay to be rude or nothing—and then started gently rubbing the wrist to make it look good.

Carlos took out his walkie-talkie—or PRC, whatever the fuck that meant. Just a fancy-ass name for walkie-talkie, far as L.J. was concerned, but he used the stupid letters to keep Carlos happy.

"Claire, it's Carlos. The motel's clear—now. Found two undead, but L.J. and I took them out."

"Nice job." Claire's voice sounded all tinny and shit over the walkie-talkie. "We'll be right down."

"Oh, and L.J. sprained his wrist."

L.J. started waving his hands back and forth. He didn't want to be examined. "It's no big, yo, just—"

Ignoring him, Carlos said, "So he might need some medical attention."

"Copy that," Claire said.

"Shit, you didn't need to be—"

Carlos interrupted L.J. "Maybe, maybe not, but you're not a doctor, and neither am I."

"And neither ain't nobody else, yo! Look, I 'preciate you lookin' out for me, but I'll be fine."

The pair of them went to the front to wait for the convoy to show up, which it did in short order. Chase, that glorious redneck motherfucker, drove the Enco

truck, and Kmart was driving the 8x8. She'd been argu-
ing with Claire about whether or not she could drive.
Claire kept saying she was too young to drive and shit.
Carlos, L.J., and pretty much everyone else pointed out
that there wasn't no DMV no more. Didn't matter, long
as she could reach the damn pedals. Besides, everybody
needed to know how to drive just in case. L.J. didn't
know why Claire had such a bug up her ass about it, but
she gave in, so Kmart got to drive the 8x8.

L.J. never had a ride like that when *he* was fourteen.
Back then, best he could do was his cousin Bodie's Lin-
coln, least until he crashed it. Bodie wouldn't let him
use nothing after that, like it was all L.J.'s fault or something.

As she hopped out of the Humvee, wearing a pair of
shades that looked disturbingly like Officer Zombie's,
Claire said, "Spread out. Find anything of use—food,
gas, ammo, you know the drill."

The ambulance pulled up behind the Humvee, and
Betty got out. "Somebody need my help?" she asked,
looking right at L.J.

"It's nothing," L.J. started, then cut himself off.
What the fuck, he was wanting to be talking to this lady
anyhow. "But if you insist," he added with a smile. As
long as she only looked at his wrist and throat.

"That's right," Betty said, walking over with her
first-aid kit. "Now, sit back and relax. I'm here to help."

She checked his throat, frowning at the bruises that
L.J. could feel forming there after Officer Zombie's attempt to choke L.J.'s ass.

"You like playing rough?"

L.J. shrugged. "Had worse."

"I'm sure," Betty said with a smile.

Carlos, whose presence L.J. had temporarily forgotten, rolled his eyes and got up. "Oh, God, I gotta go."

That was fine with L.J. He was just cramping his style.

She checked the wrist, and L.J. didn't wince in pain at anything she did—not surprising, since there was nothing wrong with it—and then said, "You'll live." She put away the kit and fixed him with a dazzling smile. "So what do you say—dinner, my place, tonight?"

Before L.J. could answer, Chase called out, "Hey, Betty, over here!"

"It's a date," L.J. said.

Betty's smile got *more* dazzling, then she gathered her stuff and ran off after Chase.

L.J. spent the next several seconds enjoying the fine booty view Betty's retreating form gave him.

Once that magnificent ass was out of sight—and it *was* out of sight—L.J. let out a long breath.

Looking around to make sure nobody could see, he gently rolled up his sleeve.

His arm hadn't buckled because of no sprained wrist.

It buckled because he'd been bit by one of them zombie-ass motherfuckers.

L.J. had seen this happen way too many times, starting with Dwayne back in Raccoon and as recently as Phil, the med tech who'd been with Betty, who got infected back in Salt Lake. He knew that he was done for. Once upon a time, there was an anti-virus, but those days was way past.

Only thing to do was to make sure he took out as many of them zombie-ass motherfuckers as he could before he became one.

Thirteen
Before

"The city of Washington, D.C., has been quarantined, and it is unclear as to the whereabouts of the president, the vice president, and the cabinet, all of whom were last reported in the White House when it was crashed, about two hours before the quarantine order came. Whom that order came from is, as yet, undetermined. The speaker of the House, who was in O'Hare Airport on her way to attend the emergency session of Congress that had been called, said at a hastily called press conference at O'Hare's Terminal 3 that she is ready to step into the breach to assume the duties of president, but she says she has yet to be informed of the status of either the president or the vice president, who, obviously, are ahead of her in the line of succession.

"In the meantime, more outbreaks of the so-called

T-virus have been reported in St. Louis, Indianapolis, and Brooklyn, New York. This is in addition to the outbreaks in Tulsa, Ann Arbor, Baltimore, Chicago, and Atlanta. A doctor from the Centers for Disease Control had this to say."

Sitting in his office in Umbrella's Detroit facility, Dr. Sam Isaacs had barely been paying attention to the news report, busy as he was finishing his report to the Committee. However, when the image switched from the concerned-looking anchor to a young dark-skinned woman wearing a lab coat, he looked up.

The title under the woman read DR. CHANDRA PATEL, CENTERS FOR DISEASE CONTROL. *"The outbreaks we've seen aren't following the vector that has been established on the West Coast and indicates that infected people are traveling by air. We're recommending—strongly recommending—that all air traffic be suspended until further notice."*

Isaacs shook his head and went back to his report as the image went back to the anchor. *"A spokesman for the FAA has said that no decision has been made regarding the CDC's recommendation—no doubt in part due to confusion over who's giving the FAA instructions. More after this."*

Rather than endure a commercial, Isaacs muted the television. He wondered if the grounding of airplanes would succeed and if it would make any difference.

His intercom buzzed, and his assistant Alissa's voice came on. *"Dr. Isaacs, Chairman Wesker on line two for you."*

That surprised Isaacs. Wesker rarely made person-to-person calls. His stock in trade had always been the terse memo, the scathing e-mail. His verbal interactions were usually only in large meetings.

He picked up the phone on his desk and touched the pad marked 2. "Mr. Chairman."

"Dr. Isaacs, I assume you've heard the latest news."

"Yes, sir, and I already have a recommendation. I believe that we should prepare for the worst."

"Explain."

Isaacs took a breath. "The T-virus is spreading at an appalling rate. We have only a limited supply of the anti-virus, and at the rate the T-virus is propagating and mutating, I can't guarantee that the anti-virus would even be one-hundred-percent effective. We have several underground bases around the globe, and I believe all of Umbrella's resources should be pressed toward turning them into bunkers where our employees can survive."

"Should our resources not be turned toward stopping the spread?"

"It would be a waste of time, Mr. Chairman. The virus *will* spread, and our efforts will serve only to cause us to lose more people like Doctors Cerota and Love." For a moment, Isaacs almost shuddered. He'd seen plenty of death in his time, and it had never fazed him, but for some reason, the sight of Jaime Cerota putting the gun to her neck and shooting her own brains out rather than be infected by the T-virus had continued to haunt him.

He went on: "Instead, we should dedicate ourselves

to survival. We have the finest minds and the deepest resources. We need to make use of those resources while they still have value and convert them to stockpiling food, medical supplies, and other equipment that will enable Umbrella to survive the coming apocalypse."

There was a distressingly long pause on the other side of the line before Wesker finally spoke. *"I agree. Several Committee members have expressed their displeasure with the notion of giving in to the worst-case scenario, but we are facing a crisis of biblical proportions. If the Four Horsemen are riding down on us, Dr. Isaacs, I prefer to stay out of their way."*

"Thank you, sir." Cradling the phone between his ear and shoulder, he put the finishing touches on his memo, then used the track ball to move the mouse to the SEND tab. "I'm e-mailing you a memo that details the very plan I just described to you."

"Good. One other thing, Doctor."

Isaacs didn't like the tone in Wesker's voice when he said that.

"Project Alice."

Ah, yes. "What of it?"

"It seems to me that someone who has the T-virus and has, to use the current vernacular, made it her bitch is someone we should have under observation, yes?"

"I don't disagree," Isaacs said. "However, she is a difficult specimen to contain."

"Perhaps, but she's a difficult one to let loose. Ms. Abernathy has contacts in the U.S. Treasury Department from her time there, and Umbrella is coming under the

scrutiny of the Secret Service. The White House being infected has mitigated the problem somewhat, but we cannot risk an investigation right now."

"I consider it highly unlikely that such an investigation will be at the top of anyone's list of priorities, Mr. Chairman."

"Regardless, Dr. Isaacs, I would prefer that Ms. Abernathy be under Umbrella's control. Bring her in. And if you can bring Dr. Ashford's daughter as well, that would be a kindness. Feel free to dispose of their friends."

"Of course, Mr. Chairman," Isaacs said. "If there's nothing else?"

"No. The end of days is come, Dr. Isaacs—let us prepare for it."

With that, the chairman hung up.

Isaacs dialed Kayanan's number. She'd been monitoring Alice whenever they'd been able to track her down. He said only three words:

"Bring her in."

Fourteen
After

As Isaacs prepared a special syringe in his lab, the image of a nine-year-old girl appeared behind him and said, *"Dr. Isaacs?"*

Isaacs winced at the voice of the White Queen. The artificial intelligence was the next upgrade from the Red Queen, the AI that ran the Hive. That computer had locked the Hive down after the T-virus spread and been a bit overzealous in her enforcement of the quarantine.

The White Queen was supposed to be an improvement, but Isaacs found her voice to be as annoying as the Red Queen's—who had been modeled after the late Angie Ashford, as a sop to her father.

For his part, Isaacs preferred computers that didn't have personalities. Not for the first time, he expressed silent gratitude at reading the report that Dr. Simon Barr, who'd developed the AIs that Umbrella used, had been killed by the T-virus a year and a half ago. Isaacs's only regret was that he hadn't been able to kill Barr himself for inflicting this lunatic girl on his life.

"What is it?" he asked.

"Another test subject has failed the training floor."

Isaacs sighed. This grew tiresome. "Where?"

"At the laser grid."

Turning, Isaacs saw an image on his flatscreen of the re-creation of the security corridor to the Red Queen's CPU in the Hive. Security Division had been a bit overzealous in its protection of the AI—which was revolutionary, about ten years beyond anything on the open market, and therefore a target, never mind the fact that its placement in the Hive made it sufficiently secure—but it proved to be a fine model for testing the Alice clones.

Or, rather, it would have been if the clones weren't proving so difficult. "Dammit, they're getting worse," he said.

"Shall I ready another?"

"Of course," Isaacs said. As if she had to ask.

"This will be the eighty-seventh."

He *definitely* preferred computers that didn't have personalities. "Your point?"

"I was merely making an observation."

Isaacs somehow managed not to snarl at the holographic image. Instead, he just said, "Tell them to take a sample of her blood." Since there was plenty of it smeared all over the glass walls, that wouldn't be a hardship. "Then prepare a vaccine from it. We'll use it on the next subject if this one doesn't perform."

Even as he instructed the White Queen, he was walking over to Hockey Jersey and injecting the syringe—which had three needles—into the back of the undead's neck. Hockey Jersey wasn't thrilled with this, but DiGennaro had done his job of securing him well, and the bonds held him steady while Isaacs injected him.

Once that took effect, it would be on to the testing stage.

Andy Timson stared at the animated corpse and wondered why he was standing in a room with one.

The corpse that Isaacs had picked out of the crowd outside for the latest experiment was now sitting docilely in a chair. He had been wearing a hockey jersey, causing Paul DiGennaro to nickname him Gretzky, which most of the rest of the staff found amusing. Timson hadn't gotten the reference, never having followed sports all that closely, but Moody explained that he was a famous hockey player. Moody also had some snide comments to make about Timson's inability to identify sports figures by name, which he thought was far lamer than Moody's inability to recognize some dumb old movie quote.

Gretzky's chair was in front of a table, on which sat a digital camera, a cell phone, and one of those kids' toys where you fit blocks into appropriately shaped holes.

Amazingly, Gretzky was very docile, just staring at the table through pustule-covered eyes.

Timson hadn't realized that the serum they'd developed to try to tame the corpses was going to have such hideous side effects. Not that the corpses were beauty-prize winners anyhow, but the boils didn't make them look any more pleasant.

Still, it seemed to keep him sedate. In a room with three living humans—Timson, Isaacs, and Moody—Gretzky showed no interest in chowing down on their living flesh and turning them into fellow animated corpses. He just sat, staring into space.

Not being stupid, they still chained him to the floor at his wrists. But the chains had some slack, so Gretzky had a certain freedom of movement.

He was staring at the three items on the table. Timson wasn't sure, but he thought that Gretzky had an almost thoughtful look in his eyes. He was obviously trying to figure out which of the three objects was of most interest.

Eventually, he reached out with decaying hands for the cell phone.

After looking at it for a few seconds, he managed to pry it open.

Then he put it to his ear.

"Amazing," Moody said, making notes on his clipboard. "He knows what it is. There's gotta be some residual memory in there of when he was alive, even though that must've been several years ago now, based on the decay of his flesh."

No sound came over the phone, of course, and Gretzky showed no inclination to speak. Even if there was a working cell tower nearby, which was unlikely, they were too far underground to get a signal.

Apparently, Gretzky realized this on some level, and he put the phone down.

Isaacs nodded. "The camera next."

Timson had had worse bosses than Isaacs. He'd also had considerably better, but at least Isaacs had been able to adjust to the changing circumstances. While the doctor did maintain a sense of discipline, he also understood that people had to let off steam, especially given the horrendous situation they found themselves in. So he let them banter and make fun of each other and generally act silly, as long as the work got done and done well.

For that reason, he and Moody toned things down in his presence. They thought it was the least they could do.

Of course, it was never clear how much Isaacs actually cared about them. He was so damn aloof—but maybe that was just his coping mechanism.

In any event, Timson followed Isaacs's instruction and pushed the digital camera toward Gretzky.

The corpse picked the camera up and started turning it over and over in his hands. Timson feared that he would just keep doing that for half an hour, but eventually he held it the right way and moved the dial on top that put the camera into the on position.

With an electronic whir, the lens cap opened. Timson broke into a huge grin. Isaacs just nodded slightly.

Moody, though, was stunned. "My God!"

Gretzky looked up and over at Moody. Moody's stunned look modulated into a frightened one, and he took a step back.

In a quiet voice, Isaacs said, "Stand your ground."

When he was sure that Isaacs wasn't looking, Timson shot Moody a grin and mouthed the word *wuss*.

Moody just glowered at Timson.

Gretzky kept staring at Moody. Timson couldn't help but wonder what, if anything, was going through his brain. Was he capable of a thought more complex than *feed*?

That was what they were trying to find out.

Then Gretzky lifted the camera in front of his face and pushed the button.

Everyone had to blink for several seconds after the flash went off.

Timson was grinning. "Unbelievable!"

Gretzky put the camera down and wandered back to the table. Timson saw Moody's face captured on the camera's small display screen. He looked like a deer caught in headlights. Timson immediately started making plans to print the picture out on the color printer and hang it on the bulletin board. Preferably with some kind of caption. Maybe even do a "Caption this!" contest. Isaacs probably wouldn't completely approve, but he wouldn't stop it, either.

That was for later, though. Right now, Timson had a job to do. He observed Gretzky, who had picked up the triangular plastic piece from the kids' toy.

Timson winced as he remembered that that toy had belonged to Humberg's son. The security man's wife and son were killed, not by the T-virus but by a tropical storm that had slammed the Gulf Coast. Nobody named this storm—by that time, the world was more concerned with staying alive—but with no government resources available, they were trapped in their Florida home when it came and were swept away. It wasn't even a particularly bad storm, not even enough to gain hurricane status, and ten years ago it would've been a minor hardship at best.

Humberg had bought the toy for his two-year-old, intending to give it to him for a third birthday present the month after the storm hit. He still had it with him when they relocated to this underground bunker. He had been reluctant to give it up at first, but eventually he had seen the wisdom of using the toy for a noble purpose.

And it was a noble purpose, Timson thought. This was the first step toward a cure.

Gretzky was looking at the triangle shape and looking at the base. Timson was still grinning. "Look at the dexterity. He has memory *and* reasoning skills."

Moody picked up the camera, staring at his own befuddled image. "It's a miracle. The serum *works*." To Isaacs, he added, "You've domesticated them—you've done it."

Timson rolled his eyes at Moody's sucking up. He was *definitely* doing a caption contest with that picture.

Looking over at Gretzky, Timson's face fell. He was trying to put the triangle into the circle.

Just when Timson was thinking that Moody needed

to ratchet back the sucking up until he actually put the triangle into the triangle-shaped hole, Gretzky started slamming the triangle down onto the base harder and harder. Timson winced as the base started to crack from the impact. He had assured Humberg that nothing would happen to the only remembrance he had of his little boy. Probably a stupid promise to make—getting attached to anything was fatally stupid in this day and age—but Timson had made it nonetheless, and he was feeling responsible.

Gretzky picked up the base and threw it across the room with an angry snarl, and Timson considered that breaking the news to Humberg was going to be the least of his problems.

Throwing his head back, Gretzky started howling with rage, a noise that Timson had never heard any of the corpses make before.

Then he grabbed Moody and ripped his head off.

Timson's entire body felt as if it were made of stone. He couldn't move, couldn't breathe. He just stood there and *watched* as Gretzky literally tore Brendan Moody's head away from his neck, as if he were popping the lid off a cheap beer bottle. Blood sprayed everywhere, including onto the camera that Moody's body was still holding.

With a supreme effort, Timson managed to turn his head. He saw Isaacs calmly walking to the door—

—and shutting it behind him!

"No!" Timson ran toward the door, but it was already sealing shut again. "Please!"

The last thing Timson saw before Grestky grabbed him was Isaacs looking on calmly.

It wasn't a coping mechanism.

In his final moments before his body was savagely devoured by the animated corpse, Timson realized that Isaacs didn't tolerate the bizarre shenanigans of his staff because he understood their difficulties.

He just didn't care.

FIFTEEN
BEFORE

Alice had been fighting for her life when she lost control.

They had found an entire enclave of undead who were pretty much taking over Purdue University in West Lafayette, Indiana. A group of students and faculty were huddled in Duhme Hall, frightened for their lives as the undead started to pound down the front door.

Carlos, L.J., Alice, and the other stragglers they'd picked up—a New York City cop named Lou Molina, a Marine named A.J. Briscoe, and a welder named Joseph King who was handy with a shotgun—were fighting off the undead who were swarming the front door to the dormitory like soldiers besieging a castle. Angie, of course, waited in the SUV with the last of their recruits, a martial arts instructor named Jisun Burton, whose job was to keep Angie safe. They had started calling themselves the strike team, traveling around the country trying to help people who'd been overwhelmed by the undead. There wasn't enough of a government left to organize national forces in that regard, so everyone was on his or her own. There wasn't anywhere in the continental United States that wasn't infected at this point. Rumors had been flying about Jill doing likewise, after helping the FBI for a while, but most of the FBI was infected, too.

Then it happened.

One moment, Alice was delivering a jumping spin kick that snapped the neck of an undead wearing a T-shirt that said UNDUE PURVERSITY.

The next, she was walking—not even running but almost sauntering—back toward the SUV.

"Alice, what the *fuck?*" Carlos cried out, even as he used his titanium knife to stab someone wearing a maintenance worker's uniform in the eye. "Where you going?"

She tried to answer Carlos, but she couldn't make her mouth work. Or stop her legs from moving.

An undead with most of the left side of his head missing and an eye socket dangling down over where his left cheek should've been crossed her path as she walked up Russell Street. Typically of the undead, he ignored her—her blood was swimming with the T-virus, and for whatever reason, that meant the undead didn't view her as a food source the way they did other living humans—but just by being in her way, he caused something to kick in. Alice grabbed the undead, gripping the back of his head with one hand and the sticky gunk of what was left of the side of his head with the other, and broke his neck.

Once the immediate perceived threat passed, Alice went back to walking toward the parking garage on Third Street where they'd put the SUV, along with King's pickup truck and Molina's minivan.

Alice focused all her concentration on trying to make herself stop walking, but nothing worked. It was as if she'd been programmed. Probably by that fucker Isaacs. He was the one who'd performed all the modifications to Alice to turn her into a freak, and he had done the same to poor Matt Addison, transforming him into some kind of monster-movie creature.

But in the end, Matt had been able to plow through the Nemesis Project programming and reassert control, sacrificing himself to save Alice and the others.

Now Alice failed to do likewise.

She kept trying, though. Matt probably had been trying to fight the programming the entire time Nemesis stomped through Raccoon City, massacring cops and people and trying to do the same to Alice. His persistence eventually paid off, and Alice's would do likewise.

At least, that was what she hoped. So she kept fighting.

Jisun was standing outside the SUV, Angie inside doing something on her laptop. "What's happening?" Jisun asked as Alice approached.

Alice desperately wanted to answer her, but her mouth refused to form the words. Worse, Jisun was standing directly between Alice and the driver's-side door to the SUV, which—based on her reaction to the undead with half a face—meant that Isaacs's programming probably would cause her to remove Jisun with extreme prejudice.

Sure enough, Alice turned her body and then leapt into a jumping side kick, aimed straight at Jisun's head.

Never was Alice more grateful for the fact that Jisun's martial arts training was as good as Alice's own. A third-degree black belt in *Kenshikai* karate, Jisun easily dodged the side kick by ducking and rolling on the parking-lot pavement. For her part, Alice instead kicked the window of the driver's-side door, shattering it. She fell to the ground, then quickly clambered to her feet. There was no pain, but there almost never was anymore. Between the T-virus and Isaacs's tampering, Alice was beyond such irrelevancies as pain now.

Physical pain, at least. Mental anguish, however, was in full bore as she and Jisun started sparring. Jisun kept trying to ask Alice what was going on between kicks and punches, but Alice said nothing, no matter how hard she tried to speak.

At one point, Jisun let loose with an axe kick; her heel slammed down onto Alice's head with a bone-jarring impact, and Alice fell to the pavement.

Only then did Jisun take out her weapon, a Glock that King had given her. "What the *hell* is going on?" she asked, her breath ragged.

Moving far faster than even Jisun could react, Alice slammed her palm heel into Jisun's nose.

No!

Alice used every erg of willpower she could gather up to try to stop herself, but nothing worked. She was convinced that she'd just killed a friend.

But then Jisun got up, blood pouring from her nose. Miraculously, Alice hadn't hit her hard enough for the skull to crack and send bone shards into the brain. Or perhaps Jisun had simply pulled her head back enough to dull the impact.

Inside the SUV, Angie was screaming. Perhaps she'd been screaming all along. Alice hadn't really noticed.

Three undead shambled toward them. Alice wanted to shoot them in the head, but she was only able to get herself to pull out her weapon. She couldn't make herself aim it at the undead.

Instead, she aimed it at Jisun.

For her part, Jisun didn't hesitate. She shot Alice in the shoulder. This time, there was pain, albeit briefly, as she felt the sizzling heat of the bullet rip through her shoulder, flesh and muscle being torn apart by the projectile.

Before Alice could retaliate, a fourth undead she hadn't noticed leapt onto Jisun's back.

Angie's screams got louder.

Jisun flipped the undead over her shoulder and shot it in the head with her Glock, but by then the damage was done—the creature had bitten into her shoulder.

Somehow, Alice's programming recognized that, and she turned, holstering her weapon and opening the door to the SUV.

"Alice, don't make me shoot you again," Jisun said.

But when Alice turned back around, Jisun was too busy fighting off the other three undead to make good on her threat.

Again, Alice tried to force herself to help rather than hurt her friend.

Again, she failed.

Instead, she got into the car, ignored the shards of broken glass on the seat, and started the SUV up.

"Alice, what's going on?" Angie asked, her screams having subsided.

She put the SUV into gear and drove out onto Third Street, working her way through various local streets until she found herself at the entrance for I-65.

For hours, she drove, first on 65 north to Gary, then east on I-94, not stopping until the gas tank was almost empty. When that happened, just outside Albion on 94, she pulled into an abandoned Enco gas station. In fact, the entire town of Albion appeared to be abandoned. It didn't take long for Alice to gimmick the pump to give her fuel, and then she got right back into the SUV.

She felt no pain in her shoulder. The bullet had gone clean through and had now completely healed. Only some leftover bloodstains and matching holes in her shirt gave any indication that she'd ever been shot.

Angie could have run when they stopped, but she was a smart kid. Where would she go? They were in a small town in Michigan, heading who knew where, and she was just a kid with no visible means of support. She was immune to the undead, it was true—they simply ignored her the way they generally ignored Alice—but she also knew that she was better off in an SUV with Alice than in the middle of Michigan by herself, even if Alice was acting strange.

Eventually, they made their way to Detroit. Amazingly, given its reputation, it was one of the few big cities that hadn't been overrun by rioting and looting and roving packs of undead.

However, there was a checkpoint at Exit 210, with police cars and large black SUVs blocking all but one lane, and several cops and Umbrella Corporation security officers blocking that lane.

Unsurprisingly, the Umbrella people were better armed and armored than the Detroit city cops.

Alice fully expected her hijacked body to plow right through the cordon, but her right foot moved to the SUV's brake.

A city cop and an Umbrella thug, whose nameplates respectively read PLEXICO and FURNARI—stood outside the driver's-side window. Alice obligingly lowered the window with the push of a button.

"I'm sorry, ma'am," Plexico started, "but this—"

Furnari interrupted. "Let her through." Alice finally placed the name; Furnari was one of the people she'd trained back in the old days when she was in Security Division. She recalled Furnari as being something of an ass kisser.

Plexico whirled around. "Say *what?* Look, we're lettin' you assholes help out as a *courtesy,* but I am *not* lettin' some bitch into town on *your* fucking say-so."

Furnari seemed unimpressed. "She's with Security

Division, and the girl in the back is an important test subject. Her presence at our facility is vital to our attempts to find a cure for the T-virus."

"You gotta be fuckin' shittin' me." Plexico let out a long breath. "All right, what-the-fuck-ever, move on." The officer grabbed the radio attached to her shoulder. "SUV, California plates, let her through." Then she looked at Furnari. "This is on *you*, fucknut."

Ignoring her, Furnari looked at Alice. "Go on through, Ms. Abernathy. Dr. Isaacs is expecting you."

More than anything, Alice wanted to punch Furnari in the nose. Instead, she drove ahead, grateful at least to have it confirmed that Isaacs was behind this.

"They'll want to kill us both."

That was the first time Angie had spoken since they left West Lafayette.

Angie went on: "They'll want to dissect us, find out why we're immune when no one else is. You've *got* to turn around."

Alice said nothing. But she imagined that if she could, she'd be crying right now.

Just as she got through the cordon, she heard a commotion behind them. Looking up at the rearview, she saw a familiar minivan barreling down 94 and not slowing for the checkpoint.

It was Molina's minivan. And Carlos was behind the wheel.

Even as Alice mentally cheered, her foot slammed down on the accelerator. She'd been to Detroit only once or twice in her life and had never really learned her way around the city, so she had no idea what streets she was taking once she got off 94, but no matter where she went, Molina's minivan—and, after a minute, several cop cars, sirens blazing—followed her.

Conveniently, there was no one else on the streets—apparently, martial law had been declared in Detroit, and no one was allowed on the streets who wasn't authorized—which meant Alice could zoom through side streets at seventy miles an hour without even seeing another car, besides the ones following her.

Turning a corner, she found herself at a giant building complex with Umbrella's older logo—a stylized U with an umbrella sticking out of the right-hand portion of the letter—atop it. The Detroit branch of the Umbrella Corporation had always been a minor facility, but with the practical elimination of all the West Coast locations, it had grown in significance.

About fifty armed members of Security Division were waiting for them at the parking-lot entrance. Four of them stepped aside to let the SUV in. Then they closed ranks and started firing on the minivan, which had just turned the corner to follow them.

Through the rearview, before going down into the underground parking garage, Alice saw the minivan fly past the entrance, Carlos at the wheel, Molina and L.J. firing at the security guards, who fired right back, riddling Molina's minivan with holes.

Alice silently wished them luck as she pulled into a spot where Isaacs and four more members of Security Division were waiting for them.

Wearing a lab coat over a dress shirt and tie, Isaacs looked staid as always. He almost smiled as he said, "Welcome home, Alice."

"Thank you, Dr. Isaacs," Alice said unwillingly.

Peering into the SUV's backseat, he added, "And I see you brought a friend. Very considerate, as we were wondering what happened to Dr. Ashford's unfortunate daughter." He sighed. "Still, I'm afraid she's not terribly useful. The form of the T-virus her late, lamented father infected her with bears very little resemblance to what's floating about in the air now. It's mutated far beyond her ability to be useful to us." Isaacs straightened up and looked right at Alice. "So I'm afraid you're going to have to kill her."

Without hesitating, Alice unholstered her weapon and aimed it right at Angie.

Sixteen
After

Claire wandered around the camp they'd set up near the Desert Trail Motel. They did this every night, not always in a town—park all the vehicles in a circle, and keep everyone inside them. Like the way they used to circle the wagons against Indian attacks in the Old West.

The difference was that the Indians were just defending their land. But Claire's homesteaders were trying to survive. In truth, they were more like the Indians, being overrun by a superior force.

It was a helluva way to fight a war. Every time the enemy got one of you, they added one to their own ranks. It was impossible to win against those odds. Claire wondered sometimes why she bothered fighting.

Then she would look at the picture of Chris on the sun visor, and she kept on going.

As she passed by them—setting up cooking fires, stretching, what have you—every member of the convoy nodded to her. She wasn't really sure how or when it had happened—she had been just another refugee that Carlos's strike team had picked up—but as time went on, she became the group's leader. She wasn't really qualified—Carlos had more experience in that regard, but even he deferred to her after a while. L.J. had called it "natural-ass charisma," which he mispronounced "ka-*razz*-muh," and Claire figured that was as good an explanation as any.

She passed by the generator and waved to Kmart, who waved back with a screwdriver. The girl was puttering about on the thing, making sure everything was working right. When they had found her, she had kept herself alive by making use of the various pieces of survival equipment the store had in proper working order, and she had become a very skilled self-taught mechanic.

Next was the Enco tanker, where Chase MacAvoy stood on the tank roof, opening the hatch. As ever, Chase wore his cowboy hat; Claire was half convinced that the thing had become chemically bonded to his scalp.

Looking up at him, she said, "Permission to come aboard?"

Chase chuckled. "Permission granted." He muttered, "Like you need it," just loud enough for her to hear.

Claire grinned as she climbed the ladder to join him on the roof. It was important to her to maintain certain protocols and rituals. In many ways, it was all they had left.

"You check out the gas station yet?" she asked as she got to the top.

Pulling out a long measuring rod from the now-open hatch, Chase shook his head. "Bone dry."

"How's it look here?"

Wincing, Chase examined the tip of the rod. It had a smattering of fuel and a lot of rust flakes.

He looked up at her. "If you can run those trucks on rust, then we're in great shape."

"Fuck." Claire also shook her head. "I'm starting to think we're gonna need to drive down to Texas and dig for oil."

Chase's face actually went pale at that. "Let's save that for last resorts, okay?"

"I was kidding, Chase," Claire said, putting a hand on his shoulder. She didn't know much about Chase's past—they'd found him in Oklahoma—but she knew he was from somewhere in Texas originally. Obviously, something had happened to him there. "Anything you wanna talk about?"

"Not any time soon." He put on a brave smile that was fake as all get-out and exaggerated his drawl. "I'll be fine, little lady, don't you worry none."

She nodded and climbed back down the ladder. He needed therapy. They all did, but it looked like the zomboids got all the shrinks.

Over at the 8x8, Otto was doling out the evening meal: cans scavenged from all over, the labels having fallen off. With a smile and a wink, Otto would grab a can at random, shake it, and announce its contents with confidence. The fact that he was talking out of his ass was of less concern than the smiles he was able to elicit.

He had probably been a great teacher.

"Pork and beans," he said to one customer, who walked. Then he grabbed another can, shook it, and handed it to Becky. "Peaches."

Next up was Ida, a little girl of about eight. Otto shook another can and said solemnly, "Cat food."

Ida's face fell.

"Just kidding!" Otto said quickly. "Pork and beans."

"Not peaches?" Ida asked, though her face had brightened.

"Maybe you can trade with Becky."

Ida grabbed the can and ran toward Becky.

"Claire Redfield!" Otto said as she approached. He grabbed a can and weighed it first. "Soup." Then he shook it. "Cream of mushroom."

Rolling her eyes, Claire said, "Bullshit." She grabbed the tab and pulled open the can.

Inside was cream of mushroom soup. She smelled it to be sure, and the wonderful fungal smell wafted to her nostrils.

"I'll be damned. How'd you do that?"

Waggling his eyebrows, Otto said, "I have my skills." Then he sighed. "Unfortunately, it's a dying art." He threw back the canvas cover to the 8x8 to reveal about four dozen cans. That would last them only a day or two.

"This is the last of it, and that includes what I scavenged here, which can be found on the empty shelf back there."

"There wasn't *anything?*"

Otto shook his head. "The cupboard was, as they say, bare. Come Wednesday, we're fucked."

Claire frowned. "I thought today was Wednesday."

"I thought it was Monday." Otto shrugged. "It's one of the ones that ends in a Y."

"Hardy har har." Claire sighed and held up the open can. "Thanks for this."

"No problemo, boss."

Peering around, Claire saw that one of the cooking fires was next to the news truck. Mikey was probably in there with the radio. A can was sitting on the cooking fire, smoke rising at a great rate. Claire took it off—it was Spam, and it was starting to burn—and put her own can of soup there.

Climbing into the news truck—which Lyndon had repurposed to be a communications center before he died—she saw Michael Faerber, wearing his usual white button-down shirt and thick plastic glasses. He held a headphone earpiece to one ear and spoke into a small microphone. "This is Claire Redfield's convoy, present location the Desert Trail Motel. Latitude 35, longitude 115. Calling any survivors. Repeat, this is Claire Redfield's convoy. Our present location is the Desert—"

At Claire's approach, he whirled around, scared at first, then breaking into a goofy grin at the sight of Claire. "Oh, uh, hi."

She handed him his Spam. "You almost burned this."

"Fuck, I forgot." He blushed. "Pardon my French."

Claire tried not to roll her eyes. "I really don't give a fuck how you talk, Mikey. The perimeter up yet?"

Mikey nodded. "Almost done."

"Who's out there?"

"Olivera."

She pictured Carlos on the quad bike that they'd liberated from Irwin, along with the sentinels. Cobbled together by Carlos, Mikey, and the now-deceased Lyndon and Emma from equipment both in this truck and taken from Irwin, the sentinels were four-foot metal poles with a bundle of electronics on top, including motion sensors, infrared video, and a battery pack that enabled each sentinel to survive for three days. The batteries were recharged each morning by the 8x8's battery, a method that was useful only as long as they had fuel.

"Give me that." Claire held out her hand, and Mikey handed her the radio mic and the headset. "Hey, Carlos."

Carlos replied a second later, the motor of the quad bike purring in the background. "Claire."

"All that smoking's been slowing you down. Get your ass in gear, old man. I want my perimeter up."

"Always a pleasure, Claire." Carlos's wry smile was clearly audible.

Chuckling, Claire handed the mic and headset back to Mikey.

"So you were a motivational speaker before?"

Mikey asked. "If not, you should've been. Mighta gotten me out of my shit job. Pardon my French."

Before Claire could, for the nine-hundredth time, tell Mikey that she didn't give a shit about language, the screens in front of Mikey lit up with the green-tinged images from the infrared cameras on the sentinels. Mostly they just showed images of the desert. A few showed what few buildings hadn't been covered over in sand.

Mikey checked over everything. "Last sentinel in place. Perimeter up and running. All motion sensors online. Cameras one hundred percent." He looked up at Claire. "We're secure."

"Good. Enjoy your Spam."

Claire went back outside the truck and liberated her can of soup from the cooking fire just as Carlos pulled up on the quad bike.

As he shut the ignition off, he indicated the truck with a nod of his head. "Any luck?"

Mikey's voice could be heard from inside, once again giving their coordinates and hoping someone would answer.

"No," Claire replied with a shake of her head. "And this place is dead. No food, no gas, nothing."

"How much farther can we go?"

She shrugged. "Maybe two more days. I don't know what to do."

Carlos put a hand on her shoulder. "We keep fighting. No matter what happens, we do *not* give up. That's what we do."

Claire looked up into Carlos's eyes. He'd been in the thick of this fight since before Claire even knew where Raccoon City *was*. She recalled seeing the story on the news about the nuclear reactor, looking at Chris, and asking him which state Raccoon was in—and Chris didn't know, either.

Since then . . .

She shook it off and gave Carlos what she prayed was an encouraging look. "Right."

He nodded and wheeled the quad bike over to the 8x8, where it was kept. Besides, Carlos hadn't gotten his nightly meal yet.

Spoons were a luxury, so Claire started sipping the soup straight out of the can.

The soup was watery, the mushrooms barely even tastable, and it was the finest meal Claire had ever had.

She headed to the Hummer. Time she got some sleep.

Carlos watched Claire head over to the Hummer and wondered if she realized how important she was. She probably didn't—that was why she was such a good leader.

For Carlos's part, he was happy to turn it over to her. He'd been a leader of men and women before, and it ended badly. Every time someone put him in charge of something, he thought about Nicholai and Yuri and J.P. and Jack and Sam and Jessica. They had been a team, and a damned good one.

That lasted right up until Carlos made a simple decision: to save a woman's life.

It was just supposed to be recon. They were doing a flyover of Raccoon to make sure that all of Umbrella's essential personnel got out. Carlos saw a woman being chased by a horde of zombies, and he went down to help her. The rest of his team followed; they were loyal.

That loyalty killed them. The helicopter flew off, and they were written off by the company as expendable.

The hell of it was, they hadn't even been able to save that woman's life.

Then, one by one, they all died: first J.P. and then Jack, both of whom were then zombified. Carlos had to shoot J.P. in the head, and Jack killed Jessica and bit Sam before the latter was able to break his neck. Sam ate her gun after that. Yuri was infected, too, and he was lost pretty soon, and then Nicholai was mauled by those fucking dogs in the school.

Six people. His team. His responsibility. All dead because Carlos wanted to save a life.

Then, when he tried it again, with the strike team, that failed, too. From Jisun, King, Molina, and Briscoe to Lyndon, Heidi, and Alex—not to mention Alice disappearing, Jill being captured in Idaho, and poor Angie— Carlos kept losing people he was responsible for.

No more. Let someone else take the heat. He'd had enough.

He went into the news truck.

Mikey was doing his thing: "—field's convoy, broadcasting for any survivors." He sighed, and a tinge of frustration leavened his usual professional tone.

"Anybody out there? Broadcasting for *any* survivors—anybody out there?"

As much to distract him as anything, Carlos asked, "Anything?"

Lowering the headset from his left ear, Mikey shook his head. "Static. Same as last week and the week before that."

Carlos nodded, muttering, "And the week before that."

"I'm starting to think there's nobody left out there. That we're the last."

Since departing California with Betty and Emilio—and nobody else on the entire West Coast—Carlos had felt exactly the same way. Somehow, he managed to bite back an agreement, though. That wouldn't do anyone any good. He screwed on an encouraging look that he hoped to a God he'd long since stopped believing in was convincing, patted Mikey on the back, and said, "Don't worry. There'll be others. There has to be."

And Carlos's words were true. There was simply no way that they could be the last thirty humans on Earth. It just didn't scan. The world was a big place, and the T-virus couldn't have gotten *everywhere*.

He clung to that hope. It was pretty much all he had left.

SEVENTEEN
BEFORE

The bullet ripped through Angela Ashford's head, splattering her brains all over the SUV's rear window.

In her mind, Alice screamed, *Nooooooooooooooooooo oooooooooo!*

But her body refused to cooperate.

At first.

Then she whirled around and shot the two security guards closest to her.

She shot at Isaacs, too, but as soon as she had turned around, he had run, and the remaining two security guards were covering him.

Alice shot them both in the head.

Then she ran after Isaacs.

Just as she turned a corner, she saw him disappear

into an elevator. Undaunted, Alice ran up to the closed doors, put her fingers at the seam where the doors joined, took a deep breath, and started to pry them apart.

It was no effort at all. With the grinding sound of stressed metal, the doors separated. Looking up, she saw that the elevator was rising.

She smiled.

She crouched and leapt into the air, her fingers clasping one of the bars on the elevator's undercarriage.

Pausing for a second to solidify her grip, she started to swing back and forth. Just as the elevator came to a halt, she built up enough momentum to swing upward, the soles of her boots slamming into the bottom of the elevator.

It took a few more of those to make a hole wide enough for her to crawl through. Once she clambered up into the elevator, she saw that it was empty. Whirling around, she saw Isaacs standing with two more security thugs by his side with MP5s aimed at Alice.

Before she could raise her own weapon, Isaacs said, "Stop."

And she did.

"Come with me." He turned around and walked down the corridor.

Obediently, Alice followed.

She tried to fight it, but she couldn't stop walking down the corridor after Isaacs. Her legs would not obey instructions.

Her arms, however, did, as she tried to raise them and surprised herself by succeeding.

Immediately, she shot one of the guards, then the other.

But when she tried to aim the weapon's muzzle at Isaacs, she couldn't.

At the sound of the shot, Isaacs turned around. "Fascinating," he said, showing no concern for his fallen employees. "Lower your weapon. Take no action without my express instruction."

Alice lowered her weapon. She couldn't raise it again.

Whatever the fucker had done to her had a more limited control than Isaacs had thought, obviously, but it also seemed to be tied directly into instructions from him.

Then an alarm went off. *"Security breach,"* said a voice over the speakers. *"All security personnel to front entrance."*

Isaacs pulled a phone out of his lab coat. "What's going on?"

"Intruders, sir," said the same voice, now sounding tinny over the phone's small speaker. *"They followed Project Alice through the cordon. Sir—one of them is Olivera."*

"Dammit," Isaacs muttered. He looked at Alice, then said into the phone, "Stop them, whatever it takes."

Alice turned and ran.

She hadn't intended to, and she couldn't stop. She heard Isaacs make a noise, as if starting to speak, but then nothing else came from him. He hadn't intended that instruction to be for her, but her now-literal-minded nervous system had responded anyhow. Apparently, he saw the benefits to that, so he let her go.

Alice tried to make herself stop, and failed.

Her only exposure to the Detroit facility had been a cursory examination of the floorplan one afternoon when she was bored while working at the mansion—the place where they'd assigned her and Spence for several months to head up security for the Hive. Despite that, she unerringly ran toward the front entrance.

She arrived to see a limping Molina, an angry Carlos, and a lot of bodies on the floor, one of which was King's. Of Briscoe and L.J. there was no sign.

"Alice!" Carlos cried upon sighting her. "What the fuck's going on?"

"Carlos, you've got to get out of here!" Her arms rose, pointing her weapon right at Carlos's face.

She lowered it a second later. Isaacs's programming was wearing off.

At least for now, absent any direct instructions from the bastard.

"Get *out* of here, Carlos!" she said. Looking at Molina, she added, "Get him some medical help, but leave here *now*."

"Not without you."

"*Yes,* without me. Just trust me, okay? If you don't leave now, more than King and Angie will be dead."

Carlos's eyes widened. "Angie's dead?"

"Yes! They killed her." It wasn't entirely a lie. "And they'll kill you, too. Get *out* of here!"

Footfalls could be heard from down the hall. "Go, *now!*"

Still, Carlos stared at her.

Molina said, "Fuck it, Olivera, she wants us gone; let's be gone! We already lost Burton and King, we can't—"

"We can't lose her, too. If we do—"

Alice interrupted, "You've already lost me, Carlos. Just *go!*"

Four security guards came running around the corner, and Alice proceeded to shoot them down in succession, blowing the head off the fourth one before the first one even hit the ground.

"Go!"

Molina was already headed out.

But Carlos kept staring at her with those intense brown eyes of his.

The two of them had been through hell together, saved each other's life a dozen times over. Alice hadn't had many friends in her life, and the few she'd had, she'd lost.

Most recently, she'd killed one with her own hand. Never mind that it was at Isaacs's direction, it was still her finger that pulled the trigger that ended Angela Ashford's life. Poor little Angie, who had, in essence, saved all of them, since they only knew about the helicopter that took them out of Raccoon before the bomb dropped because Angie's father had told them about it in exchange for rescuing his daughter.

She couldn't let that happen again. Like it or not, the strike team would have to do without her. As it was, she was directly responsible for the deaths of Jisun, Angie, and King. Who knew how many more innocents would die because of Isaacs and his ridiculous obsession with her?

No, it had to end.

Carlos must have seen *something* in Alice's blue eyes, because he finally looked away. "Fine. Let's move!" He joined Molina in heading toward the exit.

Alice ran in the other direction, refusing to let herself look back.

She just needed to make it to a room with a computer terminal and stay away from Isaacs. Without his direct instruction, she could fight this, but she had to fix things so he could never give her direct instruction again.

Which meant not finding her again. Another reason to stay away from other people.

Years ago, Alice had been recruited by Umbrella to join Security Division. She had been promised more money and more chances for advancement than she'd get in the U.S. Treasury Department. Given her inability to be assigned to the Secret Service—the whole reason she'd joined Treasury in the first place—she jumped at the opportunity.

It may well have been the stupidest decision she'd ever made. She soon learned that her new employers were a nest of vipers. And since her attempt to bring them down, with Lisa Broward's help, had failed, the human race had been hit with an extinction-level event thanks to the very deadly sins of Umbrella employees: Spence's greed, causing him to steal the T-virus and set it loose in the Hive to cover his tracks; Cain's stupidity, reopening the Hive, thus causing Raccoon City to be infected; and Isaacs's scientific curiosity, which obviously came at the expense of his humanity, experimenting on her and Matt, turning them into freaks.

And now Isaacs had taken from her the only method she had for helping people by forcing her to go off the grid and away from the only people in the world she could allow herself to trust.

Fucker.

She found a computer terminal in an empty room and started working . . .

Part Two

Fight
for
Survival

Eighteen

Alice had intended to go to sleep as soon as she made camp somewhere in Nevada, but while she ate her can of Spam, she started reading the journal she'd found next to the hanged body in the Enco station.

The last few pages of the journal were all about a place called Arcadia, Alaska. "Heard the transmission again," the journal's author had written. "They're broadcasting from a town in Alaska. No infection, no undead. They're isolated up there . . . safe."

Intermixed with the increasingly sloppy handwriting were clips from magazines about Arcadia. One was a feature about polar bears, but it had photos of Arcadia in it. The entire journal was a monument to Arcadia.

Intellectually, Alice knew there had to be places like

that. True, the infection had spread all the way across the globe, but nothing gained one-hundred-percent penetration. Isolated towns like Arcadia stood the best chance of staying free of the T-virus.

By the time she was done with the entire journal, her fire had gone almost completely out. Letting it die on its own, she lay down in the hopes of rest and sleep.

Not that she was counting on that. The last time she had a good night's sleep, Spence was sharing a bed with her.

Still, she lay on her side, closed her eyes, and hoped for the best. Besides, while the dreams had been unpleasant, they hadn't been awful for a while.

The night was quiet. Far quieter than the desert used to be. Even the animals had been affected by the T-virus.

Alice drifted off to sleep.

. . .

The bullet flew.

. . .

"Do you know what that is? It's a pen. See? You try."

"P—p—"

"Pen."

"P—pen."

"Look at me. Can you remember anything? Hm? Do you remember your name?"

"My name . . . my name . . . my name . . ."

"I want her under twenty-four-hour observation. I want a complete set of blood work and chemical and electrolyte analysis by the end of the day."

"My name . . ."

"Sir—"

"Advanced reflex testing is also a priority."

"My name . . ."

"I want her electrical impulses monito—"

"Sir!"

"What is it?"

"My name is Alice. And I remember everything."

. . .

The bullet flew threw the air.

. . .

"Looks like we get the fun job."

"Fun. Right."

"What, you don't like lounging around the nicest mansion in the state doing nothing for three months?"

"Not really. I didn't take this job to sit on my ass."

"Too bad, it's a nice ass."

. . .

The bullet flew threw the air as if in slow motion.

. . .

"What's the plan?"

"Stay alive."

"That's it?"

"That's it."

"Nice plan. Should I paint a bull's-eye on my face?"

. . .

The bullet flew threw the air as if in slow motion, firing from the muzzle.

. . .

"I failed. All of them. I failed them."

"Listen, there was nothing you could have done. The

corporation is to blame here, not you. And we finally have the proof. That means Umbrella can't get awa— Get away with this. We can—"

"What is it?"

"Aaaaaahhhhh!"

"You're infected. You'll be okay—I'm not losing you."

. . .

The bullet flew threw the air as if in slow motion, firing from the muzzle in a puff of smoke.

. . .

"Don't you understand how important you are to us? That creature is one thing, but you? You're something very, very special. Somehow you bonded with the T-virus on a cellular level. You adapted it, you changed it. You became something magnificent."

"I became a freak."

"No, far from it. You're not mutation, you're evolution. Think about it. It took five million years for us to step out of the trees. You took the next step in less than five days. With our help, just think what you can achieve. Now, who can understand that? Who can appreciate that? Us—no one else. Where else are you going to go?"

"And what about him?"

"Evolution has its dead ends. Now finish this. Take your place at my side."

. . .

The bullet flew threw the air as if in slow motion, firing from the muzzle in a puff of smoke. Angie's eyes widened.

. . .

"You don't give up, do you?"

"I'm persistent. I don't give up until I get what I want. It's what makes me good at my job."

"Good thing, 'cause you certainly won't get by on your looks."

"Hey! What about my nice ass?"

"Why do you think I was looking at your ass instead of your face?"

"Ouch! Shot to the heart."

"Don't worry, Spence—if I ever really shoot you, it'll be between the eyes."

. . .

The bullet flew threw the air as if in slow motion, firing from the muzzle in a puff of smoke. Angie's eyes widened, yet she didn't seem all that surprised.

. . .

"Why—why are you telling me this? Are you just telling me because you're going to kill me?"

"I may look like a Bond girl, Lisa, but I'm not a Bond villain. I didn't bring you here to kill you. I brought you here to talk to you."

"About what?"

"I thought that was obvious. After all, Mahmoud al-Rashan was your friend—and I can't imagine that the settlement Umbrella gave his wife did much to alleviate her grief. It took a lot of guts to do what you did. You want the virus?"

"I might."

"I can help you get the virus. I have access to security plans, surveillance codes, the works."

"But—?"

"But there's going to be a price."

"Name it."

"You have to guarantee me that you'll bring this corporation down."

. . .

The bullet flew threw the air as if in slow motion, firing from the muzzle in a puff of smoke. Angie's eyes widened, yet she didn't seem all that surprised. She'd always had a maturity far beyond her years.

. . .

"Who the fuck are you?"

"My name's Alice. We're not safe in here. That fire will spread."

"No shit. I'm Sergeant Peyton Wells of S.T.A.R.S. This is one of my best people, Officer Jill Valentine."

"I'm impressed that you stayed in town."

"Protect and serve, that's what we do."

"Weren't you suspended?"

"Yeah. I saw zombies in the Arklay Mountain forest. Everyone thought I was crazy."

"At this point, we're all a little crazy."

. . .

The bullet flew threw the air as if in slow motion, firing from the muzzle in a puff of smoke. Angie's eyes widened, yet she didn't seem all that surprised. She'd always had a maturity far beyond her years.

Then the bullet tore into her flesh.

. . .

"Get out of here, Carlos! Get him some medical help, but leave here now."

"Not without you."

"Yes, without me. Just trust me, okay? If you don't leave now, more than King and Angie will be dead."

"Angie's dead?"

"Yes! They killed her. And they'll kill you, too. Get out of here! Go, now!"

"Fuck it, Olivera, she wants us gone, let's be gone! We already lost Burton and King, we can't—"

"We can't lose her, too. If we do—"

"You've already lost me, Carlos. Just go!"

. . .

The bullet flew threw the air as if in slow motion, firing from the muzzle in a puff of smoke. Angie's eyes widened, yet she didn't seem all that surprised. She'd always had a maturity far beyond her years.

Then the bullet tore into her flesh, rending her adorable face into mulch.

. . .

"What do you think you're doing?"

"He's wounded. The infection's spreading."

"I'm fine."

"You should take care of him now."

"He's my friend."

"I understand, but it'll be more difficult later. You know that."

"No! If it comes to that—I'll take care of it myself."

"As you wish. It's nothing personal. But in an hour, maybe two, you'll be dead. Then, minutes later, you'll be one of them. You'll endanger your friends, try to kill them—maybe succeed. Sorry, but that's just the way it is."

. . .

The bullet flew threw the air as if in slow motion, firing from the muzzle in a puff of smoke. Angie's eyes widened, yet she didn't seem all that surprised. She'd always had a maturity far beyond her years.

Then the bullet tore into her flesh, rending her adorable face into mulch, drilling through her skull.

. . .

"It's a long shot."

"What's the alternative? We can sit on our asses and run from the feds. The longer we wait, the easier it'll be for Umbrella to cover this up. We gotta get people picking at the scab before it has a chance to heal."

"It's done."

"What's done?"

"I put the video online—all the footage of Raccoon City and your confession. I had to put it in two separate bits, since the website I'm using only lets me put up videos two minutes at a time."

"Angie, if they can trace it—"

"They can't. I used an untraceable e-mail address and used one of my father's programs to mask the IP address. No one'll know where it came from."

. . .

The bullet flew threw the air as if in slow motion, firing from the muzzle in a puff of smoke. Angie's eyes widened, yet she didn't seem all that surprised. She'd always had a maturity far beyond her years.

Then the bullet tore into her flesh, rending her adorable face into mulch, drilling through her skull, splattering cranial matter, flesh, and bone all across the back window of the SUV.

. . .

"I can give you the code, but first you must do something for me."

"What do you want?"

"One of your group is infected. I require her life for the code."

"The anti-virus is right there on the platform—it's right there!"

"I'm sorry, but it's a risk I cannot take."

"She's right. It's the only way. You're gonna have to kill me."

"No."

"Otherwise we all die down here."

. . .

The bullet flew threw the air as if in slow motion, firing from the muzzle in a puff of smoke. Angie's eyes widened, yet she didn't seem all that surprised. She'd always had a maturity far beyond her years.

Then the bullet tore into her flesh, rending her adorable face into mulch, drilling through her skull, splattering cranial matter, flesh, and bone all across the back window of the SUV.

Angie's body fell to the side, dead.

"Noooooooo!"

Alice sprang upward, her nine-millimeter out and ready.

All around her, fires burned. The campfire was going full bore, and several cacti were ablaze as well. Rocks and boulders and litter floated in the air—as did the BMW.

A second after she awakened, it all fell to the ground. The fires all went out.

"Shit."

She walked over to the bike, which was mangled from the impact—or maybe from Alice's burst of telekinesis. The power had scared her, and she hadn't used it much, even when it might have been useful.

But this dream, this was the worst. She wasn't sure what had triggered it—the journal, probably, and its dream of a better life—but the upshot was a nightmare as bad as she'd ever experienced.

And the sad thing was, that nightmare was simple memory.

She walked over to her radio and tuned it to a particular frequency that she'd heard many times before but never acted on.

"This is Claire Redfield's convoy, present location the Desert Trail Motel. Latitude 35, longitude 115. Calling any survivors."

Hoisting the saddlebags over her shoulders, Alice started walking toward latitude 35, longitude 115.

If nothing else, she was looking forward to seeing Carlos again.

Sam Isaacs cursed as the computer displayed the words GENETIC MATCH WITH ORIGINAL PROJECT ALICE INCOMPLETE—75% CHANCE OF SERUM FAILURE.

Which meant that Alice-86 was only twenty-five percent successful. Hardly the results that would make him—or Wesker and his merry band of lunatics—happy.

He pounded a fist on the keyboard and cursed again.

"Dr. Isaacs."

"Yes," he said testily to the White Queen, "what is it?"

"My sensors have detected a peak in psionic activity, both alpha and beta wave."

That got Isaacs to sit up in his chair. None of the clones had shown the same proclivity for psionics that the original Project Alice did. "From number eighty-seven?"

"No. The activity is not from one of the clones. It occurred outside the complex."

Instinctively, Isaacs said, "That's not possible," then realized that the words were idiotic in a world that had been overrun by animated corpses and where he spent all his time working with fully grown clones of a super-powered woman. Old habits, however, died hard.

In her usual snotty tone, the White Queen said, *"My sensors were quite clear. Massive psionic activity was detected fifteen minutes ago, centered on a desert location."*

"Triangulate immediately. I want latitude and longitude."

"Of course."

Ever since the Detroit debacle, Isaacs had been trying to track down Project Alice. She'd done something to the computers and to her implant. Isaacs was sure that if he could just get her in the same room with him, he could control her again, as he had when he had her shoot Ashford's tiresome child, but accomplishing that was proving problematic.

She had been clever, too—not using her psionic abilities overtly and staying out of satellite range.

But now, perhaps, there was a chance. And once he had Project Alice back in hand, everything else would flow far more smoothly . . .

Πίпεтεεп

L.J. checked on his wound while he sat in the ambulance waiting for Betty.

As soon as he saw the festering, bleeding mess that the zombie-ass motherfucker had made of his arm, he wished he hadn't fucking bothered.

He supposed he should've been grateful. After all, he wasn't no special shit, he was just a hustler who got lucky.

Now his luck had run right the fuck out.

All them motherfuckers disappearing and dying and shit, and L.J. kept going. First it was their whole secret society bullshit with Alice and Carlos and Angie and Jill. Then Jill got took by the feds, and they started picking people up, finally forming that strike team shit.

L.J. and Carlos was the only ones left. Alice and Jill had disappeared, and everyone else was dead.

Except these last thirty. And, soon, L.J.

Fuck.

Somebody banged on the window, scaring the living shit out of L.J. He covered up the bandage fast as he could and looked up to see Otto's dome staring at his ass.

A goofy-ass grin on his face, Otto asked, "How's it going?"

"What?"

"The date."

L.J. rolled his eyes. "Get lost, dog! Does everyone have to know my business? Can't a man get some privacy?"

"That was a joke, right? There's thirty of us, L.J. Privacy left the building a few months ago."

"Yeah, well, that just means a nigger's gotta take it where he can, you feel me? Now move your white ass."

"So, I guess I can't watch?"

"Don't you got young'uns to take care of?"

"Chase is keeping an eye on 'em."

"Yeah, another blow for modern youth. Will you move your ass?"

Otto chuckled. "Yeah, yeah. Have fun—and don't catch any diseases!"

As Otto left, L.J. felt his face fall. He hadn't even thought of that. Betty was the finest booty call he'd had in a *long* time—but what if you could transmit the T-virus through fucking? That would suck something *serious*.

Betty came in then, and L.J. forgot all about viruses

and diseases and thought about that smile. Nobody'd had any kind of shower any time recently, and L.J. had finally started getting used to it, so nobody's smell didn't bother him none, but it was hard to find someone who smelled good.

But Betty? She smelled *fine*.

The paramedic held two cans of food. "Refried beans," she said, holding one up, then the other. "Fruit salad."

"My favorite," L.J. said with a grin.

She fixed him with a look. "Aren't we forgetting something?"

L.J. stared at her for a second. Then he remembered. Reaching down into the well between the two front seats, he pulled out what was left of a candle. Wasn't like the old days, when all he needed to do was flash some cash, and bitches'd be fallin' all over his black ass. Nah, times like these called for some good old-fashioned romance. Too bad he didn't have no more Barry White CDs left.

They started eating. The refried beans tasted like they'd been refried a few dozen times, and Betty winced when she ate the fruit salad, but they both were determined to enjoy it. Beat the shit outta nothing, and that was what they was looking at soon.

A desert storm started brewing. L.J. saw some sheet lightning in the background. "Fuck."

"It's actually kinda pretty," Betty said, staring past him at the light show. "Long as it's out there."

"We'll be safe in here." L.J. hoped he sounded convincing.

Betty, unfortunately, didn't look real convinced. "Things are falling apart out there."

Trying to lighten things, L.J. said, "But we had some fun."

"Fun?" Betty was staring at him like he was flippin'.

"You know what I did before this?"

Betty shook her head, which gave L.J. time to come up with his latest previous vocation.

He looked down and saw the fine-looking leather boots Betty was wearing. They was all covered in dirt and sand, but they still looked good.

"Wal-Mart," he said. "Ladies shoes."

"Ladies shoes." Betty sounded like she didn't believe it—which made sense, since it wasn't no more true than anything else L.J. had said to folks. But he didn't think saying, "street hustler" was gonna make this any kind of real booty call. Also made it hard to take him seriously as a savior of humanity and shit.

He nodded. "Ladies shoes. So you see, this—" He waved his hand around. "It's not so bad."

Betty burst out laughing. "You are crazy, L.J."

"So I been told."

"Hey, what's it stand for?"

"What?"

"L.J."

He smiled. "Lloyd Jefferson. My momma named me after both my grandfathers. Never knew 'em—they was dead 'fore I was born—but Momma really loved both of 'em."

L.J. shook his head. He hadn't thought about

Momma in years. He'd never had the chance to make peace with her after the shit with the pyramid scheme. Now she was dead—least, that was what he figured, since she lived in Raccoon, and L.J. was pretty sure he was close personal friends with everyone who got outta that place breathin'.

Betty leaned over and rested her head on L.J.'s shoulder. It was the good one, thank God. He put his arm around her.

"Mom named me Elizabeth after the queen of England."

L.J. looked down at the top of her head. "For real?"

She nodded. "She was watchin' somethin' on TV, and she thought she looked all nice and regal. And she thought the name sounded like someone important." Snorting, she added, "That shit didn't work too good. I hated the name from when I was five. Insisted on Betty. I don't think anybody's called me anything but that since Mom died."

"How'd she die?"

"She was lucky—it was before this all happened. Cancer got her." She looked up at him. "What about your momma?"

At first, L.J. didn't want to talk about it. The fact that he and Carlos were survivors of Raccoon City wasn't something they advertised—not for any good reason, they just didn't like talking about it much. But he figured he wasn't gonna be around much longer, so he said, "She got blowed up. I'm from Raccoon City, and Momma was there when they hit it with the nuke."

Betty sat up. "That really happened? They really bombed it? It wasn't a meltdown?"

"Girl, I was *there*. Trust me, wasn't no nuclear fuckin' meltdown. That was the Umbrella Corporation dropping a fuckin' cruise missile or some shit on our asses." He shook his head. "Me and Carlos were lucky."

"Carlos is from Raccoon, too?"

He nodded.

"Shit." She lay back down in L.J.'s arms. "I was gonna ask why you didn't say, but I guess you had good reason, huh?"

"Yeah." L.J. stared at the lightning from the storm, which was moving closer. "Yeah."

She had been born Dahlia Julia Mancini, and there wasn't a single one of those names she was willing to be called in public. Her friends mostly called her D.J., but she didn't really like that, either, since it made her sound like she should be on a radio station or something stupid like that.

When everything went to hell, she'd been working in a Kmart, and eventually, she just holed up there, along with the other employees and most of the surviving citizenry of Athens.

At least, for a while.

Eventually, everyone died. There was one old guy who had a heart condition, and as soon as he died, he turned and started biting everyone else. It got worse and worse, but the survivors managed to get the upper hand, mostly thanks to the Kmart's gun counter.

But when it was all over, there was just D.J. and four others. Before too long, they all died, too, and from stupid stuff. Charlie got a broken leg, Eileen got an abcessed tooth, and both Yvonne and Willie got the flu. None of those should've been fatal, but they were.

That left D.J. to fend for herself, living off whatever supplies were left in the giant store.

When Claire Redfield and her convoy showed up, it was a lifeline that D.J. clutched.

She refused to tell them her name. This was a new beginning for her, and it started in that Kmart. Besides, being called that reminded her of the rest of the people who'd died when she survived. They lasted longer than the rest of Athens, holed up in that Kmart, and she wanted to remember them a lot more than she wanted to remember that she was named Dahlia Julia Mancini.

So when L.J. started calling her Kmart, she decided to respond to that only.

Now she woke up in the front seat of the Hummer. Something was scratching the roof.

Clambering quietly across the front seat—Claire was still asleep in the back—Kmart slowly opened the door and peered up onto the roof.

Nothing.

Letting out a breath she hadn't even realized she'd been holding, Kmart started to climb back into the car when something landed on the roof, almost causing her to fall out of the Hummer.

Trying to get her heartbeat under control, she saw that it was a crow.

But it didn't look like any crow Kmart had seen. And she'd seen plenty.

There was something in its eyes. Something deadly. Or maybe it was just the poor light.

Instinctively, she shooed the crow away, and it flew off into the predawn sky. It went past a half buried car that Kmart didn't remember seeing there before. It probably had been all buried before, but the storm last night had been pretty fierce and windy, and that probably unearthed the vehicle.

That wasn't what concerned Kmart, though. She was a lot more worried about where the crow was going. It flew and landed on the motel, right alongside several hundred other crows.

It wasn't a trick of the early morning light. They *all* had crazy eyes. Almost milky white like the zomboids.

Kmart had lived with watching the world go to hell. She'd watched all her friends and family die, many of them for really stupid reasons, she'd been menaced and almost killed by zomboids, and she never cried or screamed, not once.

At the sight of hundreds of demonic crows, she screamed.

She clambered back into the Hummer. Claire was rousing. "Claire! I think we have a problem," she said, pointing at the motel roof.

Claire followed her finger and looked at the crows. "Fuck," she muttered. Then she reached forward and grabbed the PRC. "Carlos."

"I see it." Carlos's voice sounded calm as always.

L.J.'s much less calm voice came over the PRC speakers. "What the *fuck?*"

Kmart asked, "What's wrong with their eyes?"

Frowning, Claire said, "They've been feeding on infected flesh would be my guess."

Carlos said, "Everyone stay in the trucks!"

Kmart looked up. More and more crows were arriving, perching on the motel, the motel sign, the unburied car, and anywhere else they felt like it. One or two even landed on the sentinels.

Now Chase came on the PRC. "What's going on?"

Sounding frustrated, Claire said, "Everyone just stay in your trucks. Roll up your windows and keep quiet!"

The crows kept coming. It reminded Kmart of a documentary she saw on the fairy penguins in Australia that all come in out of the ocean at sunset. The penguins just kept piling out of the water in waves (no pun intended), and that's what the crows were doing here. More and more kept coming, taking up every available surface.

Another documentary came back to her, and she said to Claire, "They're territorial. We just have to stay calm and keep quiet."

"How do you know that?"

Kmart shrugged. "Saw it on the Discovery Channel."

Claire snorted. "I hope *they* know that." Then she grabbed the PRC. "Everyone stay calm, keep quiet, and don't move. If we're lucky, they'll get bored and move on."

L.J. said, "Yeah, and if we ain't lucky, we're in a fuckin' Alfred Hitchcock movie."

Otto added, "Claire, you look a little like Tippi Hedren, actually. In fact—"

When Otto's pause went on a bit too long, Claire said, "Otto?"

Whispering into the PRC, Otto said, "We got one on the hood."

Looking over, Kmart saw that one crow had indeed landed on the school bus's hood. It seemed fascinated by the crack in the windshield, a lot more than it was with the wire mesh that protected the bus.

Again, Otto's whisper came over the radio. "Everyone stay still and quiet."

More crows started flying to the bus hood.

"Fuck," Claire said. She clambered all the way into the front, settling into the driver's seat.

Kmart sat next to her and tried very hard not to panic.

Then, for the second time in five minutes, a loud noise made her jump out of her skin. This time, it came over the radio, and it sounded like a can clanking to the floor of a school bus.

A little kid's voice—Kmart couldn't tell who it was—said, "Sorry" in a whisper over the PRC, but that was quickly drowned out by the crows on the bus hood cawing.

And then all the other crows cawed back in unison in response.

"We are *so* screwed," Kmart said, even as the crows started to fly into the air and circle the camp.

Claire was turning the Hummer's engine over. "Fire them up. Let's get out of here!"

All the other vehicles sprang to life. Chase started the Enco truck, either Betty or L.J. started the ambulance, Mikey fired up the news truck, Otto the school bus—which caused more cawing—and Carlos was probably driving the 8x8.

The crows kept circling . . .

L.J. Wayne knew he was going to die, and soon. He just didn't want it to be this way. After fighting zombie-ass motherfuckers for all these years, after surviving Raccoon getting nuked, after Idaho and Detroit and Indiana and Toronto and that goddamn fucking loony bin in Oklahoma, getting his ass taken down by crows was just *weak*.

The crazy crows were turning into some kind of tornado in the sky. As soon as Claire said the word, they was *out* of there. Betty strapped herself into the driver's seat and hit the ignition.

And nothing happened.

The engine was roarin' away, but the ambo wasn't moving. This did not give L.J. warm and fuzzy feelings.

"Dammit!" Betty yelled. L.J. could see that she was flooring the gas pedal.

"What the hell's going on?"

"We're stuck."

Peering out the window, L.J. saw that the big storm had buried the ambo in sand. Then he looked up and saw that the rest of the convoy was booking the fuck out, and they needed to follow.

He opened the door with one hand and grabbed Betty's arm with the other. "Come on!"

Betty looked at him for a second, looked at his hand on her arm, and finally nodded yes. They both ran out of the ambulance and headed toward the nearest vehicle, Otto's school bus, which had a back entrance and everything.

Outside, the crazy crows were making loud flapping noises. The only flapping L.J. had ever really heard in his life was from pigeons, so it was a noise he always figured to be annoying but not scary.

But thousands of crazy crows flapping their wings was some *scary* shit.

He couldn't help looking up and was *real* sorry he did, 'cause a bunch'a them crows was heading *right* for 'em. Whipping out his Beretta, he fired bullets into them. Betty did the same next to him, but it was like shooting into a fucking pond. Even if they did hit one or two of them birds, there was still hundreds of the motherfuckers.

One of the kids in the back saw them running and opened the emergency exit in the back for them. Betty leapt up onto the stair and ran in, L.J. right behind her fine-looking booty. Then he shut the door just as the crazy crows went crashing into the back door with a splat.

L.J. had seen some seriously disgusting shit in his time, so a bird going all kamikaze and shit into a school bus wasn't no thing, but Betty and the kids screamed like they'd seen a fucking monster.

"Fuck me!" That was Otto.

Running to the front of the bus, L.J. and Betty saw

that the rest of the birds were doing the same dive-bombing act, slamming their beaks into the windshield and the side windows. It was like it was night all over again, with them crazy crows surrounding the school bus like fucking locusts.

Then the bus lurched and crashed to a halt. L.J. stumbled forward, and half the people in the bus fell on their faces.

Otto hit his fool head on the steering wheel. Rubbing his forehead, he turned around and said, "We hit something!"

"No shit," L.J. said.

Then the windshield cracked.

Fuck.

Betty ran up to stand next to the driver's seat and held the windshield in place. L.J. was right behind her, standing in the stairwell to the front door.

"Help us!" Betty yelled.

Freddie, Jared, Blair, and Dillon all ran forward and helped Betty, Otto, and L.J. brace the windshield.

Unfortunately, some of them crazy crows got in through the side windows. Dillon broke off and pulled out his Glock and started shooting. L.J. was about to call him a crazy motherfucker when he remembered that Dillon was the one who was a better shot than Carlos.

Over the PRC, L.J. heard Kmart cry out Claire's name, and Claire responded, "Dammit!"

L.J. hoped that meant that the cavalry was getting their asses in gear.

The kids were all cowering at the back, screaming

their heads off. L.J. saw a couple of crows heading for 'em, so he ran back and grabbed them, dashing their bird brains out on the bus wall.

At least one of them. The other one started pecking at his wrist—the same one he told Carlos he'd sprained—and L.J. winced at the pain as he slammed the mother-fucking bird into the wall.

Fuck.

"Jared, no!"

L.J. turned to see Jared panic and open the bus door, running toward the motel. Freddie pulled the door shut, but they could see Jared running away and getting swarmed by a dozen or so crazy crows.

Shaking his head, L.J. realized this wasn't a Hitch-cock flick, it was a fucking biblical plague.

He also saw that what they'd hit was a telephone pole that had smashed the grille. This bus wasn't goin' nowhere.

And then Claire's beautiful voice came over the walkie-talkie. "Carlos, get that truck here, we have to evac the bus!"

"You got it," Carlos said.

About fucking time.

L.J. heard a squeal of brakes from behind the bus and saw the news truck screech to a halt behind the bus. Two seconds later, the 8x8 backed through a fence and came roaring in. That would've made L.J. laugh if he was somewhere else, 'cause Carlos was *always* showing off like he had some shit to prove or something.

Jason climbed up to where the flame thrower was

mounted on the 8x8, but then the crazy crows nailed his ass. L.J. winced, even as Kenny didn't waste no time in taking his place, while Monique opened the gas taps.

Kenny covered Carlos with the flame thrower after he ran out of the 8x8 with a twelve-gauge in his hand. Mikey threw open the back of the news truck. "The children!" he shouted. "Get them over here!"

Joel and Cliff opened the bus's back door and started shepherding the kids out. With Carlos's shotgun, Kenny's flame thrower, and Richard on the machine gun in the back of the 8x8, they kept the birds off the kids while they ran out to the news truck. Gonna be cramped as shit in there, but it beats getting eaten alive by crazy crows. They'd already lost Jason and Jared. L.J. was fucked if he was gonna let no birds take nobody else.

He'd die first. Fuck that, he was dead already. Everyone else deserved a shot to live.

Claire showed up out of nowhere and helped the kids get to Peter-Michael, Dorian, and Erica, who were with Mikey in the news truck. Crows was dropping like flies, but they kept fucking *coming*.

Hearing a scream, L.J. looked up to see Richard get taken out by about thirty crows.

Fuck!

The scream lasted only a few seconds. That made it worse.

L.J. swore he wasn't going to let nobody else die. He grabbed the last kid—little Evin, who was petrified, the poor little kid was so fucked up by all this—and carried him out.

Just as he stepped down from the back of the bus, he turned around to see Otto, Dillon, and Betty holding the windshield back. Freddie and Blair were lying dead on the floor. Fuck, L.J. hadn't even noticed them dying.

"Betty!" he cried out.

She hesitated.

From next to her, Otto said, "Go—get out of here." On the other side of her, Dillon just nodded.

Betty started to object, but Otto, who was bleeding from the head now, yelled, *"Go!"*

L.J. could see Betty gritting her teeth. Shit, L.J. was doing the same damn thing. He'd just sworn nobody else would die, and now Otto and Dillon were sacrificin' their asses.

Betty was running to the back just as the windshield started to give.

Then she stopped.

What the *fuck?*

She got down on her knees and started reaching under a seat.

Fuck—there was another kid.

The windshield collapsed, and L.J. lost sight of Otto and Dillon.

Two more to add to L.J.'s list of people who shouldn't have died while he kept on living.

"Get out of there!" he cried to Betty, but she was still reaching under the seat, even with crazy crows pecking at her.

Finally, Sebastian, who was always tugging on L.J.'s beard, climbed out.

"Come on, with me!" Betty screamed, ignoring the crows flying all around her.

Cradling Sebastian to her, she ran to the back, crows ripping her apart, pecking at her great hair and her pretty face, and there was blood fucking *everywhere*.

"Come on! Hurry!" L.J. yelled.

L.J.'s heart sank as she handed Sebastian over, and then she slammed the back door shut.

"Go," she said as she closed it.

"No!"

Tears streaming down into his beard, he picked up Sebastian and ran to the news truck.

Sebastian started pulling on L.J.'s beard.

As soon as he jumped into the crowded rear of the news truck, Carlos yelled "Go!"

The door slammed shut into L.J.'s face, and he wished the fucking virus would take his ass already, 'cause he didn't want to be living in this world no more. Fuck surviving, if this was what it meant.

The kids all safe, Carlos ran to the 8x8 even as the crows—those that weren't trapped in the bus by Betty's heroism—descended upon Kenny, who was already bloody and battered and still firing the flame thrower. Monique lay dead and bloody next to him.

As the crows overwhelmed Kenny, the flame thrower spun wildly around.

An arc of fire headed straight for Carlos.

He had only a microsecond to hope that his death would be quick.

Then, suddenly, the flame split, going around Carlos. He felt the heat on his face as the fire went around him, as if he was a rock in the middle of a river.

What the *fuck?*

Then the fire started to twist and spiral as if it had a mind of its own.

Or, rather, a mind controlling it.

Looking around, Carlos caught sight of the one person he knew who could do this sort of thing:

Alice.

She stood about twenty feet away, a bunch of saddlebags and weapons at her feet. Her arms were at her sides, and her blue eyes were fluttering back and forth like crazy.

The fire split off several more times, each tendril of flame of greater intensity than the original shot from the flame thrower that almost killed Carlos. Each shot straight at one of the crows.

Soon the sky was ablaze—literally. Strangled caws of dying crows filled the air as they all caught fire and fell to the ground, scorched and dead. Carlos held up his arms to protect his face from being singed by the ones that fell a little too close.

Seconds later, it was over.

Otto, Betty, Freddie, Dillon, Jared, Blair, Kenny, Monique, Jason, and Richard were all dead. The school bus was damaged probably beyond their ability to repair.

But the crows were gone, too.

Thanks to Alice.

Her eyes normal now, she walked over to him with that damned smirk on her face. "You miss me?"

Carlos shook his head as he stared at the woman he hadn't seen since Detroit. "Well, I'll say one thing for you, you still know how to make an entrance."

The smirk blossomed into a full smile.

Then she fell over, and Carlos reached out to catch her.

Her eyes were fluttering again, but this time it was behind closed lids. The effort of saving the lives of those few who had survived had done her in.

He shook his head and snorted a bitter laugh. "Welcome back, Alice."

Twenty

"*Another spike in alpha and beta waves detected. Forty-five-percent probability that this is Project Alice.*"

"Triangulate," Isaacs said to the White Queen in an intense tone. "Find her location."

"*I am familiar with the definition of the word 'triangulate,' Dr. Isaacs,*" the White Queen said in a snotty tone that, were she a real child, would have led Isaacs to having her drowned.

Rather than respond to the comment, he called up a graphic of the waveform of Project Alice's second psionic outburst. This one was similar, but the frequency was shorter and the amplitude much higher. Almost as if it were more focused . . .

"Impressive," he muttered. "If it is her, her development is extraordinary."

"Her powers would appear to have grown at a geometric rate since her escape from the Detroit facility."

Isaacs winced. He preferred not to be reminded of the debacle in Detroit. He wondered if the AI did that deliberately after his triangulating comment.

The door to Isaacs's lab opened then, which irked him. Only one person in this facility had the authorization to override the privacy seal, and that he had it was a source of grievance to Isaacs. Sadly, his protests had, as usual, fallen on uncaring ears.

Switching off the image of the waveform, which he had no interest in sharing, he turned to see the irritating face of that person: Alexander Slater, who was holding a digital clipboard and looked as if he'd sucked down a particularly sour lemon.

"You've made ten trips to the surface in the last twenty-four hours," Slater said without preamble. "All unauthorized. Any trip to the surface, especially to gather fresh specimens, puts my men at risk. We've already lost Timson and Moody, and we almost lost a couple more on your last trip. Why do you need so many all of a sudden?"

Isaacs snorted. *His* men, indeed. Technically, as second in command, he was in charge of personnel, but everyone on this base was Isaacs's responsibility, not Slater's.

To answer the question, since ignoring Slater would not make him go away, Isaacs said, "My research has— intensified."

"What does that mean, exactly?"

Coming to a realization, Isaacs sighed. If he didn't

give Slater *something,* he'd go over Isaacs's head to Wesker, and that simply wouldn't do. At least not yet.

So he de-opaqued the window on the far side of the lab. Now Slater could see the testing room, where fourteen undead that had been mutated by the same process that had been used on Hockey Jersey were leaping about, screaming, and throwing themselves against the walls and window. Two hit the window, causing Slater to jump back in shock.

"My God. This is madness."

"Don't worry," Isaacs said, "they're perfectly secure."

"Yeah, I'm sure Timson and Moody thought the same thing." He walked up to the window just as one of them threw a chair against the window. Made of Plasti-Glas as it was, it didn't budge. Slater shook his head. "You're supposed to be domesticating them!"

"Sometimes aggression has its uses." He saw no reason to admit to Slater that the domestication protocols had utterly failed, but sometimes the best successes came out of failure.

"What could you possibly need these things for?"

If Isaacs had ever been in any danger of mistaking Slater for an intelligent human being, that question eliminated the possibility forevermore. With the world as it was, how could anybody not see the value of such creatures?

Before he could say anything, however, the White Queen spoke up. *"Dr. Isaacs, specimen eighty-seven has reached the final stage of the test grid."*

"Perfect," Isaacs said, grateful for the distraction from Slater's stupidity. "Put her onscreen." He re-opaqued the window to the testing room.

Slater moved to stand behind Isaacs as the flat-screen monitor lit up with an image of Alice-87, wearing the red dress and boots that she had worn during the disaster in the Hive, walking down the re-creation of the Raccoon City Hospital. She pushed a gurney down a corridor and watched as the trip wire sliced the gurney in half.

At least, this one had outperformed the eighty-sixth one.

Then she sidestepped the mine, avoiding being shredded by it, which put her ahead of eighty-five as well.

Alice-87 proceeded toward the front door cautiously, as if expecting more trouble.

That was a wise thought on her part, as what would have been the door to the street opened to reveal Hockey Jersey, who screamed and leapt at Alice-87, eviscerating her with his bare hands.

Behind him, he heard Slater gasp and make a guttural noise.

While Isaacs understood the reaction—one didn't often see someone tear apart a human body by hand—the ability of Hockey Jersey to do what he just did at the slightest provocation proved remarkable. And thrilling. Did Slater truly have to ask what use these new, improved undead would have?

These weren't biohazards. These were soldiers. Soldiers who would fight in Isaacs's army.

"Is Chairman Wesker even aware of this?"

Another point against Slater, since the answer should have been blindingly obvious. "He knows what he needs to know."

"Or what you choose to tell him. You've overstepped your bounds. This is sedition."

Isaacs was unconcerned. True, Umbrella had become its own nation, for all intents and purposes, so the word *sedition* could apply, but he didn't acknowledge Slater's authority to charge him with such a crime. "My research here will change the face of everything. *Everything.*"

Slater looked at the flat-screen, then at the opaqued window, then at Isaacs. He shook his head and started to leave.

"If you pick a side," Isaacs said to his retreating form, "be sure it's the right one."

That stopped Slater in his tracks. After a second, he recovered and left the lab.

Isaacs went back to work. He would take care of Slater in due course.

Twenty-One

Alice woke up in a motel bed and wondered if she was still dreaming.

But no, she couldn't have been *still* dreaming, because she didn't dream in the first place. For the first time in a long time, she slept like the proverbial rock.

For once, she had something to thank Sam Isaacs for: her first good night's sleep in years came because she used the abilities he gave her.

She tried to avoid them where possible. The passive powers—the strength and fast healing, for example—she couldn't do much about; the active ones, she tried not to use. But when she arrived at the convoy to see an arc of fire about to fry Carlos Olivera, she acted on instinct.

Too many good people were dead. Alice couldn't bear to see another worthy soul lost.

She felt something on her arm and saw that someone had put a bracelet made of electrical wire on her wrist. Looking around, she found herself in the dilapidated remains of what used to be a lousy motel room. A young girl sat on one of the guest chairs, reading a battered, torn magazine. She had dozens of similar bracelets on her own arms.

"This belong to you?" Alice asked, kicking the blanket off.

The kid dropped the magazine onto the floor and nodded. "Gave it to you last night—for luck. Looked like you needed it."

Trying and failing to recall the last time she slept in a real bed, Alice smiled and said, "Looks like it worked. What's your name?"

"Kmart. It's where they found me—Claire and the others."

"You have a name before that?"

Shrugging, Kmart said, "Never liked it. And everyone I knew was dead. Seemed the time for a change."

Kmart couldn't have been more than fifteen years old, but she sounded like someone three times her age. Alice shuddered. This was what being a kid was now.

She heard a sound like a leaky pipe and turned to see several small children staring at her through the window. The noise had been one of them shushing the others. As soon as they realized that Alice was looking at them, they ran off.

Chuckling, Alice shook her head. "What's up with them?"

"They didn't think you were real," Kmart said with a shrug. "They tell stories about you at night, like you're Dracula, the bogeyman, something like that."

"Really?"

Kmart nodded. "Carlos used to talk about you a lot. So did Jill."

"Jill's here?" Alice blinked. She'd heard rumors about Jill but nothing solid.

Shaking her head, Kmart said, "Nah, we hooked up with her back in Atlanta, and she'd brought some folks for the convoy—Mikey was with her, and so were Dillon and Blair, two of the guys who died this morning—but she didn't stick around. Said she didn't join groups anymore."

"Sounds familiar," Alice muttered. Somehow it didn't surprise her that Jill had followed the same path as Alice. She'd been betrayed by her own back in Raccoon when her fellow cops wouldn't stand up for her after she encountered Umbrella's undead experiments in the Arklay Mountains, and that sense of betrayal by her comrades never really left. When she'd been on the run with Alice, Carlos, L.J., and Angie, Jill had always been the least trustful, and when the opportunity to leave the group came—never mind that she had little choice—she jumped at it eagerly.

Getting up from the chair, Kmart said, "Listen, we're doing a kind of memorial thing for Otto and the rest of the people who—who died. So I'm gonna go do that, okay?"

"Mind if I join you?"

Kmart just shrugged, the classic gesture of the teenager. Some things, it appeared, didn't change.

Alice followed Kmart through the halls of the Desert Trail Motel and found a gathering of about twenty people. They stood in a circle, surrounding ten wooden markers, each with a name scratched sloppily into it: FRED ANDREASSI, ELIZABETH "BETTY" GRIER, MONIQUE LANG, BLAIR MANFREDI, DILLON MATHEWS, KENNETH MINAYA, JARED PETERS, E. RICHARD PRICE, OTTO WALENSKI, and JASON WILLIAMS.

A blond-haired woman stood at the center of the circle and looked around at the survivors. "Anyone want to say something?" This, Alice assumed, was Claire Redfield.

Nobody spoke.

Ten people Alice hadn't gotten here fast enough to save.

Alice wanted to say *something,* but she didn't know any of these people. L.J. and Carlos were the only ones she did know; the rest had all joined up long after Detroit. Alice assumed that Molina and Briscoe had fallen somewhere along the way.

The survivors, who'd lived with those ten people in this convoy, couldn't bring themselves to eulogize them. Likely, there'd been so many dead that they'd run out of words.

L.J. walked over to the one labelled ELIZABETH "BETTY" GRIER and hung something that Alice couldn't make out on top of it. Tears were streaking his cheeks. L.J. had never struck Alice as the sentimental type—she recalled him saying that he once got his own mother involved in a pyramid scheme—but there he was grieving as hard as a person could grieve.

Carlos brought the leader over to Alice. "This is Claire Redfield," Carlos said, confirming what Alice had assumed. "She put together this convoy."

Alice shot Carlos a look. She had assumed Carlos to have done it. Maybe after Detroit, he lost interest in leading people in much the same way Jill had lost interest in following.

"Thank you for your help," Claire said.

"Wish I could have got here sooner."

Claire nodded. "Excuse me, I have things to attend to."

Alice watched the woman walk away. She hid it better than the rest of them, but her spirit was just as broken.

Idly, Alice wondered whether they had the sense to snap the necks of the ten corpses. Otherwise, they'd all be climbing out of their graves to wreak havoc. But Alice wasn't sure how to broach the subject, and besides, she knew for a fact that Carlos knew to do that. Mentioning it would just pour salt on the giant wound that the convoy had become.

"Don't take it personal," Carlos said, indicating Claire's retreating form with his head. "In the last six months, she's lost half the convoy."

Alice raised her eyebrow at Carlos's phrasing. He definitely had had his fill of leadership if he was talking about *Claire* losing people, rather than the convoy or Carlos himself being the ones doing the losing.

Carlos continued: "Pretty soon, there'll be more of us dead than alive."

Then Alice looked up at the sky. Something was bothering her.

"What is it?"

She checked her watch—there was still another hour before the satellite would be overhead. Letting out a breath, she said to Carlos, "Nothing."

"Alice, what happened to you?"

Overwhelmed by the sheer tonnage of the weight of the answer to that question, Alice said nothing.

"Why did you leave?" Carlos asked. "After Detroit?"

That was one she could answer. "I didn't have a choice. They were using me. I was endangering all of you."

"What do you mean?"

She thought about Jisun and Angie and King and wondered how Carlos could ask that, but he probably didn't realize just how much responsibility Alice carried for that. After all, technically, Jisun was overwhelmed by the undead, King was killed alongside Carlos trying to rescue her, and she never told him the truth about Angie.

"They were tracking me," she said after a moment. "I couldn't be around you—any of you. I'd have gotten you all killed."

"That's why you disappeared."

Alice realized that meant that Carlos had been actively looking for her after Detroit, and she wondered if his failure to find her contributed to his inability to continue leading.

"I hacked into their computers and downloaded the satellite trajectories. I stayed off the grid—ceased to exist."

"And after the world ended, why *stay* out there alone?"

In her mind's eye, she saw the bullet fly out of the muzzle in a puff of smoke and smash into Angie's skull.

She looked at Carlos, who had experienced so much death and destruction and was now partly responsible for more than a dozen children, and found she couldn't tell him the truth.

So she just shrugged and said, "Habit."

It was a weak answer, and he knew it.

"Could you be more evasive?" Carlos asked.

Now Alice smiled. "Oh, yes."

Carlos, however, refused to take the bait. Instead, he just stared at her. He knew there was more to it than she was saying.

But she would not tell him about Angie. She hadn't told *anyone* the truth about Angie.

And then there was what had just happened that morning. Isaacs had turned her into as much of a monster as Matt had become, never mind that she at least looked the same on the outside. How could she let herself be around people—worse, be around people she cared about—when she didn't even know what she was? The one person who could answer that question was also the one person she could never allow herself to get near.

"I'm better out there alone, okay?"

"You're better alone." Carlos shook his head. Obviously, it wasn't okay.

"It's just safer if I'm not around people."

Now Carlos did smile. "So why'd you come back?"

Trying to match Kmart's shrug, she said, "I lost my ride."

"That all?" Carlos prompted.

"That's all," Alice said, refusing to rise to the bait. "And I was out of smokes."

Carlos actually laughed at that. "Then you *definitely* came to the wrong place."

She burst out laughing, too, and they both just let loose with several seconds' worth of giggling, even falling into an embrace. Alice hugged him tightly for a second, not realizing until now just how long it had been since she'd had affectionate human contact. Hell, the only contact of any kind she'd had lately had been the pawing she'd gotten in Salt Lake City by those nutbars in the KLKB station.

After a few seconds, she broke the embrace. "Carlos," she said with as much finality as she could muster, "I can't stay." She didn't add, *no matter how much I want to.*

Then that nagging feeling came back. Had her watch been broken during her trek from her camp? Or had her psychic whammy screwed it up?

"What time is it?" she asked Carlos.

Carlos blinked. "Time? I don't even know what *year* it is." Looking around, he saw a man in a cowboy hat walking near an Enco fuel truck. "Chase! Time?"

Glancing at his wrist, the man in the cowboy hat

called back, "Well, Carlos, it's 12:14. You got some-place you gotta be?"

Looking at her own wrist, Alice saw that it also read 12:14. She looked up at the sky one more time, then let out a long breath. The satellite wouldn't be coming around for a while yet.

Shaking her head, she muttered, "Getting paranoid. I'm gonna go for a walk, okay?"

Carlos nodded. "I need to take care of some stuff. For one thing, we might even be able to give you a ride." Alice had a smile that didn't reach his eyes, and Carlos walked off.

After watching his retreating form for a moment, Alice started walking through the camp. Several children pulled the same act they had in the motel, staring at her and pointing and whispering. Alice marveled at the very notion of being a legend of some kind. She'd garnered a reputation in Security Division at Umbrella—Ass-Kicking Alice, they'd called her—but this was several orders of magnitude weirder.

Claire intercepted her as she passed a Hummer. "Got a minute?"

Alice nodded.

"We're all grateful for you helping us out—"

Knowing there was a *but* after that, Alice cut her off. "But how long am I going to stay?"

"Don't get me wrong," Claire said quickly. "We really are grateful. But people saw what you did. They're a little scared."

Now Alice was starting to understand why this

woman was the leader. Where Carlos was using senti-ment to argue for Alice staying, Claire was using practi-cality to argue for her quick departure. The latter was far more becoming of a leader.

In response, she said, "I don't blame them. People have a habit of dying around me."

Sourly, Claire said, "Not just you." She glanced at the ten graves, then looked back at Alice. "You want to explain what happened earlier?"

Alice sighed. "Wish I could. They did something to me. Something I can't explain, can't control." Alice as-sumed she didn't have to explain who "they" were. At this point, Umbrella's crimes had been lain bare to the world. Sadly, the world had bigger problems than prose-cuting those crimes.

Looking around at the camp, Alice went on: "So I don't blame these people for being scared. Truth is, I'm scared myself."

Claire stared at her for a second. Alice found she had trouble reading her expression, which was probably be-cause of the limited human contact she'd had the last couple of years. Finally, Claire said, "I hate to say this, but we face enough dangers every day. I don't know if I need another so close to home."

"I understand," Alice said, grateful that she'd already told Carlos she'd be going. "And I won't be staying. If I can help you, I will. Then you'll never see me again."

"What, you'll just go back out there?"

Again, Alice nodded.

"That's a hard way to live."

Alice smirked. "Takes a little getting used to."

"Everything does these days."

Now Alice had no trouble reading Claire: she was in despair. They all were, truly. Alice thought back to a red journal full of scribblings about Arcadia, Alaska, and remembered that the best cure for despair had always been a little hope.

"Claire, I found something the other day that you guys might be able to use."

Twenty-Two

Isaacs watched the images on his screen eagerly. Repositioning the satellites had done the trick. The White Queen had been able to pinpoint the two psionic bursts to the western region of what was once the United States, putting her in Utah, Nevada, California, Arizona, New Mexico, Idaho, Oregon, or Washington. The satellites then searched further, acquiring any face they could pull out.

One was with a convoy of living humans—about twenty, which was impressive for a mobile group in these dark times—in Nevada. The satellite was only able to get a partial facial identification, but the White Queen proudly declared that face to be a sixty-two-percent match with the images of Alice Abernathy that they had on file.

Isaacs allowed himself a rare smile and said, "Welcome home."

The satellite had done the same for the others with Alice, and the White Queen flagged two of them as likely being Carlos Olivera and Lloyd Jefferson Wayne, two of Project Alice's accomplices during the Raccoon disaster and its immediate aftermath.

Unfortunately, Isaacs had to contact Chairman Wesker before any sort of retrieval operation could be authorized. He could try to order the security personnel himself, but then that ass Slater would simply overrule him and bring Wesker in to enforce it.

So, as much as it galled him, he put in a request to have a private conversation with Wesker.

Within the hour, he was standing in the meeting room, speaking with Wesker's holographic image projected into the same chair as during the bigger meeting, and he filled the chairman in on what the White Queen had found.

Wesker rubbed his chin thoughtfully. "You're positive it's her?"

"Sixty-two percent—too great a chance to pass up."

In a tone that indicated disagreement with Isaacs's statement, Wesker said, "*If* it is Project Alice, she's been evading the satellite grid for years."

Detroit again. Isaacs was never to be free of reminders of that, apparently. "I've already rerouted the satellites. We can reacquire the subject, and she'll be unaware of our surveillance. I can have a strike team ready within the hour."

"No."

Isaacs had to strain every muscle in his body to keep the disappointment from showing on his face.

Wesker continued: "We'll establish a positive identification first. One hundred percent."

Gritting his teeth, Isaacs said, "The group she's with includes known associates, Olivera *and* Wayne. Besides which, the original Project Alice is vital to my research—to the whole process of domestication! Her blood, her genetic structure, is the key. The longer we leave her out there, the greater the chance we lose her again. I can't risk that."

In a low, dangerous tone that made Isaacs realize that he'd perhaps overstepped a bit, Wesker said, "That decision is not yours to make. You'll take no action till this matter has been discussed by the Committee at the next scheduled meeting."

With that, Wesker's image winked out.

"Dammit!" Isaacs yelled to the empty room. The next meeting wasn't for another three days. Project Alice could be anywhere in that time, and there was no guarantee that they'd be able to find her again.

Reaching into his lab coat, Isaacs pulled out the digital recorder. The red light was on, indicating that it was still recording. He touched a button, and the red light went off.

Returning to his lab, Isaacs once again docked the recorder, adding this conversation to the sound files he already had in a secure, password-protected folder on his hard drive that he simply called 15627, a series of numbers picked randomly. He ran a program that would carve out Wesker's voice, then isolate the individual words. The program created new files for each word, and the directory for 15627 saw several sound file icons being added, each with a file name corresponding to the word in question.

When the computer flashed the words CAPTURE COMPLETE, Isaacs sat down and called up another program, one that would compose a sound file from the individual files he created. The work was tedious and slow, but after about twenty minutes, he had a complete sound file. He played it to be sure.

Wesker's disjointed voice played over the speakers, the words sounding uneven and with odd pauses: "The, Committee, authorize, immediate, action, release, of, vehicles, and, personnel, under, command, of, Doctor, Isaacs."

Isaacs smiled.

Soon.

Very soon.

Twenty-Three

Jill Valentine had spent most of the last few days gathering up every citizen of the city of Baltimore who wasn't in the convention center.

That proved to be depressing in many ways. For one thing, the number of people she'd been able to find was only a hundred. And those she found were barely able to stand upright. They were malnourished, dehydrated, and many were on the brink of death. Worse, these people were also unarmed, unless you counted two-by-fours that were lying around abandoned row houses, which meant that when people did die—and according to Andre, they did pretty regularly—they became "zees."

Safety in numbers was a concept that they had abandoned. Many had gone to the convention center, hearing of food and shelter, but the few who made it back alive said that they shot anyone who came close—a tactic Jill had experienced firsthand. The convention center was just for "them boys."

It was hard enough for people to survive in this world, but to have them denied at least a chance by their fellow living humans?

Jill wasn't about to stand for that.

First, she needed to organize everyone, bring them all together. That proved challenging. Some were willing to be convinced. Some were too weak to argue and just went along for lack of ability to reject the notion. One person, a woman named Maureen, refused to exit her building, saying, "Last time I talked to somebody, she died and tried to eat my ass. Git!"

Jill finally persuaded Maureen to come out in exchange for food. Besides her own stores, Andre had shown her a deli that was bolted shut that nobody had been able to get into. Jill broke into the place with very little effort. While the perishables had rotted to the point where you could hardly breathe, they managed to liberate a mess of canned food and bottled water.

She had made her pitch to each person, gathering them all up in an abandoned building on Fayette Street. Most everyone said yes. The ones who didn't were so far gone that there was no helping them. They'd be dead and zombified soon.

Jill had been half tempted to shoot them in the head and have done with it.

When she asked if there was anyone left, Andre hesitated. "There's one guy, but you don't wanna be talkin' to him."

"Why not?"

"He fuckin' *crazy*."

Someone else—a boy named Marlo—said, "You talkin' about Jasper? Shit." That last word's vowel went on for several seconds. "He one crazy nigger. Back in the day, he used to be po-po, and when the shit went down, he took *all* the dope an' all the guns."

"He was a cop?" Jill asked.

"What'd I just *tell* you?" Marlo said. "Yeah, he a cop—back when they *was* cops, an' shit. Used to trade drugs for food, but he don't be doin' that no more on account'a ain't no one gettin' high no mo'."

That surprised Jill. "Nobody gets high?"

Andre shrugged. "Nothin' to get high *with*. All the junkies, they died from the DTs an' shit an' became zees. Ain't nobody left who want it."

"So where is this Jasper guy?"

It took ten minutes to pry the information out of Andre and Marlo, seeing as they thought that Jasper would shoot her in the head if she came anywhere near. Finally, Marlo said he was in the old ARM building— that was the African Revival Movement, a "black power" organization that had been founded to aid the African-American community in Baltimore. It had been shut down after a scandal involving the founder. Jill had a vague recollection of reading about it.

Nobody would go with her to the tall, gray stone building, but Jill figured it was better to go alone anyhow. She brought the Prius to a spot a few blocks away and went the rest of the way on foot, trying to stay low and out of sight. She quickly saw that the place was barricaded up, with gunsights on all the upper-floor windows. Nobody appeared to be **at** those sights, but there were ways to automate that this Jasper guy may have had access to.

Marlo and Andre and several others had said that this guy thought he had "the biggest dick in Balto City" and that he only talked to people who dealt with him, in his words, "from a position of strength." Andre was pretty sure he did exchanges with "them boys" in the convention center and that they had some kind of truce.

Jill was hoping to get him to break that truce.

Raising her nine, she took out one of the sniper muzzles.

Then she stepped forward and raised her hands. "Officer Jasper, my name is Jill Valentine. I want to talk."

"I should shoot you in the *face* for what you just did, bitch!" came a voice from the upper floors.

"That was to show you that I could. I also could've taken out the rest of your sniper rifles before you had a chance to lock and load, since I doubt you saw me coming."

"You one confident bitch, ain'tcha?"

She smiled. "I know what I'm capable of. I also know what you're capable of. And I need your help."

"Fuck off, bitch. I don't help nobody."

"Really? I was told you were a member. Didn't you swear an oath to serve and protect?"

"That's good—throwin' the badge in my face. I got me a shield, bitch, but it don't mean shit no more.

Lemme guess, you dated a cop once, so you know the lingo?"

"No, I'm a member, too. Officer Jill Valentine, S.T.A.R.S."

"Stars? The fuck is that? Wait," he said before Jill could answer, "that's those motherfuckers up in Raccoon City, right?"

"It was, yeah, back when there *was* a Raccoon City." Jill was getting tired of shouting to the rooftops. "Can I come in?"

"I know that name. Valentine. You work with an asshole name'a Wells?"

"He wasn't an asshole, but Peyton Wells was my sergeant, yeah."

"I met his ass in a conference in Seattle. Only person there who didn't have a stick up his ass."

Jill chuckled. "Yeah, that's Peyton."

"He said you were the best on his team. So I guess you okay."

Putting her hands on her hips, Jill shouted up, "That mean I can come in and talk to you?"

"Depends on what you wanna talk about."

"Right now, leaving aside the people in the convention center, there are maybe a hundred people in the entire city of Baltimore. That's the same city you once swore an oath to serve and protect. That number is dropping by the minute because the fuckers in the convention center are hoarding all the resources and killing people to get them. The city *might* stand a chance if everyone pitches in—and it could become a haven. The structure's all there, but the assholes in charge are keeping it for themselves."

Jasper finally stuck his head out the window. He had an afro that went up about a foot over his head and a thick beard. His brown eyes looked only slightly crazy, which was a lot less crazy than Jill had been figuring. "How you know about this?" Jasper asked. "They shoot anybody comes close."

"They tried. I shot 'em first."

"Good girl." Then he stuck his head back in the window.

Jill waited for something to happen. "Jasper?"

She picked up her nine. What was he—?

Then the front door opened. "Well, don't just stand there, bitch," Jasper said. Jill noticed he was armed with at least three different guns that she could see, plus a few knives and two bandoliers over his chest. "Getch'ass in here."

Smiling, Jill holstered the nine and approached the three steps that led up to the front door.

Twenty-Four

Claire stared at the select members of the convoy she'd gathered in the back of the 8x8: herself, Mikey, Carlos, and Chase. Alice was also present, having just finished telling everyone else what she'd told Claire earlier about the red journal she'd found. Normally, Claire would have included L.J., but he was still too far gone in grief over Betty to think straight.

Once Alice was finished—and while she was talking, the journal had been passed around from person to person—there was silence, aside from Mikey flipping pages.

Chase finally broke it by speaking in a dreamy voice. "A safe haven, free of infection."

Staring at a page full of pictures, Mikey said, "It's the promised land."

Claire couldn't believe what she was hearing. She had

been willing to let Alice tell the other senior-most members of the convoy about the journal, but only after Alice all but bullied her into it. "Alaska! Are you all crazy? Have you any idea what kind of journey that would be?"

Shrugging, Chase said, "Long."

"Well," Mikey said, "two thousand seven hundred and forty-six miles."

Everyone stared at him. Claire wondered for a second how he knew that, then remembered that Mikey was, at heart, a geek.

In a small voice, Mikey added, "Or thereabouts."

"And we don't have enough gas for the next *week*." Claire looked right at Alice, who, damn her, was just staring back with those fucking blue eyes of hers. "And at the end of it—what? You've no guarantee there's even anyone alive up there."

Mikey held up the journal. "These transmissions—"

"Are dated from *six months ago*. How many radio broadcasts have we responded to? How many times have we got there too late?"

Nobody replied to that. The answer to the second question was a number only slightly smaller than the answer to the first one.

Alice said, "According to the transmissions, there's no infection up there. They're isolated—safe."

Again, Claire stared at Alice, and again, Alice stared right back. "This convoy trusts me with their lives. Do you have any idea what kind of risk this would be?"

Chase said quietly, "One worth taking."

"No," Claire said firmly. She was sorry she even let

Alice talk about this. "These people don't need pipe dreams."

"Maybe that's exactly what they need."

Claire turned to look at Carlos, who hadn't said anything until those six words. "What?"

"*Look* at them, Claire," Carlos said emphatically, his honey voice sounding ragged with stress and pain. "Six months ago, there were fifty of us. Then forty. Now we're down to twenty. We buried ten people this morning alone. They're starting to give up. They *need* some hope."

"This kind of hope could get them all killed."

Carlos barked a nasty laugh. "The *world* could get them all killed, Claire! Do we really have a better chance doing what we're doing now, driving around hoping for the best and being menaced by *birds?* God, did you see it this morning? Ten people died, and nobody could even say a word. Freddie was a carpenter who had three kids, Dillon was an Army Ranger who fought in two wars, Jared was a shoe salesman, Betty was a paramedic who was studying to be a nurse, Kenny was a bank clerk who was going to school to become a lawyer, Monique was a physical therapist and a grandmother three times over, Jason was a television producer—these people had *lives,* but by the time they died in this convoy, nobody seemed to care. We need something to care about, Claire, or we may as well all eat our guns and be done with it."

Claire looked around at the others. Mikey and Chase both had the same intense desperation as Carlos. Alice—she still couldn't read Alice.

Maybe Carlos was right. At the very least, she owed it to the others to give them the option.

Ten minutes later, she'd gathered the entire convoy around the 8x8. Everyone was staring at her, waiting for her to tell them what to do.

Days like this, she wondered why they followed her. She hadn't exactly led them to freedom and safety. But then, maybe this was as good as it got now.

"We have a decision to make—it's too big, too important, for me to make it for you. There's a *chance* there are survivors in Alaska. There's a *chance* the infection hasn't reached that far. But we don't know for sure. So we have a choice: we stay as we are, or we try for Alaska." She paused for a moment, looked around at everyone. Already, she could see something different in their eyes. "For Alaska?"

Most of the twenty hands rose.

How fitting that in the middle of the desert, everyone voted for the oasis. Claire just hoped it wasn't a mirage.

"All right, then. Let's get it together." She jumped down from the 8x8 and went straight for Alice. "I hope you're right."

"Me, too," Alice said with a smirk. "But, in all seriousness, what's the alternative? Driving around and hoping for the best? At least now you have a goal."

Claire gathered all the drivers around the news truck: Mikey (the news truck), Carlos (the 8x8), Chase (the Enco truck), Claire herself (the Hummer), and Morgan, whom Claire had asked to take over the ambulance now that it had been dug out of the sand.

"Food's virtually gone," Carlos said.

Claire knew that from what Otto had told her last night. She forced herself not to think about the fact that Otto was no longer around to talk to about it. Otto had been the glue that held the convoy together, especially given how good he was with the kids. What would happen—?

She cut the thought off as Carlos went on: "Fuel tanker's almost empty."

Speaking of Otto, she'd also had some of the others siphon off gas from the school bus—which was useless to them as a vehicle now—and strip it of its armaments. They were also siphoning gas from the quad bike. Alice even offered some of the fuel she had left from her now-trashed bike, which she'd siphoned before coming here.

Mikey said, "I've got half a tank of gas—that's it. And with the added weight . . ." The news truck had taken on kid duty with the school bus gone.

"We're running on empty," Morgan said.

When Carlos prompted him, Chase said, "I don't even have empty. I got fumes, vapor." He made a show of sniffing the air. *"Parfum de gasoline."*

"So if we're going to make this trip," Carlos said, unrolling a wrinkly, beaten-up, half-faded map, "we need to resupply. These are our options."

He laid the map out on the news truck's hood. Claire looked down to see a map of Nevada that also had bits of California, Arizona, Utah, Wyoming, and New Mexico in it.

Carlos pointed at Caliente. "Nearest, safest bet is here."

Alice shook her head. "Tried a month ago—empty."

Pointing now at Mesquite, Carlos said, "Then here."

Again, Alice shook her head.

His finger hovering over Yerington, Carlos said, "Maybe—" but cut himself off at a look from Alice.

Claire's eye, however, caught another city, one she should have thought of in the first place. Well, she had thought of it but dismissed it as too dangerous, but in for a penny, in for a pound.

"Vegas."

Everyone turned to look at Claire. Most regarded her as if she were insane.

She explained herself. "It's the only place we're sure to find gasoline and supplies."

"There's a reason for that," Carlos said. "Vegas is too damn dangerous."

Chase was shaking his head. "It's lousy with them mothers."

Claire took a breath. "If we're going to go for Alaska, we're gonna need a *lot* of gasoline. And we've sucked every small-town pump dry over the last six months. We have to hit a big city again."

"She's right," Alice said. "Vegas is our best bet."

Mikey looked scared but resolved. Chase and Morgan looked resigned. Carlos still looked as if he thought Claire and Alice both needed to be locked up.

Finally, Carlos lowered his head. "Fine. Desperate times, and all that other bullshit."

"Works for me," Chase said. "Let's saddle up!"

They all moved to their respective vehicles. Claire

walked down the convoy, making sure everyone was set. As she passed the ambulance, she noticed that Morgan looked nervous in the driver's seat.

"You okay?"

"Yeah, just—" Morgan sighed. "I was thinking about becoming an EMT when, y'know, everything went to shit. Never thought I'd drive one'a these. This wasn't how I wanted it."

"We got far away from 'wanted' a long time ago, Morgan," Claire said while she put an encouraging hand on his shoulder through the open window. "Listen, how're we on antibiotics?"

"Not bad, actually, especially now that—" Morgan winced.

"Now that what?"

Morgan let out a long breath. "Now that we're down to twenty."

"Yeah." She squeezed his shoulder, then went on to the 8x8, where Alice got in next to Carlos, and Kmart got in behind Alice, staring at her as if she was some kind of goddess. Claire sighed. She supposed that it was inevitable, especially the way the stories about Alice had gotten out of hand even before she showed up and used her magic tricks to save Carlos's life.

On the one hand, Claire wished she would've shown up sooner, maybe saved a few more people who didn't make it. On the other hand, they were lucky she showed up at all.

Claire got into the Hummer. Two of the other teenagers, a girl named Tracy and a boy named Brian, sat in the backseat. "Kmart said you'd need the company," Tracy said.

Chuckling, Claire fastened her seat belt and started the ignition. "Thanks, guys."

"Thank her," Brian said sourly. "*We* wanted to be in the news truck. That's where the cool gadgets are!"

Tracy hit her brother in the arm. "Shut *up*."

Shaking her head, Claire picked up the PRC. "Everyone good to go?"

In turn, Mikey, Carlos, Morgan, and Chase all answered in the affirmative.

"Let's move."

Sitting in the passenger seat of the Enco tanker, L.J. tried not to think about how much like shit he felt.

Chase was driving. "You okay?"

L.J. shrugged it off as best he could. "Yeah, yeah, I'm fine. Pork and beans, man—lethal. Don't know how you cowboys do it."

Chase laughed.

It was gonna be over soon. L.J. knew it. He should've just walked away. It was how he do, get the fuck out before the heat hit. That was his philosophy, and it kept him going when a lot of other motherfuckers were doin' time.

But shit changed when he came out here. People was counting on his black ass. And wasn't that a kick in the motherfuckin' teeth? People *depending* on L.J. Wayne, like he was some kind of savior.

It was a weird feeling. But it was kinda cool, too.

Which made it all harder. L.J. knew he should've just walked out into the desert, let this fucking T-virus take his ass, and then he'd be a zombie-ass mother-fucker, just like Rashonda and Dwayne and those kids back in Raccoon.

But he couldn't do it. He couldn't just leave. He had to hold on so he could help some more. He had to be here for these people.

"You *sure* you're okay?"

The last thing L.J. wanted was pity. He put on a whinier version of Chase's drawl. "'You *sure* you're okay?' Not going all Brokeback on me, are you?"

"Hey, take it easy, just worried. You're my wingman. Hell, you're this *convoy's* wingman. Just makin' sure you're all right."

"I'm *fine*," L.J. said. "Just—"

"Betty, right?"

L.J. blinked. "Uh, yeah." He hadn't even thought of using his grief over Betty—who didn't deserve what she got, not that any of them did—to cover up. Shit, he *was* sick. "Yeah, that's prob'ly it. Don't wanna talk about it."

"Okay."

Chase actually shut the fuck up after that.

L.J. stared out the window of the tanker.

Alice sat in the passenger seat of the 8x8. It wasn't until they were on the road that she realized that there was a gaping hole in the floor of the army truck. The pavement went zooming by under her feet.

Looking over at Carlos, she smiled. "Nice ride."

Within minutes, they were on U.S. Route 93, headed south. A sign read LAS VEGAS 155 MILES.

Kmart leaned forward so she was between the two front seats. "What's Vegas like?"

Alice shrugged. "Used to be a fun town."

"Now?"

Turning, Alice gave Kmart as serious an expression as she could provide. "Let's hope we don't stay there long enough to find out."

They stayed on 93 for quite some time. Eventually, the rhythm of the road put Kmart to sleep in the back. As soon as she was out, Alice turned to Carlos. "You know she likes you."

Frowning, Carlos asked, "What?"

"She has a crush on you."

"Kmart?" Carlos shook his head. "She's fourteen years old."

"Old enough. Especially now."

"Yeah." The convoy passed some undead shambling down the side of the highway, seemingly without aim. "You ever think *we're* the freaks?"

"What do you mean?" Alice asked, even though she was fairly sure she knew.

"That we're the anomalies, the last of the dinosaurs. We fucked up our world, and so the world fucked us back. Look at them." He indicated the undead with his head as he drove. "This is their world now. We don't belong here."

Shaking her head, Alice said, "Believe that if you want, but I'm not ready to surrender to the new world order just yet." She reached into the pocket of the door and pulled out the journal. Flipping through, she found one of the glossy articles on Arcadia, which was attached with a paper clip. Removing both article and clip, she used the latter to attach the article—with its lovely photograph of the picturesque town—to the sun visor above her.

She looked at Carlos. "There's an end to this. I'm sure of it."

Twenty-Five

In the 1940s, Benjamin Siegel, a New York mobster who had moved to Los Angeles, decided to turn the small desert town of Las Vegas, Nevada—located in a state where gambling was legal—into the site of the greatest luxury hotel and casino the world had ever seen. The result of that dream—the Flamingo—was but the first, and by the end of the twentieth century, Las Vegas had gained a deserved reputation as a place to gamble and gambol, easily earning the nickname of Sin City.

That, however, was in the old world.

If Alice hadn't seen the sign saying WELCOME TO LAS VEGAS, and if the odometer of the 8x8 hadn't been one hundred fifty-five miles higher than it was after they passed the mile marker on the highway, she might not have believed the sign.

Claire's voice sounded over the PRC and summed it up perfectly: "Oh, my God."

Alice found herself recalling a poem she'd read in high school called *Ozymandias* by Percy Bysshe Shelley, about a kingdom that had been reclaimed by the desert, leaving only two legs from a statue erected to the long-dead King Ozymandias, the "king of kings."

Aloud, she muttered a line from the poem, "Nothing beside remains."

From behind her, Kmart asked, "Where is it?"

"Guess the desert wanted it back," she said.

Bits of Vegas were still visible over the sand dunes: the tops of the re-created Empire State Building, Statue of Liberty, Eiffel Tower, and the Sphinx outside the Luxor. Alice bitterly thought that the latter seemed a lot more appropriate now.

She shook her head. "Five years of storms and no one to hold the sand back."

Claire said, "Let's bring it to a stop, people."

After the vehicles all came to a standstill, Carlos took out his binoculars and started gazing across what was left of the city.

Over the PRC, Chase asked the question on everyone's lips. "Where are they?"

After a few more seconds, Carlos lowered the binoculars. "Nothing."

Alice couldn't believe it. Not a single sign of un-dead. That seemed impossible.

Then she saw one of those crows that had menaced the convoy flying by. She pointed at it. "Those birds must have moved through the city block by block—picked it clean."

Carlos shuddered. Behind them, Kmart said, "Fuck."

"Let's move," Claire said. "Everyone be careful."

Slowly, the convoy moved down the sandy remains of the Strip. Dead husks of palm trees lined the center divide.

"There!" L.J. said over the radio. "The Pizza San Marco."

"That's Piazza," Mikey said.

"What-the-fuck-ever, man. They got valet parking and a gas pump in there."

Alice peered ahead and saw that the Venetian was in better shape than some—you could actually enter the hotel—though the faux canals were choked with sand, the gondolas beached and useless.

"How would you know that?" Chase asked.

Having no trouble visualizing L.J.'s shrug, Alice heard him say, "Dropped two g's here back in the day."

Chase's appreciative whistle sounded bizarre over the PRC speaker. "Two grand—Mr. High Roller."

"Kiss my ass, cowboy."

Alice turned to Carlos. "You know, it brings a sense of order to the world. Everything may have gone to shit, but at least L.J.'s still L.J."

"I heard that, Abernathy. You'll get yours, girl, you feel me?"

Grabbing the radio, Alice said, "Not in your wildest dreams, L.J."

"Everybody, *stop!*"

Carlos slammed his foot on the brake at Claire's sudden order, and Alice lurched forward, the seat belt biting into her ribs.

Alice hopped out of the 8x8, Carlos right behind her, and ran past the Hummer. Claire had already gotten out, and Alice followed her gaze to the massive metal freight container blocking their path.

"We have to move it," Alice said.

Claire shot her a *no shit* look, then turned to Chase, who was just sticking his head out of the Enco tanker. "Chase, I want a lookout." She looked over to the side of the road—they were right by the Eiffel Tower. "Up there."

Alice couldn't help but smile at the crestfallen look on Chase's face as he stared up at the imposing height of the re-created Eiffel Tower. "Great."

"Could be worse," Alice said. "This one's shorter than the one in Paris."

"Rather *be* at the one in Paris right now," he muttered, then headed over to it.

The 8x8, the tanker, and the news truck all had winches in the front, and they quickly pulled all three vehicles up to the container. It would take all three to move this thing. In fact, Alice wasn't a hundred-percent sure the three would be sufficient, but the ambulance and the Hummer didn't have winches. While Alice pulled out the 8x8's hook, Claire started unspooling the cable on the news truck, with Carlos taking the tanker.

"Damn!"

Alice looked up to see Chase about halfway up the tower, shaking his hand back and forth. The metal was probably hot to the touch. After a second, he kept going.

The three of them walked up to the container, a very unsteady L.J. behind them, with his Beretta ready. Behind L.J. were the other surviving adult members of the convoy: Morgan, Dorian, Cliff, Peter-Michael, Pablo, Erica, and Joel. They were all armed and ready, too.

With Claire, Alice checked the front of the container, but there was no sign of a handle or lock or anything. It was as if it was a sealed box. "No lock, no way to open it," she said to Claire.

"Good," Claire said emphatically. From the sounds of it, she didn't want to know what was in it. "Now, let's get this done."

Just as Claire turned to hook up the winch, Alice heard a noise. Based on the way she suddenly stopped, Claire heard it, too.

She and Claire exchanged glances, then Alice put her ear to the container. It definitely sounded as if something was hitting the container from the inside.

Then she ducked as she heard an explosive noise. Looking up, she saw that it was a bolt flying off the front of the container, quickly followed by several more doing the same.

"Get back!" Alice cried, just as the front of the container fell forward onto the sandy Strip. She and Claire barely avoided being smashed by the front as it crashed to the ground.

For a second, there was silence. The inside of the container appeared dark.

Then all hell broke loose.

Ever since she saw her first undead in the Hive a lifetime ago, Alice had known that there were rules about them that they always followed. One was that they were incredibly slow. Indeed, the living's greatest advantage had always been speed. Powered only by electrical impulses being fed to dead tissue, there were limits on how fast they could ambulate.

No longer.

More than thirty undead poured out from the container, and they were moving at speeds Alice could barely keep up with, much less the others.

Alice and Claire were closest, and one leapt right at them. Without hesitating, Alice blew it away with her sawed-off. She'd hoped to hit the head, but it moved faster than anticipated, and she only got him in the chest.

Even with most of his thoracic region gone, the undead got *quickly* to his feet.

"What the hell are these things?" Claire asked as she took aim.

But these undead were too damn fast.

They attacked.

Alice got one with a clothesline across his neck that snapped bone. This time, it didn't get back up.

That was something: they had the same vulnerabilities.

Several convoy members took shots, but they weren't all as good as Carlos or Alice herself—or Jill, whose marksmanship Alice found herself missing horribly right about now—and they couldn't seem to make head shots.

"Run!" Alice screamed, not that she needed to tell anyone twice. Claire was heading for the Hummer, L.J. and Carlos covering her.

Alice ran and fought and shot, but there were so many of them. One literally ripped Morgan in half. Another punched Pablo, his fist going right through Pablo's chest, thrusting his heart out through his back. Two more grabbed Cliff's retreating form and pulled him to the ground, beating him into a bloody pulp.

L.J. barely made it into the 8x8 in time, slamming the door in an undead's face. The monster kept pounding on the door, though, putting huge dents in it, then went for the window. As it shattered, L.J. screamed to the backseat, where Alice assumed Kmart still to be, "Get in the back!"

First Alice heard Kmart say, "Forget that." Then she heard a distinctive pumping sound.

Then she saw the undead get blown back out the window following the report of a shotgun.

Looking over at the Piazza San Marco, Alice saw Joel and Peter-Michael being chased onto the Venetian bridge by two more undead. Alice ran after them, pulling out the Kukris she'd taken from the fuckers at KLKB.

She'd been looking forward to a chance to use these things.

Her first swing sliced open one undead's arm. Her second, with the other one, carved into the other undead's neck but wasn't a fatal blow.

It was enough to get the undead to focus their attention on Alice instead of Peter-Michael and Joel, however. They ran. Alice stayed and smiled at the undead.

Carlos kept firing until both his .45s dry-clicked. He made sure that Claire got into the Hummer and that Mikey got into the news truck. When Peter-Michael and Joel ran down from the Venetian Hotel, Carlos made sure they made it into the ambulance. Unfortunately, he hadn't been able to help Pablo, Cliff, or Morgan, and he couldn't see Dorian or Erica. Chase was still up the tower, and the occasional bullet from above meant that he was doing his part. The kids were all in the ambulance with Joel and Peter-Michael. They were all safe.

Carlos, however, wasn't. The undead that had been blown out of the 8x8 was now on Carlos, and his .45s were both empty. With no time to reload, he instead dove to the ground and rolled under the 8x8.

Reaching into his ammo pouch with sweaty fingers, he kicked at the two undead who clawed at his boots. He let the empty clip fall to the ground and struggled to slam the full one into the barrel.

One was right near his calf, opening its mouth to bite.

Finally, Carlos slammed the clip in and fired on the

undead, blowing his head off, then doing the same for the next a second later.

He let himself breathe a sigh of relief.

Turning his head, he saw another undead face snarling right at him, its decaying breath blowing right into his nose.

Then it moved to bite him . . .

Isaacs stood in the tent they'd set up in what used to be Las Vegas. A helicopter sat next to the tent, ready to evac at a moment's notice in case things went wrong. The last few years had taught Sam Isaacs that it was best to assume that the worst would happen, because all too often it did.

With him were two of the people working under him whom Isaacs came closest to trusting, mostly by virtue of having overheard them say disparaging things about Slater. One was Kim Pinto, a technician who was adept with Umbrella's satellite network, the other was Dr. Howard Margolin, who'd supervised the mass production of the serum that had made these new creatures and had also been aiding Isaacs with his other formula.

He'd also been the one to coin the phrase *Super Undead* to describe them, a neologism that spread through the entire complex before Isaacs had had a chance to put a stop to it.

Besides them were DiGennaro and Lobachevski from Security Division. A pilot, Alan Kistler, was waiting in the helicopter, along with Perroneau from security.

In front of him on one of the plasma-screen monitors, Isaacs watched the satellite feed that showed the battle on the Strip. In another, he got what Pinto had referred to as "Alice-cam"—this was a direct view of what Alice was seeing, thanks to the implant that Isaacs had placed in her skull back in San Francisco before her "escape." Below them were smaller monitors that provided various bits of data about Alice's health.

Once they'd found Project Alice heading with Olivera, Wayne, and eighteen other survivors toward Las Vegas, it was a simple matter to place an obstruction on the only road that was still passable in that fabled city: the so-called Strip, where Project Alice and her compatriots were all but guaranteed to find it.

And now they had. The Super Undead were performing beyond expectations. It was a pity that people had to die to test the Super Undead, but given Isaacs's long-term goals, a smaller living population was preferred.

Alice apparently had gotten her hands on some exotic weaponry in her travels. As he watched the two plasma screens, he saw her use a pair of Nepalese blades on two of the Super Undead.

Or, rather, try to. One blade became embedded in a Super Undead's shoulder, and the other one ducked a swing of Alice's. The follow-through resulted in the blade slamming into the wall of one of the vulgar hotels that used to dominate this metropolis, breaking off the blade's tip.

Still, Alice fought on. Her heart rate, respiration, and EEG all remained at the same level they had been at before the fight began. This wasn't much of an effort for Alice—or, rather, even if it was, that effort wasn't taking a great deal out of her. Her heart rate was only a marginal percentage higher than it usually was—though that still made it far faster than normal—and her EEG remained stable.

One Super Undead fell to the ground, and it took Isaacs a moment to realize that she'd beheaded the creature with her remaining blade. It had happened so fast that Isaacs had almost missed it.

"She really is magnificent," he muttered. Then he turned to Margolin. "When she's dead, make sure you move in fast. I need a sample of her blood while it's still warm."

Margolin nodded.

Looking at the plasma-screen, he watched Alice dispatch the other Super Undead. Then she retrieved her blade from its shoulder.

Isaacs had seen enough. To Pinto, he asked, "Satellite in position?"

"Yes, sir," Pinto replied.

"Then shut her down."

Pinto entered some commands into her keyboard. Seconds later, Alice stopped moving, her arms going limp, the blades dangling loosely in her weakened grip.

Isaacs smiled.

Mikey Faerber knew, rationally, that no one could possibly think the world was better now than it was. Most of the population of the United States was dead, as far as he'd been able to determine, the rest of the world was only in marginally better shape, and he had absolutely no idea from day to day if he'd have such basics as food and shelter.

But he didn't exactly miss his old life, either. He worked as a computer programmer for a bank. True, he worked long hours, but at least the pay was dreadful. He was underappreciated at his job, and his social life would have had to have improved by several orders of magnitude before it would reach the lofty heights of pathetic.

He'd been home sick with mono when the zomboids started showing up in Tampa. By the time he recovered, everyone in his apartment complex was dead, and only the dead bolt on his door had kept him safe. The next living human being he saw was a woman named Jill Valentine, who offered to let him come along with her and the others she'd picked up throughout the Gulf Coast. They went down to Key West, then headed north.

In Atlanta, Jill had met up with Claire and Carlos and dumped everyone off with them, saying she was sick of people. At first, Mikey had thought that he'd annoyed her too much—and admittedly, his attempts to hit on her were lame as hell, but she'd literally saved his life, and it was hard not to be grateful and smitten at the same time, especially with someone as amazing-looking as Jill—but Carlos had assured him that Jill had always been like that.

He'd quickly proven his use to the convoy with his programming skills. For the first time in his entire life, he was appreciated, wanted, needed, and even liked.

Pity it took the end of the world to happen.

His love life hadn't gotten any worse, not that there was anywhere to go from zero. If only those women who'd all told him they wouldn't date him if he were the last man on Earth were here now, he could call their bluff.

That, however, was the least of his concerns right now. It had been bad enough dealing with all the zomboids. At this point, Mikey had pretty much gotten used to them. But crows? And now these souped-up zomboids—it was just *wrong*.

Carlos had covered Mikey's retreat into the news truck. The kids had all been put in the ambulance, leaving Mikey alone in the truck, which suited him fine. He didn't say anything, but he'd never liked kids and hadn't relished the idea of his truck—his refuge, his haven, his Fortress of Solitude—replacing the school bus for babysitting duty.

And now it was just as well, because one of the big, scary monsters was heading right for the truck.

Slamming it into reverse, Mikey backed the truck away, not bothering to look where he was going. Besides, the side-views were all covered in sand.

He winced as the truck collided with—something. It didn't keep the truck from moving, so he didn't care all that much.

Then it slammed into something that jolted him right out of his seat, bringing the truck to a sudden and painful halt.

Throwing it back into drive, he floored it.

The truck didn't move.

"Come on, come *on!*" To quote nobody in the world except geeks like him, Mikey put the pedal to the metal, but nothing happened. He could hear the back wheels spinning, probably on sand.

Mikey was really learning to hate sand.

A rhythmic pounding indicated that the zomboids were now taking out their frustrations on the truck itself. Within seconds, and with an ear-splitting rending of metal and shattering of glass, they removed both doors, one window, and an entire side panel. Mikey tried not to think about how impossible it would be to replace the equipment they were shredding—which proved easy, as his primary thoughts were of how he was going to live another ten seconds.

Then he remembered—he had guns! Thanks to Carlos, he even knew how to use them! Bringing up the .22s he'd been entrusted with—Carlos had said that anything more powerful would be "unwise"—he fired them at the two nearest zomboids.

Four more took their place.

Whirling around, Mikey saw that there were no undead at the rear door. Jumping out of his seat, he made a beeline for the back. He threw the back doors open and ran as fast as he'd ever run in his life. Faster even than he had when Butch Mowbry went after him in search of lunch money. (And who named their kid Butch, anyhow? That was his given name, on his birth certificate and everything. He'd grown up to be a janitor, which Mikey had always considered poetic justice. Mikey wondered if he survived the apocalypse. He hoped not.)

Something crashed into Mikey's back, and he fell to the floor, hated, evil sand getting into his nose and mouth and eyes. The weight on him was tremendous, and for the first time in his life, Mikey understood the phrase *dead weight*.

A big woman zomboid rolled Mikey over and craned her mouth open, ready to feed on him.

Then her head exploded.

Looking past the decapitated zomboid, Mikey saw Claire holding a smoking gun.

"Mikey! Over here!" she screamed.

As if he had to be told twice. Mikey had been secretly in love with Claire Redfield from the moment he first met her but hadn't said anything, burned as he'd been by a lifetime of rejection. But he swore if he got out of this alive, he was asking her to marry him.

Clambering to his feet, Mikey ran toward the Hummer, even as Claire turned and shot another zomboid.

Then another impact, this on his side.

And another.

And another.

Overwhelming agony, worse than anything Butch had inflicted on him in an entire childhood of bullying torture, wracked Mikey's body as the zomboids literally ripped him apart.

His last thoughts were of Claire.

The last thing he heard was Kmart calling his name.

• • •

Kmart would have thought that after all the people she'd seen die, she'd get used to it.

As she watched the monster zombies tear Mikey—poor, sweet Mikey, who never hurt another human being in his entire life—to pieces, after having seen them do the same to Cliff, Pablo, and Morgan, she realized that she hadn't. And this less than a day after losing Otto, Betty, Dillon, and the others.

Kmart didn't think she could take any more heartbreak.

Whirling around, she stared into the milky-white eyes and open mouth of L.J.

L.J. had turned into a zombie-ass motherfucker.

Screaming, Kmart tried to bring around her shotgun—oh, God, how could she shoot L.J., *how?*—but it was too cramped. L.J. leaned in to bite her, and she scrambled back, forced to abandon the shotgun.

Then another pair of hands grabbed her from below.

At first, she thought it was another zomboid, but it was just Carlos, climbing up through the hole in the floor. He pushed Kmart out of the way—

—and then L.J. bit *him* in the shoulder.

Carlos screamed, and so did Kmart.

Raising his .45, Carlos shot L.J. in the face.

L.J.'s head snapped back, and he slumped in the front seat.

Kmart couldn't believe it. L.J. was the one who'd first *called* her Kmart. He'd been the one who always joked, always had a story for the kids, the one who kept them going. He couldn't be dead, he just *couldn't*.

She turned to look at Carlos, whom she had to admit to having a *huge* crush on, though that seemed immature and stupid right now. He had a big wound in his shoulder.

He was gonna die, too.

Bile rising in her throat, Kmart realized that they were all going to die here in this place that Alice said used to be a fun town.

Twenty-Six

Alice fought.

It had been a while since Detroit, which was the last time that the Umbrella Corporation had her under their control. It had been a while since she had to fight them.

Last time, she hadn't been able to do it until after they made her kill Angie Ashford.

This time, she fought harder.

Alice had already been a hard woman, forged by her years in Treasury and as head of security for the Hive, tempered by the years since the T-virus spread, both through the Earth and through her veins.

She would *not* let herself be subject to Isaacs's whims ever again.

For all the people who died in the Hive, from the five hundred employees to One and his commando team.

For Matt and Lisa, crusaders who wanted to bring Umbrella down.

For the entire population of Raccoon City, sacrificed on Umbrella's altar of superiority.

For the people of this convoy who'd given their lives in an attempt to survive.

And for Angie.

Her eyes still worked, and she watched as the monsters tore the news truck apart and then did the same to Mikey.

She watched as L.J. turned and Carlos shot him in the face.

She watched as four more of the undead headed toward the ambulance, Peter-Michael and Joel managing to kill all four with their pistols, but not before one of them literally tore Peter-Michael's head off.

She watched Dorian and Erica run toward the Eiffel Tower, hoping it would provide the same sanctuary that it had for Chase. One of the undead grabbed Erica's leg, sending her crashing to the ground, killing her instantly. Dorian, wisely, kept running.

Alice could do nothing.

So she fought.

Pinto frowned. "Sir?"

Isaacs had been discussing the latest version of the formula with Margolin when Pinto interrupted. "What is it?"

"She's fighting the conditioning."

Dammit! He had been afraid of this. "Boost the control signal." Her EEG was now flying about like mad.

Pinto nodded and typed more commands in.

Then the image on the plasma-screen jumped and faded away, replaced with the words SATELLITE OFF-LINE. The other monitors went to static.

"What is it?" Isaacs asked angrily.

Shaking her head, Pinto entered some commands, then pounded the keyboard in frustration. She shifted her chair over to another control station. "It's the satellite—some kind of malfunction." Turning around, she said, "It's not like we've been able to do maintenance on the things."

"Can you move another satellite into place?"

Nodding, Pinto said, "Already on it. Satellite 5 will be in place in six minutes."

Tensely, Isaacs watched the technician work. The seconds ticked by agonizingly. Luckily, he'd already gotten "authorization" from Wesker for this operation, so Pinto's commands would be automatically authorized without the need for oversight. Moving a satellite would have taken far longer otherwise.

After Isaacs was certain six minutes had passed, he testily asked, "How long?"

"New feed coming online in fifteen seconds."

Perhaps it was only five minutes and forty-five seconds. Isaacs sighed. He didn't mind waiting, but he hated not *knowing* . . .

Alice felt control come back to her limbs. She'd done it. It had taken all her focus, but she'd concentrated on the

Umbrella satellite that was monitoring them and managed to burn out just one microchip. Such a small chip, yet destroying it had such catastrophic consequences.

At least, they were catastrophic if your name was Sam Isaacs. For Alice, it was liberation. She raised her Kukris and looked at the undead that remained.

She smiled. "I think you boys are looking for me."

If you had told Chase MacAvoy ten years ago that he'd be hanging off the Eiffel Tower in Vegas shooting at horror-movie rejects that had murdered several of his closest friends, he'd have sent you to the rubber room.

Or at least put you under arrest. He'd been able to do that during his all-too-brief tenure as a county sheriff in Texas.

That reign had been brief, ended by a scandal that had been caused by an error in judgment on Chase's part. That error was in thinking that the quarterback on the high school football team wasn't above the law. The state religion in Texas was football, and nobody messed with that. If the quarterback raped and killed one of the cheerleaders, well, that was a tragedy, true, but the state championships were coming up. Chase hadn't seen it that way, and he'd put the quarterback under arrest.

Suddenly, there were pictures. They'd been Photoshopped, but try explaining that to an angry populace who wanted their star quarterback on the field, and besides, that little slut was asking for it, wearing that short skirt and tight sweater . . .

After the special election kicked him out of office,

Chase got in his truck and drove north. When he crossed the border into Oklahoma, he swore he'd never set foot in the great state of Texas again.

Thus far, he'd kept that vow. Though at this point, he had a certain interest in heading back there to see if any of his fellow townsfolk were still alive.

Chase hoped they weren't, and he hoped they died in considerable pain.

But he could be a vindictive sumbitch when he put his mind to it.

Now, though, Texas and quarterbacks and sheriff's duties were the last thing on his mind. Dorian and Erica had been chased all over the Strip. They caught Erica, but Dorian was now climbing up the tower. Seven of the big, scary monsters were climbing up after her, and Chase could *not* get a good shot. He winged the tower a bunch of times, hit shoulders and chests, but couldn't get himself a head shot. And nothing short of a head shot'd kill these bastards.

That Alice dame came outta nowhere, then, and threw something at four of the monsters, hitting them right in the back. Whatever they were, they worked, as the four of them fell to the ground. Alice then leapt way faster and farther than people were supposed to and landed on the tower. She started to climb.

Just as Dorian was getting near Chase, one of the monsters grabbed her ankle. Bending over as far as he could without losing his grip on the metal rod, Chase inserted the muzzle of his gun into the monster's mouth and pulled the trigger.

"Climb!" he said before the gun's blast finished echoing.

Nodding, Dorian climbed past him.

Chase tried to shoot the other two, but they moved too damn fast. He wasn't used to that—the monsters were supposed to be *slow!*

One of them grabbed his leg and pulled, yanking Chase hard enough for him to lose his grip.

As he fell toward the ground, he decided that this was a shitty way to die.

Alice watched as Chase fell past her, then climbed faster. The final two undead were almost on top of Dorian, and Alice was determined to save *somebody*'s life today. She did a flying leap across the beams, slicing through one of the undead as she landed. The other one was grabbing a screaming Dorian, and Alice took care of him, too.

The four pieces of what was once two undead fell to the ground, landing right next to the three undead who were feasting on Chase's corpse.

From her vantage point, Alice realized that these were the only three left.

Carlos and Claire ran out of their respective vehicles and took on those last three, blowing their heads off.

Too late, sadly, for Chase.

She looked around and saw thirty-five undead bodies around the Strip. There had been thirty-six, but she didn't see any sign of the last one. Her view wasn't complete—perhaps it was under a truck or a sand dune.

At least, she hoped so.

Turning to Dorian, Alice asked, "You okay?"

Dorian stared at her. "You're fucking kidding me, right?" She shook her head. "Shit, I'm alive. That's as okay as I'm likely to fucking get. Jesus."

"Come on, let's get down."

Slowly but surely—Alice could have gone faster, but she went at Dorian's pace—they climbed down the Eiffel Tower.

Before she and Dorian even landed, Claire asked, "What the *fuck* were those?"

"There's only one company depraved enough to experiment on the undead," Alice said. "And they're also the only company that can control me, even for a minute."

"Control you?" Claire asked.

"Remember when I said they did something to me?" Alice asked, which got her a nod from Claire. "They can control my mind sometimes. They did it for a few minutes during the fight, but I managed to break it." She looked around. "I might have been able to save Chase, Erica, and Peter-Michael if—"

Carlos held up his hand. "No. We're not responsible. They are." He shook his head. "Umbrella. The world's gone to hell, and they find a way to make it worse."

Alice tried to smile but couldn't. "Should be the company slogan."

"So now what?" Claire asked. She looked around. The ambulance's engine had been smashed by the creatures, the news truck was a complete wreck, and the

Hummer and 8x8 were in pretty bad shape. Even if there was gas in the Venetian Hotel, there wasn't much left to put it in. The Enco tanker was the only vehicle that was still more or less intact.

Now Alice could smile, but it was a nasty one. "Oh, I have some thoughts in that regard. Give me a second."

She concentrated, sending her mind outward. It wasn't something she'd done very often, but luckily she knew what she was looking for, and there weren't very many active minds in the area.

Then she found it. "Bingo."

Running toward the Venetian's parking garage, she said, "Follow me!"

Behind her, she heard Claire tell Dorian to go to the ambulance and help Joel watch the kids. Carlos, Claire, and Kmart followed her, though Alice put considerable distance between herself and them in short order. Eventually, she slowed down enough so that she stayed in eyesight of the other three.

She ran up the parking garage's stairs on the far end, reached the roof, and ran across.

There it was.

An Umbrella tent and an Umbrella helicopter.

Just as she was about to jump down to the ground, she felt it.

They were trying to regain control.

Fuck that.

She gripped the Kukris by the blade, the edges slicing into her skin, the pain giving her more focus. There wouldn't be another life she couldn't save because

Isaacs was fucking with her mind. There wouldn't be another Erica, another Chase, another Peter-Michael.

There wouldn't be another Angie.

Jumping down from the parking garage, she landed on the ground, bending her knees with the impact. She could feel them trying to take control, but she would not let them.

As she ran toward the tent, she could hear voices.

"She's still coming!"

"Shut her down, dammit!"

"I'm trying, but there's interference!"

"Boost the control signal!"

"It's already at max! She's resisting command protocols."

None of the voices belonged to Isaacs.

Ripping open the tent, she saw four people. She recognized one of the security guards, Paul DiGennaro—he'd been the one shouting to shut her down—but she didn't know the other security guard, the man in the lab coat, or the woman at the computer station.

The security guard she didn't know raised a machine gun. Alice threw a Kukri right at his chest.

As he died, impaled on the support pole behind him, his finger spasmed on his weapon's trigger, which was apparently set to automatic, and bullets sprayed all across the tent, taking out computers and screens and killing the technician and DiGennaro instantly.

The man in the lab coat was also shot but not dead yet. Alice grabbed him by the throat.

"Where is he?"

Then she heard the whirl of helicopter blades.

"Fuck." She dropped the dying doctor to the floor and ran out.

Twelve seconds after she said she'd have the satellite online in fifteen seconds, Pinto said, "Online in three—two—one."

One of the plasma-screens flickered to life. Isaacs, pleased with his foresight in bringing Pinto along, immediately scanned the screen for signs of Alice. Or anyone.

All he saw were unmoving bodies, including what appeared to be almost all, if not all, of the Super Undead. Plenty of human corpses as well, but none was Project Alice.

"Dammit, where is she?"

Pinto said, "Live feed from Project Alice coming online now."

Isaacs nodded in satisfaction. The so-called Alicecam would do the trick.

The other plasma screen lit up to show the interior of a parking garage. Tarnished signs that had worn into illegibility were visible on the walls. "Where the hell is she going?" Isaacs asked.

She turned and ran up a flight of stairs, putting her on the roof of the garage.

Then she looked out and down at this very tent.

"Oh, shit!" Pinto said, a sentiment Isaacs could get behind.

"Shut her down—*now!*" Isaacs said.

But even as Pinto entered commands, Isaacs knew

that it was over. Alice had already broken the programming several times, and he simply could not trust that she wouldn't do it this time.

Turning to DiGennaro, he said, "Stop her," and left the tent before he could say anything.

He ran straight for the helicopter. As he climbed aboard, he said to Kistler, "Back to the base, *now!*"

"But what about—" Kistler started, but Isaacs ignored him and turned to close the door behind him.

As he did so, a meaty hand grabbed his arm. Looking up, he saw Gretzky.

This was a complication Isaacs did *not* need.

Before Isaacs could do or say anything, Gretzky leaned in and bit into Isaacs's shoulder.

Sam Isaacs had lived the sedentary life of a scientist. Oh, he'd felt pain before, of course, most notably when Project Alice had broken his arm and thrown him into a tank. That arm still throbbed occasionally, particularly when the air conditioning in the facility malfunctioned or when it rained.

This pain was several orders of magnitude worse than anything he'd ever felt before.

A defeaning report from a machine gun cut through the pain, and Gretzky's head exploded a second later. Perroneau had shot the Super Undead.

Isaacs could feel his grip on consciousness eluding him, and he gritted his teeth, trying to force himself awake. He let Perroneau guide him inside the helicopter, and then, after closing the door, the security guard applied a pressure bandage to his wound.

Somehow, Isaacs made his lips move. "The anti-virus! Get me the anti-virus!" He couldn't tell if the words he spoke were comprehensible or not.

Apparently, they were. Perroneau moved Isaacs's own hand to the pressure bandage. Then she reached down under one of the seats to pull out an emergency first-aid kit. She pulled a hypo filled with the beautiful green of the anti-virus and injected Isaacs with it.

As Kistler took off, Perroneau moved to the front of the helicopter.

Once she was out of sight, Isaacs lifted the pressure bandage.

The bleeding had stopped—far sooner than it should have, given the severity of the injury—and the wound was already starting to itch, indicating the healing process.

Isaacs smiled.

Twenty-Seven

Alice watched as the helicopter took off. She jumped up in the hopes of nabbing the landing struts, but it was too far in the air for even her to reach, and she came crashing to the ground, rolling with the impact.

Dusting herself off and cursing not so silently, she ran back into the tent.

Kmart, Carlos, and Claire had caught up and were entering the tent just as Alice got back. To Kmart, Alice said, "See if any of these computers still work. I want to know where that chopper's headed."

Nodding, Kmart ran over to the computer.

Claire looked around at the four corpses that littered the tent. Then she looked up at Alice. "You weren't kidding."

"About what?" Alice asked.

"That death follows you around like a lost puppy."

"Claire," Carlos said in a stern tone.

Alice, however, waved Carlos off. "No, she's right." Alice shook her head. "I never should have come to you."

"Damn right, you shouldn't have. If you hadn't shown up with your fucking journal and your fucking Alaska pipe dreams, we wouldn't have come to Vegas. These assholes set this ambush up for *you*, didn't they?"

Alice said nothing.

"Didn't they?"

Finally, Alice nodded. Claire was absolutely right.

Carlos, gripping his wounded shoulder tightly, said, "And if she hadn't shown up, *we'd all be dead.*"

Angrily, Claire whirled on Carlos. "On what planet? She—"

"She didn't send those crows."

That brought Claire up short. Alice, too, as she'd temporarily forgotten about the mutated birds.

"They were literally eating us alive. If Alice hadn't shown up when she did, everyone—not just the ones who died today but *everyone*—would've been killed by those things!"

The tent got quiet after that. Claire was fuming, and Alice couldn't blame her. She was lashing out at Alice because the vast majority of the convoy for which she had taken on responsibility was dead, and Alice was a convenient target—and not an entirely illegitimate one, Carlos's protestations notwithstanding. Carlos just stared at Claire, blood dripping down his arm from where he'd been injured.

In a small voice, Kmart said, "Uh, excuse me?"

Alice looked over at the teenager. The monitor in front of her was active.

"Sorry to interrupt your bickering, but that chopper's headed for a weather station in the salt flats. I can print out the map."

"Good," Alice said. "That's where I'm heading."

"That's where *we're* heading," Claire said.

"Claire, no," Alice said. "Carlos was right, but so were you. I can't ask you to follow me."

"It's not your choice." She held up her hands, indicating the tent. "If this is just what they have for a little outdoor excursion, that base probably has equipment up the wazoo. This is the best resupply possibility we've found. Shit, they've got a *helicopter*. Maybe more than one." She smirked in a frightening impersonation of Alice's own facial expression. "That'd get us to Alaska in a heartbeat."

"It's Umbrella," Carlos said. "They'll have security."

"I can take care of their security," Alice said.

"Not by yourself," Carlos said.

Before Alice could respond, Claire said, "She won't be by herself." Then she turned to Kmart. "Salvage anything from here that we can use, and print out the schematics of that Umbrella base. We're heading back to the convoy. We're gonna bury our dead, salvage what we can from here, and then we're going Umbrella hunting."

Hours later, after they'd picked the tent apart and gathered fuel from as many valet parking garages in Vegas that they could find, Alice stood next to Carlos, blood still dripping down his hand from the wound inflicted on him by L.J. More graves had been dug, names scrawled on the makeshift crosses: MICHAEL FAERBER, CLIFF NADANER, PABLO VILLANUEVA, MORGAN HERTWECK, CHASE MACAVOY, PETER-MICHAEL SULLIVAN, ERICA SIMONE, and LLOYD JEFFERSON WAYNE.

Alice took Carlos's bloody hand in hers. "I can't believe L.J. didn't make it."

"Yeah." Carlos shook his head. "God, when I think of everything the two of us went through, all the people who died all around us, and he was still right there with that goofy smile and talking about busting a cap in the zombie-ass motherfuckers' asses . . ."

Unable to help it, Alice chuckled. She almost felt guilty about it but then decided that it was the best way to remember L.J. From what Carlos had told her, he had taken on the role of morale officer in their convoy, always making sure everyone was distracted from the nightmare they'd come to live in. Perhaps because L.J. had seen the worst of it back in Raccoon City and was one of the few to make it out alive, it gave him a perspective the others needed.

Or maybe he was just the kind of asshole who thrived in lousy conditions.

At least for a while.

Alexander Slater had just about hit the end of his rope.

It had been bad enough being assigned to work with Sam Isaacs. Slater had never been overly impressed with the doctor's work, thinking him to be a hack with delusions of grandeur, but that didn't prepare him for the megalomania.

Now, though, he'd finally taken that step over the line that Slater knew had just been a matter of time. Isaacs had thought himself so clever, smuggling a digital recorder into the meetings with Wesker, but Slater knew he'd been doing it. He could have reported it. In fact, according to regulations, he should have reported it. But regulations were guidelines more than anything, and especially now, Slater felt a more Darwinian approach was called for. Let Isaacs dig his own grave.

Sure enough, he'd done it. Using the recordings he'd made, he put together "orders" to allow him to leave the facility and pursue Project Alice—this after Wesker expressly forbade him to do so.

Naturally, Slater wasn't going to let that stand. He let Isaacs do what he wished on the surface; leaving aside any other considerations, he might come back with Project Alice, which would change things. However, he returned empty-handed—and without four of the people he'd taken with him. Slater assumed that Margolin, Pinto, DiGennaro, and Lobachevski were as dead as Timson and Moody. The security guards were less of a concern, but Margolin, Pinto, Timson, and Moody were people they could ill afford to lose. Indeed, they couldn't afford to lose *anybody* right now, and Isaacs's callous disregard for Umbrella's needs—not to mention for human life— was something that could no longer be tolerated.

Upon his return, Slater ordered Perroneau to confine Isaacs to his lab and showed him the written orders from Chairman Wesker that ceded authority over this facility to him and removed Isaacs from his position as head of Umbrella's Science Division.

After spending some time with Rosenbaum in the IT Department to make sure that all the computer protocols had been changed so that Isaacs no longer had access, Slater went to Isaacs's lab, where Humberg was waiting for him.

"How is he?" Slater asked the guard.

Shrugging, Humberg said, "Under house arrest, as you instructed. He's been quiet. He was infected by one of those enhanced biohazards, though, so he's had to have the anti-virus."

"I thought he got a shot in the plane."

Humberg hesitated. "He's had several shots, sir. I thought you knew."

Sighing, Slater entered the lab. Perroneau and Finnerty were standing guard over Isaacs, who sat at his desk, injecting himself with the anti-virus. Several empty vials lay on the table next to him. He looked pale and un-well. A bloody bandage was on his shoulder where one of the enhanced biohazards had attacked him.

His eyes widening, Slater asked, "How much of this have you used?"

In a maddeningly calm voice, Isaacs said, "Her blood increased the creatures' powers. But it also in-creased the strength of the infection. I needed it."

"You have no idea what this will do to you."

Isaacs smiled, though on his pale, sweaty face, it was like a rictus. "Oh, I have an idea."

Shaking his head, Slater turned away from Isaacs's ghoulish countenance. "You're out of control. Well, this ends here." Taking out his Glock, Slater pointed it right at Isaacs's chest. "Under Executive Order 1345, issued by Chairman Wesker at 5:29 P.M. Pacific Standard Time on this date, for insubordination and gross misconduct in the field, I sentence you to summary liquidation."

Isaacs raised an eyebrow. "Liquidation?"

Slater had to admit that the euphemism was silly. So he tilted his head, aimed the pistol, said, "Just die," and squeezed the trigger.

Looking down at the wound, Isaacs seemed surprised. "But—"

"You always were an arrogant sonofabitch."

To be sure, Slater shot him twice more.

For a moment, Isaacs convulsed with the impacts, then he slumped forward, eyes closed.

It was the most beautiful sight Slater had ever seen.

The world was in danger of total collapse, and that required leadership, not fostering personal agendas. Umbrella was going to lead the world out of the darkness, Slater was sure of it. But that would never happen as long as Isaacs was alive.

With him gone, things were, he was sure, going to run a lot more smoothly.

He turned to leave the lab. "Take the body to the surface," he said to Humberg, "and dispose of it. Then bring up all the stats of Project Alice. I want to see what harm he's done."

Humberg said nothing. Instead, he was staring ahead, his mouth hanging open.

Confused, Slater turned around.

Sam Isaacs was standing upright, smiling that awful smile, three big bloody holes in his chest.

"Don't look so shocked." Isaacs's voice sounded different—deeper.

That wasn't the only thing different. Slater could see something slithering in his chest wound.

Isaacs raised his right arm, and then it split open. Slater felt the mustard on the sandwich he'd had for lunch rise into the back of his throat as the flesh of Isaacs's arm peeled back to reveal several green tentacles.

The tentacles lashed out in all directions, piercing through flesh and body armor and equipment.

Two went straight for Slater's eyes.

He didn't have time to scream.

The corpses of four men lay at Sam Isaacs's feet.

No, not Sam Isaacs. That was the name of a human. He was more than that now.

He was Tyrant.

That had been the name of the project that had been aborted in favor of Nemesis when Cain had brought in Alice Abernathy and Matt Addison. But Isaacs had never abandoned Tyrant, because the T-virus had, he was sure, been the key to it.

The so-called Super Undead had been the first step.

The anti-virus was the next, mixed with the formula he'd developed with the late Dr. Margolin. It had done its work, changing Isaacs as the T-virus had changed Alice Abernathy.

He looked down at Alexander Slater's corpse. It was the most beautiful sight Isaacs had ever seen.

No, not Isaacs.

Tyrant.

Twenty-Eight

Peanut couldn't believe what he was seeing.

He'd pulled sentry duty today, which already pissed him off. He hated standin' around with his MAC-10 lookin' like a fool. But after that crazy bitch in the Prius killed Motown and Cowboy, Peanut couldn't really do his usual routine about how the sentry shit was stupid.

Next to him, Bee was pickin' at his fingernail. "Yo, Bee, you see what I'm seein'?"

Bee looked up. "Looks like one'a them junkies."

"Maybe he a zee."

The junkie was shufflin' toward them like he *was* some kinda zee, and Peanut figured his day was lookin' up if he got to do a zee.

But then the junkie held his hands up. He had a can in one'a them. "I ain't lookin' for no trouble, yo! Jus' lookin' t'talk, a'ight?"

Aiming his Glock at the junkie's head, Bee said, "You ain't welcome here, motherfucker!"

But Peanut was lookin' at the thing in the junkie's hand. "What's that?"

"What's what?"

"In y'*hand,* nigger, what *is* that?"

The junkie looked up at his hand. "It's a food can. Take a look." He bent over and rolled it down the cracked pavement toward Peanut.

It hit a pothole and stopped. "Cover me, yo," Peanut said to Bee, and he ran forward to grab it.

The can was pristine. The label wasn't faded or ripped or nothing.

"The fuck you find this?"

"There's a whole store full of 'em, yo, I ain't playin' you."

Peanut raised his MAC-10. "Where?"

"Look, I'll tell you, I promise, I ain't playin' you, but you gots to be givin' me somethin', a'ight?"

"Only thing I'm givin' yo' ass is a bullet in the brain, you feel me? Now, tell me *where,* motherfucker!"

"I'll tell you," the junkie said, "but you gots to be lettin' me in."

"No fuckin' chance."

"Then shoot me, 'cause I ain't telling you fuck-all 'til you get me inside. I can't be livin' out here no more. Ain't nowhere safe from them zees."

Bee cocked his Glock. "Nigger, *shoot* his ass."

Peanut turned around. "This a *fresh* can, yo!"

"So?"

"So it means this nigger found himself a mother-lode!" They had plenty of water and guns and ammo, but the food was starting to get light. Fewer pigeons came by lately—in fact, the only one they'd had in a month turned out to be that crazy bitch with the Prius. Only thing she did to help was give 'em two less mouths to feed. Last ones to come by were those people in that minivan. Lotsa food, no guns. Peanut shot their leader in the back of the neck his own self.

But they needed more food.

This needed to go to the Council. "Keep y'hands in the air, and move yo' ass inside."

The Council consisted of the five people who'd been with the group longest. With Motown dead (Cowboy wasn't on the Council), that meant Peanut, Snoopy, Riot, String, and Dog Meat. The chairmanship rotated, and right now it was Dog Meat. LaWanda had gone out to join Bee on sentry duty, which meant that Bee'd spend the whole time staring at LaWanda's ass, but that was LaWanda's problem.

With Motown, Cowboy, and Yolanda dead—Yolanda got bit by a zee that broke through the perimeter—they was only twelve now. Pretty soon there'd be more Council than no Council.

The junkie, whose name was Andre, was in the meeting, too, telling everybody about a deli that they couldn't get into for the longest time, but he'd found a way in. "Don't nobody know about it 'cept for me, and it'll stay that way. You got my word."

"Yeah," Riot said, " 'cause your word means so much *shit,* don't it?"

String said, "Look, we need *food*. We can't be hopin' more pigeons'll show up, that's a forlorn fuckin' hope. Ain't nobody left."

"We *ain't* the only ones left," Snoopy said with his annoying lisp.

"Maybe not," String said, "but by now? Only folks that ain't zees are gonna be like that bitch the other day—hard. Only ones left'll be *survivors,* and—"

"And if they come by," Riot said, "we'll shoot they asses. Fuck this shit, let's just get the food and go."

Peanut asked, "What about *this* motherfucker?"

"I'll take you there," Andre said.

"You can't tell us where it is?" Snoopy asked.

"I could. But I ain't gonna. 'Sides, you ain't gonna know the way in 'less I tell you."

Dog Meat finally spoke. "We vote. The motion is to let this junkie motherfucker into the group if he shows us where to find this food. All in favor?"

Riot kept his hand down, but everyone else raised theirs.

"A'ight." Dog Meat looked around. "We send six. One to keep an eye on *this* motherfucker." He pointed at Andre. "Three to gather the food. Two to keep an eye out for zees."

"No," String said. "Nigger, that's almost half'a what we got left."

Andre said, "You gonna need at least that many to carry the shit."

"Safety in numbers," Dog Meat said. "Anybody else disagree?" He looked around at the Council.

Peanut actually thought they should take more, but he wasn't about to say nothin' to piss off String. If he did, Peanut'd be sleepin' alone tonight, and he didn't want that. String was the only one who could suck him off right.

Nobody else disagreed with Dog Meat. String sighed. "Fine, what-the-fuck-ever, but I ain't goin'."

"I'll go," Riot said. "I'll be the nigger keepin' an eye on *this* asshole." He grabbed Andre by the front of his battered coat.

"It'll be me," Dog Meat said, "Riot, Peanut, Robbie, Tish, and Omar."

Peanut had been hoping he wouldn't be picked, but he was the one who used that workout equipment they'd taken from one of the hotels the most, so Dog Meat'd probably have him carrying the food back. That was cool. Long as they didn't find more zees.

"One thing, motherfucker," Dog Meat said to Andre.

"What?" Andre asked, sounding scared.

"You join up, you be takin' a shower, you feel me? Don't want no stink in our house."

Andre grinned. "Shit, I don't even 'member what that *feels* like, but I bet it'll be *fine*."

"Let's go."

Peanut was throwing cans into garbage bags when he heard the voice say, "Drop it, asshole."

Andre had been on the up-and-up. The deli was way the fuck over in West Baltimore, but it really was the fucking motherlode. Riot was bitching that it smelled like pussy, but nobody else gave a shit. There was enough food in here to last 'em at least another six months, especially what was in the basement.

But then he heard that voice.

Omar and Tish were outside, keepin' an eye out for zees and stray junkies, but that voice didn't belong to neither one'a them.

"Fuck you, bitch!" That was Omar.

A whole mess'a gunshots came after that. Peanut dropped his garbage bag, which made a lotta noise when it hit the floor, and took out his MAC-10. Everyone else took out their pieces, too, aimin' 'em at the door—except for Riot, who put his Beretta at Andre's temple.

"The fuck?" Dog Meat asked.

"Uh, Dog Meat?" Riot sounded all funky when he said that.

Peanut turned around to see that somebody had a gun at the back of Riot's neck. After a second, he recognized the motherfucker.

Dog Meat said, "Jasper, what the *fuck?* Thought we was—"

"We ain't *shit,* asshole," Jasper said with a big-ass grin on his face. "Drop your fuckin' weapons."

"I'd do it," said another voice. Peanut turned back to see that it was some white bitch. She had two guns out. "Those two fuckers out front didn't, and they're just as dead as the *other* two fuckers I shot the other day."

Dog Meat said, "You're the bitch in the Prius?"

She smiled. "The very bitch. You guys are fucking idiots—and also the luckiest assholes on the face of the planet. But your luck just ran out."

Riot tried to raise his Beretta. "Fuck yo—"

Jasper splattered Riot's brains all over the refrigerator door and Andre. Andre didn't move.

Peanut dropped his MAC-10 on the floor.

Nobody else was that smart.

Bullets flew all over. It was the loudest fucking thing Peanut had ever heard. He closed his eyes and covered his ears.

After a few seconds, it was over. Peanut had been shot a few times, back in the day, and he remembered what it felt like, so he knew he ain't been shot this time.

He decided to open his eyes.

Jasper and the white bitch were standing there, their gun muzzles all smoking. Andre was, too, but he didn't have no gun. Riot, Dog Meat, and Robbie was dead on the floor.

The white bitch repeated herself. "You guys are fucking idiots."

"Shit," Peanut said. "What just happened?"

"You lost, Peanut," Jasper said.

"How many are left?" the white bitch asked.

"What?" Peanut was still kinda dazed.

"Don't make me ask twice, asswipe, how many of you are left?"

"They—they was fifteen. You killed Motown and Cowboy, and Yolanda got bit by a zee, and now these five, so—"

"Seven." The white bitch lowered her guns. "Son of a holy bitch, there were only *fifteen* of you? Over a hundred people out here, and you couldn't summon the will to share what you have. Jasper tells me you have food, medical supplies—"

Peanut couldn't believe that *that* was what this was about. "That shit's *ours,* bitch! The fuck we got to be sharin' it for?"

"Because there aren't that many people left. The zees are taking over, and the only way the human race is gonna survive is if they work *together*. A friend of mine is part of a big convoy—got like thirty, forty people. They're traveling, staying alive, staying ahead of the zees. You guys have a lot more than they do, and—"

Jasper interrupted. "Valentine, shut the fuck up and shoot this asshole, will you?"

"No."

Peanut had no idea where this bitch suddenly got a conscience, but he'd take it.

"Whaddaya mean, no?"

"I mean, he dropped his gun when we told him to. I don't kill people unless they threaten me. This asshole hasn't threatened me." Then she looked at him and smiled, as if Peanut was a meal she was about to chow down on. "Yet."

"I ain't threatenin' shit, lady."

"Peanut's cool," Andre said. "He the one that told the Council t'listen t'me, an' shit."

"Good for him," Valentine said. "Let's see if he can keep his cool factor high. Besides the two on the road, where are your other sentries?"

Peanut frowned. "Whatchoo talkin' 'bout, bitch?"

"Other sentries. Where are they?"

This bitch was crazy. "We don't got no 'other' sentries. Shit, what the fuck for? We blocked off all the other roads. Don't nobody come 'cept that way. Then we step to."

"And if someone, say, walked up from the Inner Harbor?"

"Don't nobody do that." Was this bitch mental or some shit? "How the fuck they get there? Ain't nobody but zees and junkies in this town left. Everybody else, they take the road."

Valentine looked at Jasper. "You *dealt* with these guys?"

Jasper shrugged. "Only game in town."

"No, *you* were the only game in town. They were just playacting, and everyone bought it. Jesus, fifteen people? You could've taken them down in a heartbeat instead of doing your hermit act."

Again, Jasper shrugged. "I thought there were more."

Peanut didn't say nothing. They always tried to make it seem as if there were about fifty of them whenever Jasper was around. String always put that shit together.

"Well, your reign of terror is over. Officer Jill Valentine has come to town."

Now it all made sense. "Shit, another cop? Damn."

"Not just a cop," Jasper said. "S.T.A.R.S. You don't fuck with them."

Valentine grinned.

Jill was amazed at how easy it was.

She and Jasper moved around to the Inner Harbor—having to shoot their way through a few "zees" on the way—and approached the convention center from the rear entrance. It took them five minutes of walking up stairs and through corridors and down escalators before they finally found a supply room—unguarded, amazingly—and then another minute before they saw a person, who surrendered right away.

Only one person resisted, and Jill shot her between the eyes. That left six. One guy, who called himself String and who Peanut had said would likely be the leader of the ones left, agreed to Jill and Jasper's terms: Open up the convention center to everyone, or get shot.

Andre led the rest of the survivors from the row house on Fayette to the convention center. The stronger ones (which weren't very many) carried the food from the deli. A few wouldn't come past a certain point until they saw that nobody would shoot them.

That night, Jill organized a huge feast. It was all canned food and water from the convention center's supply.

Jasper walked over to her during the feast. "Nice job."

"Thanks."

"No, thank you. It was easier to stay put in the ARM building, do my business, and forget the rest of the world. But this—" He shook his head. "Shit, this is why I *became* a cop."

Jill grinned. "Not just so you could carry a gun?"

"Nah, I hate guns."

"Really?" Jill's eyes widened in surprise.

"Yeah. Was always a good shot, but I hate the fucking things. I'd rather talk. But the real world's the real world, so fuck it, I use my guns. But, nah, I became a cop 'cause I wanted to help people." He shook his head. "That's some sappy shit, ain't it?"

Jill shrugged. "But it works. This"—she indicated the large convention center floor where they were holding the feast for more than a hundred of the remaining living Baltimoreans—"is better than what there was before. Everyone together instead of in three different factions. And maybe someday someone'll come up with a cure."

Jasper snorted. "You believe that?"

"I have to." Jill looked away. "The alternative's too shitty to think about." She looked back at Jasper. "You take care of these people, okay?"

"Excuse me?"

"I'm heading out. The—"

"Fuck that, bitch!" Jasper said it loudly enough so that several people, including Andre, heard him and looked up in shock.

"It's okay," Jill said, holding up her hands. "We're

good. Keep eating." She turned back to Jasper. "I can't stay. I did the thing where I followed, and—"

"Who said shit about following? Bitch, you started this, you for goddamn sure finishing it. These people need a leader—not that Council bullshit and not some asshole who's been living in a building by himself. They need someone who's been in the world, someone who can show them how to survive. And if some asshole does have a cure, someone's gotta get it to them. That's *you*, Officer Valentine."

Jill opened her mouth, then closed it. She'd just assumed that Jasper would take over. He was a cop. He was suited to it.

But he was right. He'd been holed up alone for years. He wouldn't know what to do.

Would she?

She thought about the last words she said to Carlos in the It'll Do Motel in Idaho several billion years ago: "Besides, this *needs* to be done, and I'm the best person to do it."

It was true then, and it was true now.

"All right," she said. "I'll stay."

Twenty-Nine

Carlos looked down at the thousands of undead, all clambering toward the fence that surrounded the old weather station. Also inside the fence's perimeter were a ditch, a watchtower, and a helicopter pad, complete with the same helicopter that had taken Sam Isaacs away.

Isaacs had never really reached Carlos's radar during his time at Umbrella. He'd come across the scientist a few times, and he'd always struck Carlos as a cold fish on those rare occasions when Carlos had given him any thought.

Now, as he lay on a ridge overlooking Isaacs's haven, Carlos found himself wishing he'd spent more energy hating the man. Especially given that he was the one who'd turned Alice into something that caused her to stay away from him for so long.

He looked over at Alice, who was watching through a

pair of binoculars. Carlos wasn't sure what he was feeling for her—he'd never understood love back when there was a world, and nowadays, there just wasn't any kind of time for it—but he knew that Alice had been important to him from the moment they'd met in the basement of Angie's school. That was why he'd burned out of West Lafayette like a bat out of hell and chased her all the way to Detroit.

And now they'd finally been reunited—just in time for him to die.

"Definitely the worst vacation ever," he muttered.

Alice put her binoculars down. "What?"

"Nothing."

Behind them, Kmart pointed at the helicopter and asked Claire, "You can really fly one of those?"

Claire nodded. "I logged two hundred hours of flight time—"

"Wow."

"—on Flight School Pro," Claire added, sounding more sheepish.

Kmart stared at her.

Shrugging, Claire said, "PSP."

"Great."

"C'mon," Claire said, "how hard can it be?"

Carlos was about to comment that this wasn't the best time to be quoting Indiana Jones, when he was seized with another coughing fit. Putting the back of his hand in front of his mouth, he coughed hard enough to almost dislodge his rib cage for several seconds.

When he pulled his hand away, there was fresh blood on the back of his hand.

Alice was there, comforting him. "Hold on. They have the anti-virus down there."

Snorting, Carlos said, "Too late, and you know it. Infection's gone too far. And you need someone to get you in there." Then he smiled. "Besides, I have a plan."

"Well, that makes everything okay," Alice said wryly.

Claire asked, "Does this plan get us through the remake of *28 Days Later* down there?"

"If it goes right."

Kmart frowned. "If it doesn't?"

"If it doesn't," Carlos said, "I won't care all that much, 'cause I'll be dead either way."

"What do you mean, either way?" Kmart asked, her voice rising.

Carlos walked up to Kmart, putting his less bloody hand on her shoulder. She looked up at him with tears welling in her eyes. "I'm already dead, Dahlia. This way, at least, I get to accomplish something when I go."

"How—how'd you know my name?" Kmart asked with a sniff.

"Magic." Carlos smiled.

Claire sighed. "Let's go gather everyone up."

A few minutes later, Carlos faced the rest of the convoy—what was left of it. Besides the kids—and that they'd kept them alive was just about the only thing Carlos took pride in right now—the only survivors were Claire, Kmart, Joel, Dorian, Alice, and Carlos himself. Some of the kids were crying; hell, so were most of the adults.

He outlined his plan. "Once I set off the tanker,

there'll be a clear path to the weather station. When you get down there, you make for the helicopter. Alice is right—we can't be the only ones left." He thought about Jill, driving all across the country and dropping survivors with Carlos and Claire. He thought about the red journal. He thought about this fenced-in base, which couldn't have been the only haven from the zomboids. "There are others like us out there, somewhere. You make it to Alaska—to safety."

Without another word, Carlos turned and climbed into the tanker.

Alice intercepted him before he could shut the door. She took his hand and pressed something into it. Looking down, he saw it was a pack of American Spirit cigarettes.

"Found these," Alice said with a conspiratorial grin. "Don't tell Claire."

He handed them back. "Thanks, but they don't count."

Shrugging, Alice said, "Just as well—those things'll kill you."

It was a terrible joke, and Carlos laughed so hard he coughed again.

When the coughing fit ended, Alice was staring at him with those damnably amazing blue eyes of hers. "Carlos, I know we—"

Shaking his head, Carlos said, "Save it. Just promise me one thing. When you get in there . . ."

He trailed off, but he knew that she knew what he meant.

"Consider it done."

Nodding, he closed the door and started the tanker up. Looking down between the two front seats, he saw the fuse that led to the explosives they'd taken from the Umbrella tent. Combined with the gasoline they'd put in the tanker, it'd cause a nice big bang once Carlos lit it.

Glancing into the side-view as he drove ahead, he saw Alice saluting him as she climbed into the Hummer with Claire, Kmart, and the rest.

He returned the salute, then looked ahead.

No point in looking back anymore.

Cliché dictated that Carlos's life would flash before his eyes, but it didn't now. Not that there was much of a life. Childhood was constantly moving around Texas while *Papi* tried to find work. As soon as Carlos graduated from high school and could get as far away from *Papi*'s indolence and *Mami*'s misery, he enlisted in the Air Force. After serving his bit there, he joined Umbrella, rising quickly through the ranks of the Security Division.

Every attempt he'd made to have a proper childhood had been shitcanned by *Papi* moving them somewhere new, forcing him to make new friends. As an adult, service had been his life.

If it came to that, the same could be said for what happened after he quit Umbrella. He and L.J. and Jill and Angie and Alice, and later Molina and Jisun and King and Briscoe, and still later Claire and Chase and all the others—they'd fought to keep humanity alive in the face of the most overwhelming odds the species had ever faced.

Maybe it wasn't such a bad life after all.

He sighed. "Wish I had a smoke."

Now he could see the backs of the zomboids, all shoving forward toward the only sign of live flesh in the general area. Some of them turned around at the sound of the approaching vehicles. Checking the side-view, he saw the Hummer way behind him, far enough away that it wouldn't be hit by the explosion.

Carlos slammed his foot down on the accelerator, and the tanker rammed into the tide of zomboids.

It was easy going at first, but the density of animated corpses started to slow the tanker down, and Carlos found he had to fight for control of the wheel.

"Just a little bit more . . ."

Suddenly, the tanker jolted, sending Carlos flying upward, just as the tanker itself started to list to the right.

With a bone-jarring impact, Carlos went flying across the cab, his head striking against the passenger-side door. Belatedly, Carlos realized that fastening his seat belt might not have been a bad idea.

The tanker skidded on its side along the ground, finally coming to a halt. The zomboids swarmed all over the truck, making it impossible for Carlos to see how close he was to the fence.

He hoped it was close enough.

Something caught his eye on the passenger-side sun visor. Reaching up, he pulled it down to see a half-full pack of cigarettes, along with a purple cigarette lighter that was inscribed with the words BAD MOTHER-FUCKER.

Carlos couldn't help it. He laughed. "I'll be damned. L.J., you sneaky sonofabitch. Always had *something* going on the side . . ."

The zomboids started to claw their way into the cab. Carlos ignored them, instead lighting L.J.'s distinctive lighter.

First he lit the fuse.

Then he lit the cigarette.

Not a bad life, after all.

After he took a long, satisfying drag on the cigarette, the world exploded.

Alice braced herself in the passenger seat of the Hummer as it plowed forward into the burning ground left by the destroyed tanker. Luckily, this was the only surviving vehicle. The ambulance never would have made it through this, and with that big hole in its floor, neither would the 8x8.

Joel and Dorian kept the kids calm in the cramped confines of the back. Kmart was wedged in between Claire in the driver's seat and Alice.

As they drove their bumpy way through the inferno, Alice saw tears in Kmart's eyes. "Hold on!" she cried.

Kmart, though, turned her head as they went through. By the time the Hummer slammed through the perimeter fence, she was completely turned around.

Looking at Carlos.

The Hummer came to a halt at the helicopter. Claire and Kmart ran ahead to open it; Dorian went about halfway between the Hummer and the chopper; Joel stayed in the Hummer, and the three of them herded the kids in while Claire went to the controls.

For her part, Alice held her sawed-off in one hand and the red journal in the other, keeping an eye on the undead. They were starting to work their way through the tanker's fire, making a beeline for the new hole in the fence.

The rotors sprang to life. Alice heard Claire say, "That was the easy bit."

Once the kids were all on board, Dorian and Joel got in behind them. That left just Kmart and Alice outside. "C'mon," Kmart said.

Instead, Alice handed Kmart the journal. "Here."

Frowning, Kmart said, "You're not coming?"

She shook her head. For one thing, she'd made a silent promise to Carlos. For another, Claire had indeed been right. If she stuck around, more people would die. She was better off alone.

"Take care of the others," she said to the teenager who would need to assume the roles L.J. and Carlos had assumed in the convoy, helping Claire to keep it all together. "They need you."

With that, she turned and ran toward the weather station. The undead started pouring through the hole in the fence. Alice took out two of them.

Turning around, she saw the helicopter lift off, Claire's semi-steady hand at the controls. It wasn't a smooth takeoff, but it got the job done.

Alice wished them godspeed and luck. Without her around, they might just make it.

Then she turned and headed toward the weather station—when something caught her eye.

It was a big ditch, ringed with lime. In it were dozens of corpses.

Every one of them looked like her. In fact, they all seemed to be wearing the same red dress she wore when she'd been in the Hive with Spence, Matt, and One and his team.

What the *fuck?*

Alice had thought she couldn't possibly have been more angry at Dr. Sam Isaacs.

She was wrong.

Pulling out her Kukris, she headed into the weather station. Kmart had found the full schematics for this station, including how to operate the hydraulic elevator, so it was the work of only a moment for Alice to summon it and have it bring her down into Umbrella's complex.

She arrived to a darkened corridor, which split into two. The one on the left was smeared with blood. As she drew closer, she saw bloody handprints on the walls.

There was a fight here. A vicious one. Quite possibly some of the undead who'd been set loose on Vegas had gotten free and killed everyone. That was Alice's ideal scenario, and she found herself entertained by the notion of Isaacs being torn to tiny pieces by his own monsters. If anyone deserved the Frankenstein ending of being destroyed by his own creation, it was Sam Isaacs.

Following the bloody corridor, she found the door to a storage room opened. Peering inside, she saw that the light fixtures had been smashed, bullet holes riddled the walls, and blood was everywhere.

But no bodies.

She looked up and saw that a ventilation duct had been smashed open. There was blood all over the hole, and Alice wondered if bodies had been carried up there.

Out of the corner of her eye, she sensed movement, and she whirled around with her sawed-off and shot.

The shot went straight through the hologram of a little girl, one that looked eerily similar to Angela Ashford.

"I'm sorry, I didn't mean to startle you. I am the artificial intelligence which—"

"I know what you are," Alice said with disgust. She'd lived with the Red Queen every day of her life as head of security for the Hive and had been sentenced to death by that same computer. She'd had her fill of Umbrella's little-kid answer to Hal-2000. "I knew your sister. She was a homicidal bitch."

Using the same prissy tone that the Red Queen had used—but which Alice had never heard from Angie—the computer said, *"My sister computer was merely following the most logical path for the preservation of human life."*

"Kill a few, save a lot?"

"Put simply, that was her goal."

Unable to resist the shot, Alice said, "Didn't quite work out, did it?"

"We cannot control the vagaries of human behavior."

That was a particularly euphemistic way to refer to Timothy Cain's psychosis. Rather than get into a protracted discussion on the subject—which wasn't something Alice was all too eager to dwell on in any case—she went on a different tack. "What happened down here?"

"Dr. Isaacs returned in an infected state. He was bitten by a creature that had been treated with a newly developed serum—a serum derived from your blood. The resulting infection has caused massive mutation."

"My blood?" Suddenly, the ditch full of Alice clones made a sick sort of sense.

"Your blood has bonded with the T-virus. Dr. Isaacs correctly deduced that it could be used to reverse the process of infection. To cure or destroy the biohazard for good."

Alice blinked. "My blood is the cure for all this?"

"Correct."

Had this facility belonged to any other company, she would have asked why this cure hadn't been mass-distributed. But that wasn't Umbrella's style.

Remembering the devil's bargain she'd been forced to make with the Red Queen in the Hive, Alice asked, "And why are you helping me?"

"Like my sister, I was programmed to preserve human life. My satellites show that there are one million, seven hundred thirty-three thousand, five hundred forty-eight human survivors still alive on the surface of the Earth."

Alice found that that news made her almost giddy. She had honestly been convinced that there weren't even a thousand people still alive, much less a million. And it also gave her hope that Claire and her group would find fellow survivors in Arcadia.

The computer went on: *"Your blood is pure, and this facility contains all the laboratory equipment you will require to synthesize a cure."*

"This could all end?" Alice asked cautiously.

"Correct. There is, however, a small problem."

Now Alice smiled. "Let me guess—Isaacs?"

"Yes. Continue down this corridor, and take the emergency stairs to level seven. That is as far as my program is able to control."

Not liking the sound of that, Alice did as the AI instructed, eventually finding herself at a giant steel door labelled LEVEL 7. The AI's face appeared on a flatscreen near the door, which Alice found only marginally less annoying than the hologram.

"I have him contained on the lower levels, but this is where the laboratories are located. Once you cross the threshold, I cannot help you. He altered my protocols, locking me out from this level."

Now Alice understood. In order to synthesize the cure, Isaacs had to be taken care of, and the AI couldn't do that as long as he was down there. The best she could do was contain him, which was fine if that was the only goal.

But a cure was down there.

So Alice nodded to the AI, grabbed a flashlight from a nearby rack, and slid the door open with a metallic grinding.

Just before she stepped over the threshold, the AI said, *"Alice—good luck."*

Stepping in, she saw more smashed light fixtures,

with only Alice's own flashlight and dim blue emergency lights providing illumination. In the center of the space was a pile of human bodies. The pile was surprisingly neat. Most were wearing Umbrella security garb; some wore lab coats. If this was Isaacs, he seemed to have carved a swath through his own employees.

Well, as she herself knew quite well, employee loyalty wasn't high on Umbrella's list of important things to consider.

Muttering, "Someone's been busy," she moved on through the lab.

She kept getting a sense of movement in the room but nothing she could *see*. Either she was imagining things—unlikely—or there was something in here that was inhumanly fast—very likely.

Then she saw the tank.

Alice had woken up in one of Isaacs's labs in a tank just like that one in San Francisco.

And like that tank, this one had Alice in it.

Another clone.

Moving the flashlight to the left, she saw that there were more of them—dozens of Alice clones in tanks.

"Well—this is different."

Then the movement came closer.

Without warning, something struck Alice, knocking her to the floor and sending her flashlight flying.

In the remaining light, she could barely make out the form, but she caught a glimpse of a face.

For the most part, it looked like Isaacs. The blood staining his teeth was new, as was the maniacal gleam in his eyes. Not to mention the enhanced muscles in his torso and the arms that weren't so much arms as tentacles. *Dozens* of them.

He struck again, but this time Alice was ready. She ducked under the strike and elbowed his shoulder, dislocating it.

It didn't even slow Isaacs down. He grabbed her and—in a move quite similar to what she did to him back in San Francisco—threw her into one of the tanks.

Green fluid mixed with broken glass poured all over Alice, and she had to push the dead weight of her own cloned body off her. Managing to get to her knees, she reared back and threw one of her Kukris at Isaacs.

It sliced through Isaacs's shoulder, a blow that would have killed a human.

Next to her, the clone coughed and stammered and shivered, looking befuddled and frightened. Alice couldn't blame her.

Alice looked up, but Isaacs was gone. She'd only turned away for a second.

He was as fast as she. Faster, perhaps.

Her attention was grabbed again by the clone, who started to cough and convulse even harder, her blue eyes widening in obvious agony. Alice put her arms around her twin's shoulder and whispered, "It's okay. It's gonna be okay."

Then the clone put the lie to those words by dying in her arms.

Snarling with rage, Alice got up and ran out of the lab to the nearest corridor, the only way Isaacs could have gone. There was a door there, marked with the words TEST FACILITY. Throwing it open—

—Alice found her world turning upside down. She was back in the mansion.

Built by an eccentric old millionaire in the 1960s, the mansion had been taken over by Umbrella and used as the gateway to the Hive. Security Division always posted two people there, posing as a reclusive married couple, to serve as the gatekeepers.

The last two people to hold that position had been Spence Parks and Alice herself.

For reasons passing understanding, Isaacs had re-created at least the hallway here.

Walking over to the table, she saw the "wedding photo" of her and Spence.

Spence. The man who started all of this with his greed. If only he were alive, so Alice could kill him again.

The glass reflected the window behind her. In the real mansion, those windows had been shattered by the arrival of One and his team.

Now she saw movement reflected in it.

Diving out of the way, she just missed being punched by Isaacs. Instead, his blow destroyed the table on which the picture had sat.

Alice sliced upward with her other Kukri, the one that had had its tip knocked off in Vegas, and it made a ragged cut through Isaacs's chest.

Then, before her eyes, the wound healed.

This, she realized, was going to be a problem.

Her shock at seeing that gave Isaacs an opening to

backhand her, sending her flying across the hallway toward where, in the real mansion, the access door to the Hive had been.

Isaacs spoke, finally, his voice sounding deeper but still the same irritating voice that tried to tell her what a pen was all those years ago. "You can't kill me. They already tried. To think, I actually *feared* you."

He stepped forward and wrapped a tentacle around her neck, strangling her.

A part of her wanted to just give up. Carlos was dead. L.J. was dead. Angie was dead. Jill was God knows where. What was left?

The cure. There was that. And only she had it.

As spots formed in front of her eyes, she caught sight of the Kukri, which had embedded itself upright into the faux mansion's floor. It was just in reach, if she could grab the hilt . . .

Somehow, even as consciousness started to fade, her fingers managed to close around it, and she sliced straight through the tentacle, severing it from Isaacs's body. Isaacs howled in pain and stumbled backward several steps.

The tentacle fell to the floor. Alice took several quick, deep breaths.

Isaacs stopped screaming and looked down at the stump where the tentacle had been.

Two more tentacles grew out of the stump to full extension.

Turning to Alice, Isaacs smiled. "Now I have an idea what it feels like to be you—the *power*."

"You have no idea," Alice said.

The tentacles lashed out toward her, and Alice realized there was only one way to win this fight.

Reaching out with her mind, she froze the tentacles in midair. Then she ripped up the floorboards on which Isaacs stood, sending him careening into the wall.

Then Alice collapsed, spent. The day's exertions were starting to catch up even to her enhanced metabolism.

But Isaacs just climbed out from the wall, plaster dust crumbling at his feet. "I told you, I can't die," he said with a hollow laugh.

Then the floor and windows and walls all exploded with similar psychic force. But Alice wasn't doing it. It was Isaacs. Alice felt herself picked up and thrown at the mansion's front door—and through it.

She landed on a glass floor. Trying and failing to clamber to her feet, she saw that the door led to another re-creation, this from the Hive itself: the corridor to the Red Queen's CPU, where One, Drew, Warner, and Danilova were sliced to pieces while Alice watched.

Isaacs strode in and looked down at her broken, bleeding form. "So weak, so pathetic."

Gathering every inch, every aching, pain-wracked muscle, Alice got to her feet. If she was going to die, it would be standing up.

And she didn't intend to die, unless she took the fucker who made her shoot Angie with her. If she was lucky, the room would provide that any second now, assuming they really had re-created this room to the letter.

She punched him, a weak lunge that Isaacs probably

would have seen coming even before he was mutated. He grabbed the fist and threw her behind him, back toward the far end of the corridor.

Just as she'd hoped. The pain was beyond agonizing, but she didn't care anymore.

"For so long," Isaacs said as he slowly walked toward her, "I thought you were the future. How wrong I was. *I* am the future."

"No," Alice said contemptuously, "you're just another asshole."

The lights dimmed. Finally!

"And we're both going to die down here."

A laser lit up at the end of the corridor behind Isaacs. A horizontal beam of death headed straight for him.

Then, not bothering with the first two steps, the laser spread into a diagonal grid that left no room to run, no room to duck, no room to hide.

No room to live.

When One was confronted with the laser grid, he stood and took it, allowing himself only one final muttered curse before he died. But he knew he had no choice, and he faced it head-on.

When Isaacs was confronted with the laser grid, he screamed, "Nooooo!" in a tone that sounded much whinier than his earlier pronouncements of superiority.

The laser sliced through him, literally cubing him.

It moved inexorably on toward Alice.

She was ready to die.

Then she felt it.

Another mind. But the *same* mind, somehow. Images flooded her brain, and she realized that she was being telepathically contacted by the clone that she thought had died in her arms in Isaacs's lab.

The clone was standing at Isaacs's computer workstation and inputting commands into a keyboard. In front of her, the screen displayed the words LASER SYSTEM DEACTIVATED.

In front of her, the laser grid fizzled out, and the lights in the room returned to normal.

Speaking simultaneously, both Alices said, "Yeah, you're the future, all right."

The clone asked, *So what happens now? Is it over?*

Alice thought about the dozens, if not hundreds, of clones Isaacs had created in his desire to turn himself into the future.

The AI had pointed her the way to a cure. Now she also had a way to exact revenge.

No, she said to her sister, *it's only just begun.*

EPILOGUE

Somewhere over Canada, Claire Redfield flew an Umbrella Corporation helicopter with increasing confidence. The snowcapped Rocky Mountains below her, she was heading straight for what she hoped was a haven.

Next to her, Kmart was reading through the journal.

Looking up, Claire saw the picture of Chris. She had no idea if her brother was still alive, but now she had something better than a bunch of ground vehicles. Maybe now she'd find him.

Quickly glancing back, she saw Dorian, Joel, and the kids all fast asleep, exhausted from the ordeals they'd suffered.

She thought about all those who died. Carlos had been right; it wasn't Alice's fault. If it weren't for Alice, they'd *all* have died at the Desert Trail Motel, and if it weren't for Alice, they wouldn't be in a helicopter en route to Arcadia.

For the first time in a long time, Claire Redfield had hope.

In Baltimore, Maureen came running up the escalator to where Jill was smoking a cigarette. After being the most reluctant to follow Jill's plan of organization and takeover of the convention center, she'd become one of the firebrands of the survivors, organizing, scheduling, inventorying, and generally being one of the most useful members of this new society Jill found herself in the process of building.

"Jasper says we got us a van coming. Looks like seven people."

The ex-cop didn't play well with others, as he himself had predicted, so he mostly did sentry duty, which put his skills to use. Unlike the previous occupants' sentries, he didn't shoot people on sight. Living people, anyhow. Zees were taken down without hesitation, of course.

"Okay. See what they got, what they might be willing to trade, and if they need a place to stay. The usual drill."

Maureen nodded and ran back down the escalator. Anyone who came by was offered a free night's stay, but after that, they had to contribute something, trade something, or be gently turned away. It was harsh but not as harsh as it used to be—and also necessary for survival.

Seeing that it was about noontime—which she saw by the height of the sun in the sky streaming through the huge windows—Jill went into one of the small conference rooms, where Andre was playing with the radio.

"Anything?" she asked, same as she did every day.

Shaking his head, Andre said, "Nah," same as he did every day. "But I'll keep tryin'. You never know, you know?"

Jill smiled. It was a real smile, something she found herself doing a lot more these days. "I know. We'll find more people. I'm sure of it."

In truth, she wasn't sure of it. She hadn't heard boo from Carlos or Alice or L.J. or anyone. For all she knew, they were dead. For all she knew, these hundred people in Baltimore were all that was left.

But no, a van was coming. That meant more people. That meant there was hope.

Jill left the conference room for her next task. She had work to do.

Albert Wesker sat at the head of the conference-room table in Umbrella's Japanese headquarters. Surrounding him at the table were holograms of the remaining members of the Committee.

Dr. Sam Isaacs was conspicuous by his absence, as was his theoretical replacement, Alexander Slater.

Adjusting his sunglasses, Wesker said to the others, "All attempts to contact the North American complex continue to fail."

Colin Wainwright's hologram made a *tch* noise. "How long have they been off the air?"

"Seventy-two hours. We must consider them lost.

But our plans remain unchanged. All data have been transferred to this facility, and the research will continue under my personal supervision."

In retrospect, he should have done this in the first place. Wesker had assumed Isaacs to be a rational, intelligent person. He now realized that Isaacs had only seemed that way in comparison to the man he'd replaced, Timothy Cain. However, while Isaacs lacked Cain's fundamental inability to think a plan through, he more than made up for it in personal ambition. Cain was loyal to the company but also spectacularly incompetent. Isaacs was supercompetent but loyal only to himself. Wesker had hoped that Slater would have neither of those defects, but that seemed to be a dead issue.

He continued: "I expect results within one month, two at the mo—"

"Oh, you won't have to wait that long, boys."

Wesker frowned. That voice didn't belong to any of the Committee members—who, for their part, looked just as confused as he felt.

Then a hologram appeared in the seat that had been Isaacs's and was supposed to have been Slater's.

The image was of Alice Abernathy.

Somehow Wesker just knew that this was the orignal Project Alice. It seemed Isaacs had been correct in that his sixty-two-percent match was the original. Unfortunately, it seemed that Isaacs had tragically underestimated the power of his hold on her.

Alice was smiling. "You see, I'm coming for you, and I'm going to be bringing a few friends."

She looked over at the large screen on the north wall. Wesker followed her gaze.

The screen lit up with Alice sitting in a chair in a wrecked laboratory. Behind her was another woman who looked just like her.

Behind them were dozens of tanks, all containing clones of Alice.

Hundreds.

Wesker's authorization was only for one hundred Alice clones. Eighty-seven of them had failed, so there should have been only thirteen left.

From what Wesker could see, there may well have been thirteen *hundred* clones of Alice, all with her enhanced ability.

And now, apparently, all under the direction of their source.

Alice smiled. "Have a nice day, boys."

Her image winked out.

TO BE CONTINUED . . .

About the Author

Keith R.A. DeCandido returns to the world of *Resident Evil* with *Extinction*, having novelized *Resident Evil: Genesis* and *Resident Evil: Apocalypse* in 2004. His other novelizations include *Serenity, Darkness Falls, Buffy the Vampire Slayer: The Xander Years* Volume 1, and *Gargantua*. He's written tons of novels, short stories, and eBooks based on video games (*World of Warcraft, StarCraft, Command and Conquer*), television shows (*Star Trek* in all its incarnations, *Buffy the Vampire Slayer, Supernatural, Doctor Who, CSI: NY Farscape, Gene Roddenberry's Andromeda*), comic books (Spider-Man, X-Men, the Hulk, the Silver Surfer), and more. He's also a veteran anthologist; the editor in charge of the monthly *Star Trek* eBook line; a professional percussionist, having performed with the

Boogie Knights, the Randy Bandits, and the Don't Quit Your Day Job Players, both onstage and in the studio; and a practitioner of *Kenshikai* karate. Find out less about Keith at his official website at www.DeCandido.net, or read his inane ramblings at kradical.livejournal.com.